CW01669768

MADEIRA

Pearl of the Atlantic

The Complete Guide

MADEIRA
Pearl of the Atlantic
The Complete Guide

John & Susan Farrow

ROBERT HALE · LONDON

© *John & Susan Farrow 1987*
First published in Great Britain 1987

Robert Hale Limited
Clerkenwell House
Clerkenwell Green
London EC1R 0HT

British Library Cataloguing in Publication Data

Farrow, John
Madeira: pearl of the Atlantic
1. Madeira—Description and travel
I. Title II. Farrow, Susan
914.69'80444 DP702.M16

ISBN 0-7090-3159-9

Photoset in North Wales by
Derek Doyle & Associates, Mold, Clwyd
Printed in Great Britain by
St Edmundsbury Press Ltd, Bury St Edmunds, Suffolk
Bound by Hunter and Foulis Limited

Contents

List of Illustrations

Colour Plates

Between pages 88 and 89

Picture credits
All colour photographs by Eduardo Perestrelo and João Pestana

Black and White Plates

Between pages 64 and 65

Picture credits

Authors' collection: 1-4, 6, 38; Direcção Regional dos Assuntos Culturais: 5, 7-8, 11-14; Eduardo Perestrelo and João Pestano: 9-10, 15-37

List of Maps and Plans

Acknowledgements

We wish to acknowledge the help and assistance in the provision of photographs for this book given by Senhor Eduardo Perestrelo and Senhor João Pestana. We would also like to thank DRAC (Direcção Regional de Assuntos Culturais) for permission to reproduce photographs from the Vicente Collection.

To Ross, our long-suffering son.

Introduction

Many people have heard the word 'Madeira'. To some it may conjure up madeira wine or madeira cake; fewer people have heard of the island of Madeira or know of its location; fewer still have actually visited this floral paradise. Madeira, 'the Pearl of the Atlantic', covers an area of 270 square kilometres, which makes it slightly larger than the Isle of Man. It is located some 978 kilometres south-west of Lisbon in the Atlantic Ocean, on a similar latitude to Bermuda, Los Angeles and Jerusalem.

Whether you arrive in Madeira by air or by sea, it is an awe-inspiring and breathtaking sight. We have never forgotten our first arrival in Madeira by sea. It was late one autumn afternoon. A speck of dust on the horizon slowly became larger and larger until the entire eye picture was filled with mountains running down to meet the sea. Then we were in the harbour of Funchal, and the vista of the town was before us – the white-walled buildings with their red-tiled roofs – and behind, in the amphitheatre of Funchal, the green backcloth of the mountains and their grey summits contrasting with the blue of sea and sky.

By air, the arrival is no less dramatic and can be a little nerve-racking if the air currents are strong. The peaks of the mountains rise up out of the clouds to meet you, then it's through the cloud and down in a wide sweep over the sea and along the coast past Santa Cruz, so close to the mountains you think the wing tips are touching them. And then suddenly you are down and the engines are switched off. You emerge from the aircraft to the smell of warm fresh air tinged with the aroma of flowers. For this is an island of flowers; they grow in great profusion by the roadsides, in gardens and in thousands of plant pots.

Madeira was in at the birth of tourism some 150 years ago and yet does not appear to be very commercially developed. This is one of its charms, as is the friendliness of the people. Tourism mixes amicably with the Madeiran way of life. No doubt the island will change. It changed after the opening of the airport in 1965, and since 1980 this change has accelerated. Planned developments make change inevitable, and in the whole island, not just Funchal. New roads opening up other parts of the

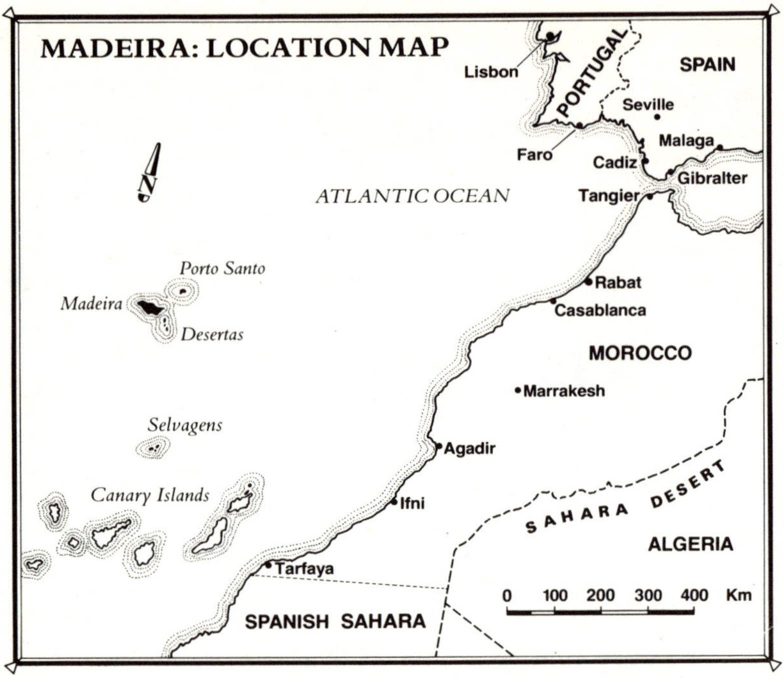

island and relief roads, to ease the congestion in Funchal, are planned; with help from the Common Market, they will come to fruition, as also will the multi-storey car-parks in Funchal, and the new hotels in the country.

Although there are a number of glossy pictorial books about the island of Madeira and specialist flower and walking guides, there has not been a comprehensive travel book written about the island for over a quarter of a century. We hope this book will help fill this need and enable those who have already visited the island and those who may do so in the future to know and understand 'the Pearl of the Atlantic'.

1 *Discovery and Early History*

There is no doubt that João Gonçalves Zarco and Tristão Vaz were the official discoverers of the Madeira archipelago in the early part of the fifteenth century. However, the islands had probably already been visited accidentally by earlier sailors, prior to the official discovery in 1418 of the island of Porto Santo and in 1420 of nearby Madeira.

At the beginning of the Christian era, the Romans had knowledge of some islands far off the African coast. Pliny wrote about 'the Fortunate Islands', and his description makes them recognizable as the Canaries. He also wrote of 'the Purple Islands' whose geographical position in relation to the Fortunate Islands suggests them to be the Madeira group. In a 1351 Genoese map known as the Medici map, the island appears as 'Isola della Lolegname' which is a direct translation of the Portuguese 'Island of Wood' or 'Island of Madeira'. A map of 1385 does not show the Atlantic islands, however.

Whoever first discovered Madeira, civilization began here only with Zarco's discovery.

Legends also abound in connection with the islands of remarkable voyages such as that of the Englishman Robert Machim, in the reigns of Edward III of England and King João I of Portugal (mid-fourteenth century). The young Robert Machim fell in love with Anne d'Arfet (or d'Orset or d'Eufet or Dorset), an extremely beautiful and talented young lady from a wealthy noble family. Family pride meant that permission was refused for her to make an inferior match with Machim. Instead, her family forced her to marry a nobleman of high rank and great wealth whom she disliked. A warrant was obtained from the King to keep Machim imprisoned until after the wedding had taken place. Immediately after, Machim was released and the husband took his bride away to his family seat, a strong castle in the Bristol area. With a band of chosen friends, Machim went to Bristol. One of his friends gained entry to the castle and made known to Anne Machim's continued love for her, as well as a plan for their escape.

Taking Anne, they set sail from Bristol in a small ship destined for

France. A storm blew up and, with no qualified navigator on board, they missed France and were driven into the ocean and tossed around helplessly. On the fourteenth day they arrived exhausted at Madeira, where they landed in a beautiful wooded bay. However, before anything could be moved ashore, the badly anchored ship was swept away in another storm. Anne, dejected and weary, despaired and died in her lover's arms. She was buried at the foot of an altar under a large and beautiful tree, against which was placed a carved cedarwood cross. Machim himself died a few days later of a broken heart and, at his request, he was buried in the same grave as Anne. An inscription was put nearby, dictated by Machim, containing the sad story and asking, if there were future Christian settlers in the island, that they should build a church on that site and consecrate it to the Redeemer of Mankind.

After Machim's death, those remaining found some means of leaving the island – accounts differ as to whether this was in their small boat or in some kind of canoe or raft which they made themselves. However, when they reached the Barbary Coast, they were captured and kept in slavery in Morocco – where they met the rest of the crew, presumed lost when the ship had been blown away in the storm. Here the slaves often talked over their past adventures, and these were heard by a fellow slave, Juan de Morales, a skilful Spanish seaman and experienced navigator. Soon afterwards his ransom was paid by the King of Spain, but on his way home Morales was captured off the Algarve coast and taken to Lisbon by João Gonçalves Zarco, to whom he related the story. It is thus that Zarco is said to have developed the idea of looking for the island and suggested it to Prince Henry the Navigator. Anyway, that is the legend and it goes back a few hundred years.

João Gonçalves Zarco, born in 1395 at Santarem, had fought as a cavalryman and sailed the seas around the Algarve at war against the Castilians and Moors. Tristão Vaz had been a soldier in North Africa. Both were lieutenants of the talented and far-sighted Prince Henry the Navigator, son of King João I of Portugal and Philippa of Lancaster, the daughter of John of Gaunt. In 1418 Zarco and Vaz were exploring the coast of Guinea for Prince Henry when a violent storm blew them off course and, after some time, cast them up on an island which gave them shelter and which they called Porto Santo. When they returned on their second voyage those who had remained in Porto Santo talked of a strange cloud formation on the horizon which they thought might mark the end of the world. Zarco and Vaz went to investigate and, in 1420, discovered the island of Madeira.

Bartolomeu Perestrelo, an Italian interested in the economic possibilities of the new lands, joined them on their second voyage. He stayed in Porto Santo and became Governor of that island. Perhaps he traded in 'Dragon's Blood', a resin from the dragon tree which was sold in Europe for use in weaving and dying.

Meanwhile Zarco and Vaz took possession of the island of Madeira which, along with Porto Santo, had no indigenous population (nor have any signs of earlier settlement ever been found). Vaz and Zarco were given half the island each to govern by Prince Henry: the eastern part from Caniço (with its administrative centre in Machico) was for Tristão Vaz, and the western part (with its centre in Funchal) for João Gonçalves Zarco. Zarco ruled wisely for the rest of his life, and the governorships (Donatory Captaincies) were held in unbroken line by his descendants until the Spanish occupation in 1580. When he died, aged eighty, he was buried in Santa Clara Church in Funchal.

In the City Museum (Museu da Cidade) is a sword, given by a Mr Hinton, on whose blade are marks which say it belonged to Pedro del Monte in the sixteenth century. According to tradition, however, this sword was originally Zarco's, and it is labelled in the museum as his.

Captive Moors and slaves from the Canary Islands and Africa, as well as a number of condemned Portuguese criminals, were sent to populate the island. Poor farmers, refugees and adventurers also came from Portugal in search of a better life. To form an aristocracy, four young noblemen arrived to marry Zarco's four daughters. Then came representatives of other Portuguese noble families – Menezes, Freitas, Mendonça, Pinto, Barros, Bettencourt, Cunha, Sousa, Silva, Aguiar, Almeida, Correia, Ornelas, Leal etc. The first children born were twins, a boy and a girl, to Gonçalo Ayres Ferreira, who named them Adam and Eve.

The Portuguese settlers were joined, shortly after they began colonizing the islands, by adventurers from Flanders, Genoa, Poland, France, England, Scotland and what is now Germany, and they adopted Portuguese versions of their own names. For example, Sir John Drummond, Lord of Stobhall, brother of Annabella, Queen of Robert III of Scotland, came to Madeira in 1425. He was probably a refugee – in any case he revealed his real name only on his deathbed. His descendants today are called Escócio, Escorcio or Drummond.

The forest which covered most of Madeira had to be cut down and burnt for the colonization to proceed. Parts of it were fired, and tradition has it that a fire raged for seven years, though this is unlikely: at the most there may have been pockets of fire over a seven-year period.

Zarco had to organize the basic conditions necessary for civilization. Homes and places of worship had to be built, land allocated, fields sown, animals bred and administration organized. Porto Santo soon showed itself to be barren and arid. Machico and Funchal, however, flourished. Zarco and Teixeira (Vaz had adopted the name of his wife, Branca Teixeira) had their own mini-Courts where they reigned supreme. Zarco's province had the best agricultural land and climatic conditions, the large, naturally protected bay of Funchal and easier communications between settlements on the southern side, advantages which gave rise to an economic shift in favour of Funchal, and from these early times the history of Madeira has been synonymous with that of Funchal.

Up to the end of the fifteenth century, grants of land were in great demand amongst men of high birth who hoped to make their fortunes in Madeira. They lived on estates worked by settlers or slaves (from North Africa mainly), and large fortunes were quickly made. At the end of the fifteenth and at the beginning of the sixteenth century, the landed gentry began to prefer the pleasures of town life and left the estates in the hands of their tenants. The landowners wasted their money on prestigious two-storey houses in Funchal, imported furniture and Flemish paintings. Funchal has been a city since 1508.

The people of Porto Santo are often referred to as *Profétas* – Prophets. The reason for this goes back to 1533, when Fernando (or Fernão) Nunes and his seventeen-year-old niece Filipa left their home in the north of Porto Santo and declared themselves prophets. They quickly gathered a large following of people from all stations in life, rich and poor, learned and ignorant. The people were impressed that Filipa, who had been paralysed for many years, could walk again and that Fernão Nunes seemed able to pinpoint each person's sins. There were large public gatherings and fasting, and the movement quickly became fanatical. When, at one of the public gatherings, João Calaça, a public notary, was seen reading from a prayer book, Fernão Nunes declared that anyone who needed a book to pray from must be filled with the devil, whereupon the crowd set upon Calaça and killed him.

The Prophets and their followers caused much concern among the authorities in Madeira and in mainland Portugal, and so João Fonseca, a magistrate, and two clerks arrived at Porto Santo on 10 March 1533 to deal with the movement. The Prophets and the clergy involved were all arrested and taken to Madeira. The clergy were punished by the Bishop, and the Prophets were condemned and sent to mainland Portugal. Part of their punishment was to sit on the steps of the cathedral at Evora wearing a type of dunce's cap, labelled 'Prophet of Porto Santo'. The Prophets never returned to Porto Santo, and there seems to be no record as to what finally happened to them.

In 1478 Christopher Columbus came to Madeira to buy sugar. The local merchants refused to load it until it was paid for in full. While negotiations proceeded, he stayed some time in the house of Jean d'Esmenaut (João Esmeraldo), a rich Flemish merchant, in Rua do Sabão. (Unfortunately the house no longer exists.) He also married, at some uncertain date, Filipa Moniz, daughter of Bartolomeu Perestrelo, the first Governor of Porto Santo. This part of the Columbus story is fact, the rest may or may not be true. It is said that Filipa and Columbus lived for some time in Porto Santo in the house of Filipa's father and that their son Diogo was born here. During this time Columbus studied his father-in-law's maps and charts and closely observed the debris washed up on the beaches of Porto Santo – debris which is said to have convinced him that there was indeed land across the ocean. He certainly left the archipelago long before he set off on his voyages of discovery.

On 30 May 1513 João de Cáceres was commissioned to build a town wall with ramparts round Funchal. Cáceres was the stonemason for royal building works and lived in Madeira. In 1528 the wall was still incomplete when a Biscayan ship attacked and robbed two other ships off Funchal. Therefore the people of Funchal petitioned the Crown to finish the wall. By 1542 the original plan was completed. The wall had two gates, one facing the sea and one on the western side facing inland.

In 1566 the Frenchman Bertrand de Montluc arrived at Funchal with a squadron of ships. It is not known if they arrived by chance, were blown ashore by a storm or lured by rumours of riches in Funchal. (He is often erroneously described as a Huguenot, a French Protestant. In fact, he was the son of Marshal de Montluc, a fierce enemy of the Huguenots.)

Montluc and his men landed at Praia Formosa (just to the west of Funchal) and marched on the city in two columns. They met little resistance at the western gate and entered the city. The new defences had soon proved inadequate. Inside the Palace of São Lourenço, the attackers put to the sword all the occupants, some 250 people in all – armed men, local merchants and their families, and the temporary governor and his family. The French occupied the island for several days and carried out much pillage and destruction. When they heard that help was on the way from Lisbon, they loaded all the available treasure and vast quantities of wine and set sail, but Montluc himself had died of a leg wound received during the looting.

Soon after the 1566 attack by the French, Jesuits came to Funchal. They created a good impression and in 1569 King Sebastião gave permission for the founding of a Jesuit College. On 18 March 1570 several members of the Order arrived and by 1574 they had acquired all the land where the Colégio Church adjoining the College stand today in Praça do Município.

Between 1580 and 1640 mainland Portugal and Madeira were under Spanish occupation. Under the Spanish the island began to be governed as one unit when, in 1582, King Philip appointed Dom Agostinho Governor. It has been one unit ever since. When the Spanish Armada set sail against England in 1588, many of the ships were built of, or internally decorated, with the dark brown wood of the giant *tils* and the mahogany-like wood of the tall *vinháticos* from Madeira.

The Spanish completed many fortification works, including the Fort of São Tiago and Pico Fort and the extension of the Fort of São Laurenço. In 1640 the Portuguese revolted against Spain and restored their own monarchy by placing John, Duke of Braganza, on the throne. Some time later Portugal gained its full independence and regained possession of Madeira. The Spanish had started to keep a garrison on Madeira because of the dangers of invasion by pirates, and the Portuguese continued this once they regained control of the islands.

The island of Porto Santo, with its long sandy beach, was an invitation to pirates. In 1595, for instance, English vessels under Captain Amias Preston attacked Porto Santo in retaliation for the ill-treatment they said they had previously received. The main town was burned, although the inhabitants had offered to ransom it, and the villages too were all burned. With few people to defend the island and no fortifications, the population of Porto Santo regularly took to the hills in the fifteenth to eighteenth centuries, pursued by Algerian and Moorish corsairs or by French or English pirates. As a result of the constant attacks, many people left the island for the relative safety of Madeira.

In 1552, according to Fructuoso, there were some 2,700 slaves in Madeira, the total population having risen from 16,000 in 1500 to 28,345 in 1614. By the end of the sixteenth century the number of slaves had risen to almost 3,000 – about one tenth of the population of the island at that time. The men worked in the fields and in the sugarmills, and the women as house servants. These slaves were mainly African Negroes, but there were also slaves from the Canary Islands and Morocco. Funchal even had a *mouraria* a Negro quarter, and this name still persists in the name of one of the streets (Rua do Mouraria). In 1773 the Duke of Pombal, an important Minister in mainland Portugal, became alarmed by the number of slaves in Portugal and issued a decree to abolish slavery, which was published in Funchal in April 1775.

2 *Modern History*

In 1662, when Catherine of Braganza was preparing to marry Charles II of England, there was a great danger of Madeira's being ceded to England as part of the dowry. The Queen Regent Luiza of Portugal was so anxious for this alliance that a secret treaty was drawn up in case England's Parliament did not consider Tangier and Bombay sufficient as Catherine's dowry, in which Madeira too would have been ceded to England. Exactly why it was not included in the treaty is unclear. Some stories say the scribe who drew up the document for the Queen Regent was a Madeiran and that he deliberately forgot to include Madeira. Other stories say that the Queen Regent became afraid of a public outcry should it be found out that she had even contemplated giving up such a prize. Anyway she never needed to play her trump card, and Madeira remained Portuguese. After the marriage, many British merchants began to settle in Madeira to take advantage of Charles II's protectionist policies which were embodied in an Act of 1665 banning the export of European goods to the English colonies. This was designed to build up English exports, to encourage English shipping and increase England's share of the carrying trade, of which the Dutch had the lion's share at that time. This ban did not include Madeira and so British merchants were able to ship wine from Madeira to the American colonies.

In the seventeenth century a new era commenced, with Madeira at the centre of the trade routes between Europe and Africa, the East and West Indies and North and South America. It became the last stop for taking on provisions for the large convoys of merchant and naval ships crossing the Atlantic.

On Captain Cook's first voyage in the *Endeavour*, he anchored at Madeira between 14 and 19 September 1768, after seventeen days sail from England. The ship was welcomed by the British Consul, Cheap. Captain Cook was accompanied by a group of scientists including Joseph Banks (1743-1820), later Sir Joseph Banks. He was one of the greatest benefactors of the British Museum and devoted much wealth and time to the pursuit of science. On his visit to Madeira he and other scientists collected plants and investigated the lifestyles of the inhabitants. On this visit, Mr Weir, the mate, is said to have become entangled in the buoy rope when the anchor was being dropped and was dragged to the bottom and drowned. On Commodore John Byron's voyage in search of new land in the southern Atlantic (1764-6), he called at Madeira between 13 and 19 July 1764 in command of two British naval ships, the *Delfim* and the *Tamar*. The island was also of interest to geologists, botanists, zoologists and other scientists. (See Appendix I.)

The three main rivers through Funchal were often the cause of serious flooding. By 1803 the river beds, in some parts of the city, were two or three metres above the city. In 1803, after there had been no rain for several months, it began to rain incessantly and at about 8 p.m. on 9 October the rivers burst their banks. All the bridges were swept away, except the one on which the surveyor's house was built, and part of the defensive wall was destroyed. Several houses were flooded and the doors could not be forced because there was so much water inside. The inhabitants were on the upper floors calling for help but, before anything could be done for them, the houses disintegrated and the people were all lost in the flood. One house, inhabited by a British family called Tatlock, was carried out to sea whole. It remained floating for some minutes, with lights burning at the upper windows and people shouting for help, and then finally sank.

When the floods subsided, the streets were littered with bodies, choked with rubble from the ruins, and there were heaps of dead oxen, sheep and domestic animals. The victims were laid out in the churches to be claimed by relatives, many, reportedly, still showing a spark of life which was ignored in the general rush to clear up. Afterwards all the bodies were burned and all the pitch and tar in Funchal were requisitioned to fumigate the streets with bonfires. In all, some 600 people were lost.

On 19 February 1804 Brigadier Engineer Reynaldo Oudinot, a Frenchman who had taken Portuguese nationality, arrived in Funchal to look into the problems of flooding in the city. Although he died in 1807, he had by then planned the 'canalization' of the three rivers and the construction of the walls alongside them which can still be seen today.

Madeira did not escape the effects of the Napoleonic Wars. In 1801 a British force occupied the island to safeguard the port as a vital revictualling point for the Navy. Troops commanded by Lieutenant-Colonel Sir William Henry Clinton stayed for some months co-operating with the Portuguese garrison.

In 1807 the British again returned to Madeira under the command of

General Sir William Carr Beresford, who had already won a great reputation whilst still under forty years of age. This occupation, which continued until peace was concluded with France in 1814, was friendly, as Britain had no territorial designs on the island. The arrival of the British had been impressive: on 24 December 1807 a squadron had anchored in Funchal under the command of Admiral Samuel Hood and consisted of four ships of the line, four frigates and sixteen ships for transporting troops, carrying two regiments of infantry and two companies of artillery. The British flag was raised on all fortifications in Funchal. In 1808 Beresford and half the force returned to Lisbon. The British troops were very friendly with the Madeirans and many courted the local girls, which is said to explain why so many fair-haired and blue-eyed men and women of obvious Anglo-Saxon ancestry are to be seen in Madeira.

A reaction against the occupation by the British began to develop after an incident in December 1813 when the then British commander, Major-General Gordon, condemned to death a British soldier for insubordination and the murder of a sergeant. The Portuguese Governor intervened and said such an execution on Portuguese soil would be an insult to the Portuguese Crown. When the execution was carried out in the Fort of Penha de França, the people of Madeira showed their disgust by turning their heads away from the fort whenever they passed it.

On 23 August 1815 HMS *Northumberland*, commanded by Admiral Cockburn, anchored in Funchal harbour, bound for the island of St Helena and taking Napoleon into exile. Only the British Consul, Henry Veitch, was allowed on board while the ship was in Madeira. A quantity of fruit, books and old madeira wine was taken on board. It is not known which lodge supplied the wine nor whether it was Napoleon or one of his party who ordered it. This, however, gives rise to two legends: firstly that it was paid for by Napoleon in gold louis to Mr Veitch, who later buried the coins under the foundation stone of the English church; and secondly that the wine was never drunk by Napoleon but returned to Madeira after his death to be bottled in 1840 by Blandy's. A bottle of this wine was opened at Reid's Hotel in 1950 when the British community gave a dinner in honour of Sir Winston Churchill's visit. Sir Winston, when told the story of the wine, insisted on serving each guest at the table himself. 'Do you realize,' he asked, 'that when this wine was made, Marie Antoinette was alive?'

Consul Veitch was later removed from his post for addressing Napoleon as 'Your Majesty' instead of 'General', as he had been instructed by London.

On 26 August 1823 a new Governor, accompanied by a regiment of the Seventh Infantry, was sent to Madeira by King João VI, who had recently been proclaimed absolute monarch. When in 1826, the *Carta Constitucional* (Constitutional Letter) was published, the Bishop of Funchal ignored the directives of the Ministry of Justice refusing to explain them to his flock. This led to insubordination amongst the Seventh Infantry who attacked the Governor and wounded one of the officers who accompanied him. On 27 April 1827 a new Governor, Captain-General José Lúcio Travassos Valdez, arrived to calm the situation.

In Portugal, in May 1828, a rival claimant to the throne, Dom Miguel, proclaimed himself absolute monarch, and the following month Portuguese ships appeared off Madeira, bringing the new Miguelist governor, José Maria Monteiro. In August 1828, after a small exchange of fire, Monteiro landed with a thousand troops under Colonel José António de Azevedo Lemos. Some British officers had been sent to help the Madeirans with their resistance, but they had arrived only a few days before the Portuguese troops landed and had not had time to organize. The Governor, Valdez, and his family and many locally important people fled to Britain on board the frigate *Alligator*. The Miguelist forces entered Funchal, and some 146 people and twenty-one clergy were arrested and imprisoned, sent to Lisbon and deported for life to the Portuguese colonies.

Over the years many sailing ships were wrecked on the rocky shores of Madeira, driven there by foul weather. In 1842 six ships were at anchor in Funchal Bay when a hurricane blew them all onto the shore. In 1863 the 200-ton brig *Comet* sank at her Funchal anchorage, and in 1877 the schooner *Patagonia* went ashore near Ponta São Lourenço. Salvage from sailing ships was an important additional income for the local people, but ceased with the coming of the steamships as they could stand out to sea in a storm. In the autumn of 1852, the first failure of the vines coincided with extensive disease in the potato crop, and the people faced famine. A committee was appointed by the Portuguese Government to receive and distribute food to those in distress, but there were still many deaths. In the summer of 1856, an epidemic of cholera broke out and over 7,000 people died in the course of a few weeks. In many parts of the island there was total disorganization as a result, and the government had to install many new officials to replace those who had died or fled.

In 1916 Portugal seized some German ships in Lisbon harbour, at which Germany declared war on Portugal. On Sunday 3 December 1916 a German U-boat sank the French warship *La Surprise* and two other ships anchored in Funchal Bay and then lightly shelled the town. Some houses were damaged and a shell fell on the church of Santa Clara. There were few casualties on shore but forty-five seamen lost their lives when their ships sank. In 1917 Funchal was again attacked by a German U-boat, but little damage was caused.

During the Second World War Portugal was neutral. Most of the Madeirans were sympathetic to the Allies and those who were sympathetic to the Germans (*Germanófilos* as they were colloquially called) were unpopular. There were hardships on the island due to supply problems from Lisbon of goods such as petroleum, car tyres and spare parts and other imported commodities. But, as in most places, shortages were eased by ingenious home-made car parts and machinery, by pooling transport where possible and, for instance, easing the salt shortage by extracting it from the sea. The tourist trade was practically non-existent and Reid's Hotel was closed during the War. Madeira became, however, the temporary home for 2,000 Gibraltarians evacuated to Funchal and their arrival relieved what might have been a financially distressing situation resulting from the lack of tourists. The evacuees filled most of the small hotels and the Savoy, many of them financially supported by the British Government. Always referred to by the locals as 'the Spanish', they had their own school (where the Hotel Monte Carlo is now situated) and the New Year's Eve parties here were particularly popular. The Gibraltarians liked to drink coffee in the open air cafés and the women loved to knit – occupations new to the Madeirans but which rapidly became and remain popular pastimes. After the War a few who had married in the island remained, but the majority returned to Gibraltar.

With the overthrow of the Portuguese monarchy in 1910, Portugal became a republic. Internal dissension continued until 1926, when a military dictatorship gained control. Dr Antonio d'Oliveira Salazar, an economics professor from Coimbra, was appointed Finance Minister. In 1932 he became Prime Minister and in 1933 Dictator, a situation which continued until his retirement due to a massive stroke in 1968. He was followed by Dr Marcello Caetano, a law professor, who remained in power until the popular Revolution of 1974 when the army overthrew the dictatorship. At this time the colonial wars in Africa, which were destroying Portugal's economy, were abandoned and free elections were introduced. The deposed leaders, president Américo Tomás and Prime Minister Caetano, stopped at Madeira on their way to exile in Brazil. They were allowed ashore but were kept in the sixteenth-century São Lourenço fortress during their stay.

During the Salazar dictatorship Madeira fared badly, particularly after the revolt in the island in 1931. About 300 political prisoners had been deported from Lisbon to Madeira in the autumn and winter of 1930, and they were to be important in the trouble which followed. On 26 January 1931 the so-called 'Hunger Law' was published which gave the monopoly on imported flour to a small group of mill-owners. This caused the bankruptcy of two of the most important local banks where the majority of Madeirans had their money deposited. On 6 February there was a spontaneous strike by the stevedores, and this quickly became a general strike, with the mills being attacked. The Lisbon government reacted unusually promptly, and on 9 February Colonel Silva Leal arrived with some 300 soldiers and six pieces of light artillery to put an end to the trouble. He immediately began harsh repressive measures and many Madeirans were deported to the Azores and some to the Cape Verde.

On Saturday 4 April the 300 deportees, the island garrison and some of the troops from Lisbon staged a *coup*, and the following day declared a military dictatorship. The Civil and Military Governors and many officers were imprisoned, and General Sousa Dias (one of the deportees) was proclaimed Dictator. Commerce was paralysed, the telephones were cut, there was strict censorship of all correspondence and telegrams, and careful control of the port. This revolt soon spread to the Azores and Cape Verde, where there were more deportees from Lisbon.

On 8 April the British cruiser *London* arrived, having come from Gibraltar in twenty-four hours. The commander explained to the Dictator that the ship had come only to ensure the safety of British subjects and not to interfere in the situation in Madeira. The British Consul, Brown, advised all British visitors to return home in case the island was blockaded, and a large group left the island on the *Edinburgh Castle*, including an important delegation from Britain's Grand Masonic Lodge which had been in the island to attend the inauguration of a new Masonic temple.

The situation was quiet, with just a few soldiers in the street, for the next few days. The Lisbon Government tried to avoid bloodshed by starving out the rebels and blockading the island. On 28 April the Lisbon forces disembarked at Ponta de São Laurenço under cover of firing from the ships. The Madeirans replied and claimed to have forced the troops back on board ship. Men from the British cruisers *London* and *Curlew* protected the foreigners who were concentrated in the neutral zone of the Hotels Reid's, Atlantic and Savoy. British fusiliers and marines also protected the British Consulate and the homes and businesses of British residents.

On Thursday 31 April 700 Lisbon soldiers disembarked at Caniçal and, aided by fog, took the town of Machico and forced the rebels into the hills to the west. By 2-3 May, General Sousa Dias realized he and the rebels had lost the battle and surrendered. All the officers, except Dias himself and two others, sought asylum either with the British Consul (and went on board the *London*) or in the neutral zone in the hotels. The toll on the Lisbon troops was one dead and seven wounded and for the rebels three dead and fifteen wounded, including one civilian. The rebel soldiers were imprisoned and taken to Lisbon.

The Revolution of 25 April 1974 was greeted enthusiastically in Madeira. There was a period of unrest and excessive zeal, of settling old scores and family feuds – all very mild, really. Some people left the island quickly in chartered planes to Brazil. Some have since returned and lead quiet lives. Various regional movements emerged, some of which became political parties. The Madeirans were worried, in particular, in case a post-revolutionary Communist dictatorship should install itself in Lisbon. The revolution deterred visitors to Madeira and adversely affected the already fragile economy. The *Jornal da Madeira*, owned by the Diocese and directed by Dr Alberto João Jardim, became the centre of Madeiran democratic resistance against Communism. In 1976 a constitution was drawn up in Lisbon which designated Madeira an Autonomous Political Region.

Today, under the leadership of Dr Alberto João Jardim, President of the Autonomous Regional Government, Madeira is responsible for most of the administration of affairs that affect the Region and can initiate legislation in certain areas. However, the island remains very much a part of Portugal and receives annual funds from the central government.

Since the first democratic regional elections took place in 1976, the Region has been governed by an overwhelming Popular Social Democratic majority. The PSD party is a national, slightly right of centre, party which in July 1987 won an absolute majority in Portugal. In Madeira the local branch of it is dominated by the charismatic figure of Dr Alberto João Jardim and at any election, national or local, the party can count on between sixty-five and seventy per cent of the votes cast in the island. As well as an overwhelming majority in the Regional Parliament it controls all the municipal local authorities. The opposition is led by PS, the Socialist party, which is strongest in the urban areas around Funchal. The CDS, which is more right wing than the PSD, has one deputy in the Regional Parliament. The Communists, PCP also have one member and their colleagues, UDP or United Democratic Party, have two members and draw most of their support from the Machico area. Since the Revolution of 1974 and the opening of the Regional

Government and Parliament granted by the new constitution in 1976, vast improvements have been made to the infrastructure of the islands and to the living standards of the people.

3 *Emigration*

Emigration and tourism have long been the main contributors to the economy of Madeira, emigration being the older. The emigration of Madeirans to far-flung places, where they worked hard and sent back funds to support their families in the island, is almost as old as the colonization of the island itself.

When the islands were first settled, the population began to increase rapidly and the number of inhabitants soon exceeded the resources, prompting emigration to other Portuguese lands. Whenever the flow of emigrants slowed, the government in Lisbon encouraged it again. In 1676 a royal decree ordered the transportation of between three and four thousand people from Madeira to Brazil.

The majority of the islanders lived at subsistence level. Their main preoccupation was how to feed their families, as the availability and price of imported wheat, maize and dried fish varied greatly. Emigration in search of better living conditions increased whenever there was a crisis in the production or exportation of wine, upon which the island's economy depended.

In 1836 the population of the archipelago was 115,446 (1,618 of these in Porto Santo). The continued increase in population accentuated the hardships for the peasants: a great variety of taxes to pay; the price of imported wheat continually rising, when most peasants could manage to grow only enough food to last them three months; and the vines and potatoes suffered blight and disease. Nineteenth-century Madeira had many problems similar to those of nineteenth-century Ireland, and many people emigrated in search of a better life.

No precise official figure on emigration exists before the end of the nineteenth century. It is, however, estimated that between 1835 and 1855 about 40,000 people left Madeira, and between 1890 and 1910 about 38,500 – but the total population of the islands remained constant. There was a decline in the island's population in the mid-1850s associated with many people emigrating at the time of the *oidium* disease of the vines. In 1843 the total population was 117,372 but this had declined to 107,088 by 1854 and to 98,620 in 1858. By 1900 it was back up to 148,263 and rising again. Although the Madeiran knew about the hardships of emigration, it remained an attractive proposition when he saw an emigrant return well dressed, with shoes on his feet, money in his pocket and stories of success.

The early emigrants went to Brazil and the Portuguese African colonies (popular because of the common language). As time went on, they also went to British Guiana, the Hawaiian Islands, North America and Curaçāo. More recent destinations have been South Africa, Venezuela, Australia and Europe.

The abolition of the Slave Trade by Britain in 1807 created shortages of manual labourers in the plantations of colonies such as British Guiana. In 1841 the Madeiran Press published an advertisement, by the Governor of British Guiana, Sir Henry George Macleod, for an agent in Madeira and offered rewards for settlers who went to British Guiana. So many people wanted to emigrate in answer to this that the local authorities feared that the traditional system of agriculture in Madeira as well as the new industries, would be endangered by a shortage of artisans and workers. They therefore published terrible stories about the hardships of emigration and the problems which had befallen many emigrants. The authorities also tightened up on illegal emigration – the coastal areas were patrolled and hiding-places for illegal emigrants were found in central Funchal; those responsible were arrested, tried and sentenced.

The would-be emigrant faced many difficulties. First of all there was the paperwork: it was necessary to obtain permission from the head of the family, to have a certificate of baptism for each emigrant, to obtain exemption from military service for males, to have no criminal record and to prove how the voyage would be paid for. These were significant problems for the majority, who were both illiterate and poor. Then there were the hardships of the voyage itself. For example, the sailing ship *Thomas Bell*, which left Funchal on 8 November 1887 and arrived in Hawaii on 14 April 1888 (156 days via Cape Horn), had 400 emigrants on board and they suffered a great deal from sea-sickness and hunger. During the voyage there were fights and illnesses, seven babies were born, eleven people died and there was one marriage and a miscarriage.

Emigration began to Curaçāo in the Dutch West Indies in the 1930s, when the Madeirans went to work in the petroleum industry there. In the 1940s there was an agent in Madeira for recruiting emigrants, and he gave would-be emigrants a medical examination and enquired into their marital status, number of children, qualifications and so on. The ships were very full, with large numbers of emigrants and a doctor on board. During the Second World War the Portuguese Government tried to insist that only neutral ships be used, but this was often ignored.

On the night of 16-17 March 1944, for example, a ship left Funchal with a doctor and 1,206 Madeirans, all bound for Curaçâo, their passage having been paid by the petroleum company. On arrival they were given simple accommodation in the company camp and received their meals from the centralized kitchen. After four years of service they could return home for a holiday with the family or bring out their wives and children, providing they had found accommodation for them. (Many emigrants chose to bring out their wives, and in 1948 and 1950, for example, ships arrived bringing women only from Madeira and the Azores.) After ten years of service, providing there had been no problems, the emigrant could continue living in Curaçâo without working for the petroleum company, providing he had a job. The year of maximum emigration to Curaçâo was 1945, when 2,769 emigrated, this being forty-six per cent of the total number of Madeiran emigrants in that year. Between 1952 and 1970 the number of emigrants to Curaçâo declined and then stopped, largely because other places increasingly appeared more attractive to the emigrant.

In the 1960s the oil boom made Venezuela the country to emigrate to, and it was a common occurrence for the emigrant who made good to hire a large American car (Cadillac or similar) and to return to Madeira by ship with the car. He would drive round his home village for a couple of weeks, impress his family and friends with the car, cigars and drinks and pick his future wife. He would then marry her and return with her to Venezuela, where he would return his hire car and take his new wife to his humble home. Sometimes an emigrant would advertise in the newspaper in Madeira for a suitable wife, marry her by proxy and pay for her passage out to join him when he could afford it. Even today the emigrant returning for a visit is expected to spend a fair amount of money entertaining family and friends.

Today many Madeirans live and work in Venezuela. They started work in the restaurants, supermarkets and hotels, and many still work in such establishments. Some have done well and now own the businesses in which they were once employed or have opened their own. There are, at the present time, 190,000 Madeirans in Venezuela.

South Africa has also been very popular with Madeiran emigrants. Today there are some 600,000 Portuguese there, half of them from this small island. Many of the emigrants to South Africa were from middle-class families and are now in the professions there. Some have done very well indeed – for example, the Pestana family who now own the recently extended Madeira Sheraton Hotel as well as the Casino Park Hotel. Another success story is that of Joe Berardo – 'Joe Gold' – who left Madeira some twenty years ago and started work in a greengrocer's shop. Eventually he owned a greengrocery business which he then mortgaged to buy spoil heaps across the road from the gold mines, which had been there since mining began, on the assumption that the equipment a hundred years ago was not as efficient at finding gold as today's modern machinery. He hired some plant and employed a geologist and found a lot of gold in those old spoil heaps. Today he owns, amongst other companies, two gold mines and a diamond mine. He is a large shareholder in a bank and has companies in Australia and Canada, as well as investments in Madeira. He has never forgotten his island of birth and returns three or four times every year.

Surprisingly enough, the small island of Jersey has been host to about 5,000 Madeirans, many of them contract workers in the hotels for the season. However, many have settled and stayed in the island. The professionalism of the Madeiran hotel and restaurant workers has certainly something to do with the high standard of hotels and restaurants to be found in Jersey.

In fact, there are few corners of the world where Madeirans are not to be found: from Alaska to Australia, from California to Macau. In Madeira, to stand behind a little old peasant lady, dressed in black, in the bank cashing her cheques from family worldwide is quite an experience. She is an expert in exchange rates, with her cheques in many different currency denominations. She may not be able to read or write but she can convert dollars, francs, rand, etc into escudos!

4 *Landscape and Climate*

Climate

The island of Madeira enjoys one of the most equable climates in the world. It is warm all year round, with warm summers, mild winters and moderate rainfall. Summer temperatures rarely exceed 27°C (86°F) and winter temperatures never fall below 10°C (52°F). Within this general analysis there is a considerable variety of micro-climates – as one might expect on a small island in the Atlantic with altitudes from sea-level to 1,800 metres.

Precipitation of about 550mm per annum (in Funchal) usually comes in short but very heavy showers. March usually has the heaviest rainfall, just over 100mm on average. From May to September, there is almost no rain; from October to February, rain falls on average on five to seven days per month. In the winter, snow or, more usually, hail can fall on the tops of the highest mountains and yet one hour's drive down in Funchal people are swimming and sunbathing. Between December and April, the temperature averages between 15°C and 21°C (59°F to 70°F); it then gradually increases to around 21°C to 24°C (70°F to 75°F) between July and September, and drops again to an average between October and December of 18°C to 21°C (64°F to 70°F). This equable climate has long appealed to people from northern Europe (especially the United Kingdom) as a place to escape to from the rigours of a cold winter. During June and July, heavy cloud may at times build up and the weather can become very humid.

Prevailing winds from the north-east (the Trade Winds) very occasionally bring a *leste*, a hot, dry wind which blows from the desert areas of North Africa. This normally happens only in the summer and lasts for an average of one to five days. The sky turns greyish-brown and the air is filled with fine red-brown dust. During these times the temperature may rise to as much as 40°C (104°F) and the humidity drop to below ten per cent.

The temperature of the sea water is at its highest in September (21°C, 70°F) and falls to 16°C (61°F) in March.

The weather in the mountains can change very rapidly, and mists can descend suddenly, particularly in the winter months. Very often the day starts clear and bright in the mountains, and this continues until about 11 a.m., when misty cloud develops between altitudes of 500m and 1,200m. This is caused by condensation in the air which moves upwards as the temperature at lower altitudes rises. The reverse process often takes place in the evening, and the mountains become clear and sharp again. Above 1,200m you can often enjoy beautiful weather and look down on a sea of white clouds, with the occasional peak protruding through. The impression is one of being on the roof of the world.

Thomas Stanford, in his book *Leaves from a Madeira Garden*, states (with regard to the changing climate and scenery) that in Madeira one can travel in the space of an hour from a sub-tropical region to the Riviera, from the Riviera to Bournemouth, from Bournemouth to Caernarvonshire, and from Caernarvonshire to the Alps. It truly is an island of contrasts.

Porto Santo, being smaller and lower than Madeira, has a different climate. The wind sweeps unhindered across the plains, and there is very little precipitation. It is dry and arid. Between July and October it is usually very hot, with little rest from the blazing sun – an ideal holiday place for worshippers of sun, sand and sea.

Location

The archipelago of Madeira consists of the islands of Madeira, Porto Santo, the Desertas and the Selvagens. Madeira is situated between latitudes 32°22'20"N and 33°6'50"N, and between longitudes 16°16'30"W and 17°16'38"W. Its maximum east-west length is 57km, and the maximum north-south width 23km. The population of the island of Madeira is 260,000, including 90,000 in the city of Funchal. Of the total island population, eighty-six per cent live on the south side and only fourteen per cent on the north.

Porto Santo is the second largest island in the Madeira group, and the only other one which is populated. It is 64km north-east of Funchal and 36km from the nearest point on Madeira. It is 12km long and 7km wide and has a resident population of 2,700.

Looking east from Funchal, you can see three islands called the Desertas. These islands are uninhabited, except for a few wild goats, rabbits and birds. At the nearest point they are 30km away from the island of Madeira. From left to right (when viewed from Madeira), we see Ilhéu Chão, Deserta Grande and Bugio. Ilhéu Chão is about 100m

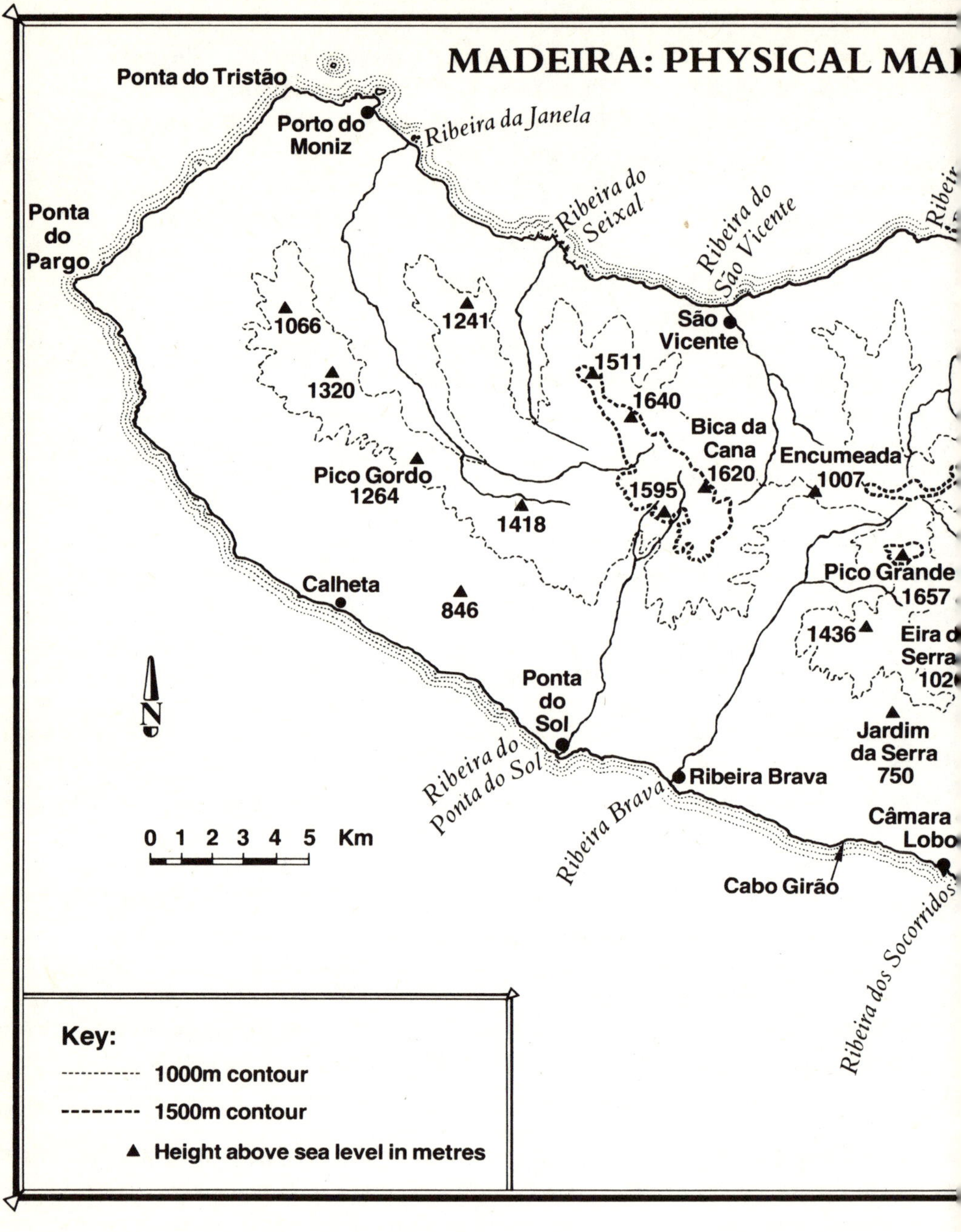
MADEIRA: PHYSICAL MA
Ponta do Tristão
Porto do Moniz
Ribeira da Janela
Ponta do Pargo
Ribeira do Seixal
Ribeira do São Vicente
São Vicente
1066
1241
1320
1511
1640
Bica da Cana
1620
Encumeada
1007
Pico Gordo
1264
1595
1418
Pico Grande
1657
Calheta
846
1436
Eira d
Serra
102
Ponta do Sol
Jardim da Serra
750
Ribeira do Ponta do Sol
Ribeira Brava
Ribeira Brava
Câmara
Lobo
Cabo Girão
Ribeira dos Socorridos
N
0 1 2 3 4 5 Km
Key:
1000m contour
1500m contour
Height above sea level in metres

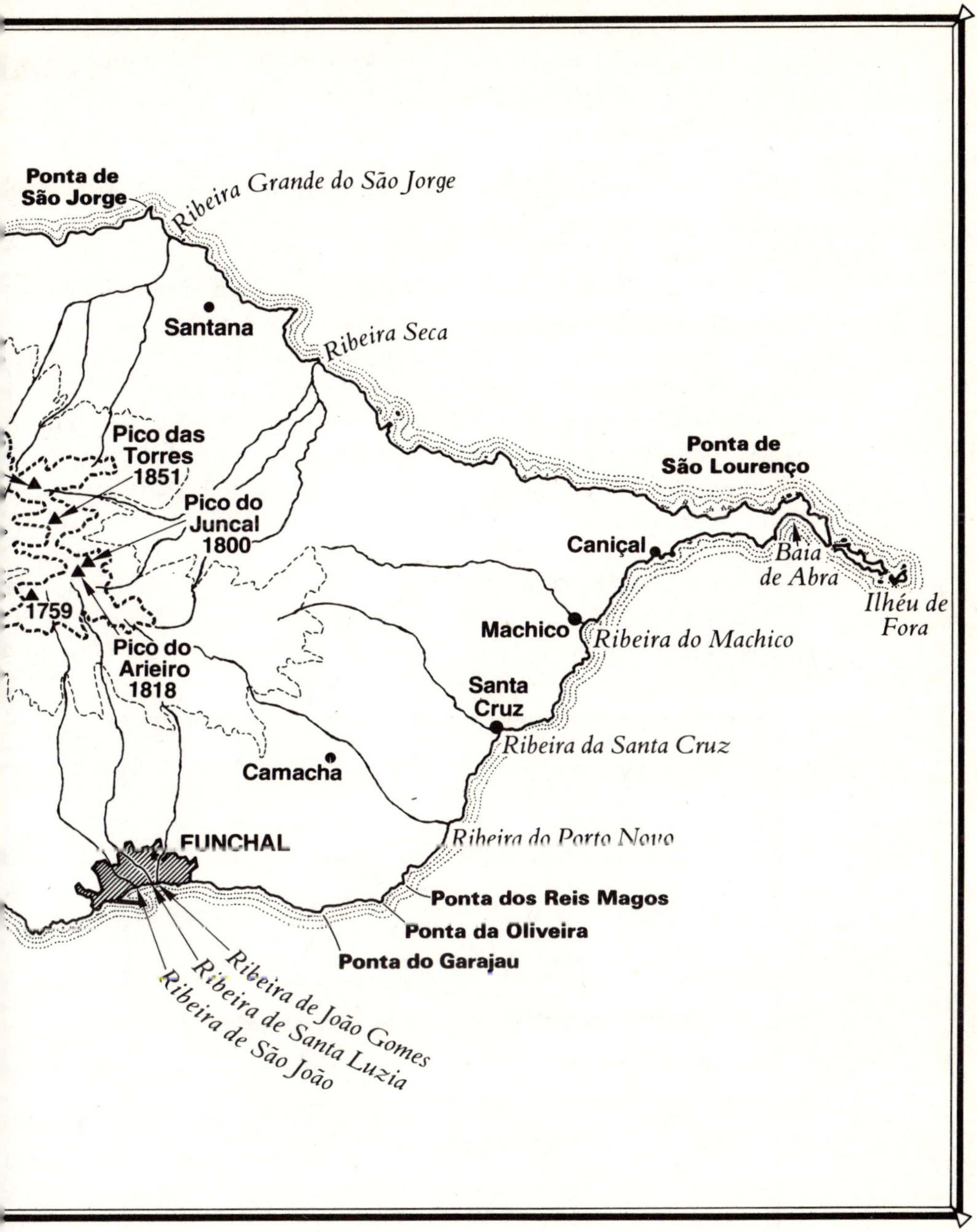
Ponta de São Jorge
Ribeira Grande do São Jorge
Santana
Ribeira Seca
Ponta de São Lourenço
Pico das Torres 1851
Pico do Juncal 1800
1759
Pico do Arieiro 1818
Caniçal
Baía de Abra
Ilhéu de Fora
Machico
Ribeira do Machico
Santa Cruz
Ribeira da Santa Cruz
Camacha
FUNCHAL
Ribeira do Porto Novo
Ponta dos Reis Magos
Ponta da Oliveira
Ponta do Garajau
Ribeira de João Gomes
Ribeira de Santa Luzia
Ribeira de São João

high, 1,500m long and flat-topped. To the north of this island is a pinnacle-shaped stack known as Sail Rock because it looks somewhat like a ship under sail. Legend has it that it was once fired on by a warship because it failed to reply to a signal! Deserta Grande is 10km long and 1,500m wide, has only one practical landing place and used to be inhabited. Today it is sometimes visited by sportsmen in search of wild goats. Bugio is 7.2km long and 750m wide. The Desertas are now a bird sanctuary.

The fourth part of the Madeiran archipelago is a group of three islands and reefs called the Selvagens. They are 250km from Funchal and are, in fact, nearer to the Canaries than to Madeira. They have the effect of increasing the territorial waters of Madeira (Portugal). Great Selvagem is 2.5km long by 2.2km. It is used by fishermen and is designated a bird sanctuary. The other main islands are named Great and Little Piton. Great Selvagem is where the pirate Captain Kidd (1645-1701) is said to have buried his treasure. In 1830 a search was made by a British Government expedition, but nothing was found. In 1890 a private expedition was also disappointed.

There is another slightly different version of the story of treasure in the Selvagens. On his way to the South Pole, Shackleton called in at Madeira

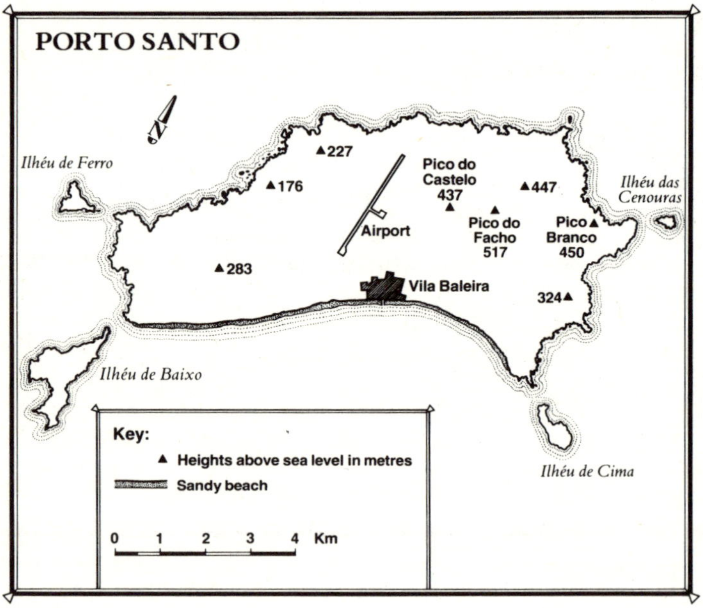

between 16 and 19 October 1921. He persuaded the then owner of the Selvagens to allow him, on his return journey, to search for the treasure, which would be split between them. According to Shackleton, the treasure was from a French pirate ship which had been wrecked on the island, proof of which, found in the British Admiralty, was an account by one of the survivors of the wreck. Unfortunately Shackleton died whilst still in the Antarctic on 5 January 1922, and so he never did search for the treasure.

Geomorphology

Geomorphologically speaking, the island of Madeira can be divided into three main areas: the central mass, the western part and the eastern area.

The central area is volcanic in origin. Eruptions started under the sea, probably in the Miocene period some 20 million years ago. These successive submarine eruptions built up layers of material which eventually emerged above the ocean's surface as a small island, and coral reefs formed around its edge. The island was uplifted and igneous intrusions took place. It then became elongated west-north-west/east-south-east by successive eruptions of lava and ash from volcanic cones along the top of the ridge. The maximum height thought to have been reached during this period is 2,000m. The island became covered with vegetation, fossils of which are sometimes found in the volcanic ashes. The volcanic eruptions are thought to have finished some 1.7 million years ago, and the volcanoes are considered extinct.

The western part of the island is separated from the central mass by the deep ravines between Ribeira Brava and São Vicente. It is made up of volcanic formations deposited in a north-west/south-east direction, the plateau of Paúl da Serra being the main core. This plateau is about 17 km long, 6km wide and 1,200 to 1,500m high. In the west it is heavily dissected by the Ribeira da Janela and the Ribeira do Seixal, both of which flow to the north coast.

The eastern part of the island, ending in the narrow, curving peninsula of Ponta de São Lourenço, consists of the small plateaux of Poiso, Chão das Feiteiras and Santo da Serra. These small plateaux, covered in basaltic lavas, are similar in formation to that of Paúl da Serra to the west of the central mass. Shell sand, blown into the area between Caniçal and the end of the island in recent geological times, contains fossil shells and root- and branch-shaped concretions of the vegetation which existed at that time.

The volcanic rocks of the island of Madeira (tufas and volcanic ashes interbedded with basaltic lavas) have long been subject to the effects of

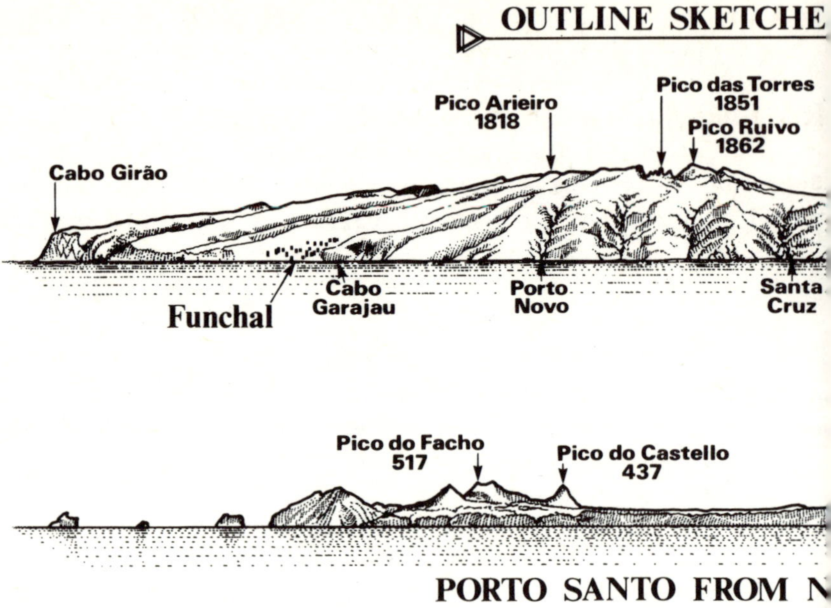

Outlines of Madeiran Islands

rain and rivers. Differential erosion of the rocks has resulted in the hard rocks being left as peaks separated by deeply eroded valleys and ravines. Curral das Freiras may look like an old volcanic crater but it was, in fact, formed by the headwater erosion of the Ribeira dos Socorridos. The shape and direction of the valleys have been influenced by the location of the more easily eroded volcanic material. Today Madeira consists of a curving longitudinal ridge with numerous minor ridges running north and south from it. All valleys are deep, with steep, often precipitous, sides. Between the mouths of the rivers are high cliffs, some of the highest in the world, with vertical columns of basalt and layers of red and yellow tufa exposed in some places. The central mountains of Madeira are about 1,860m above sea-level, the three highest peaks being Pico Ruivo (1,862m), Pico das Torrinhas or Torres (1,851m) and Pico Arieiro (1,818m).

One of the best descriptions of the landscape of Madeira is that given by White and Johnson (*Madeira: Its Climate and Scenery*, 1860): 'When Columbus was asked by Queen Isabella to give her some notion of the configuration of Jamaica, it is said that he took up a sheet of paper, and after crushing it in his hand, partly opened it out; then placing it on the table, he told her Majesty that she would derive a better idea of the island

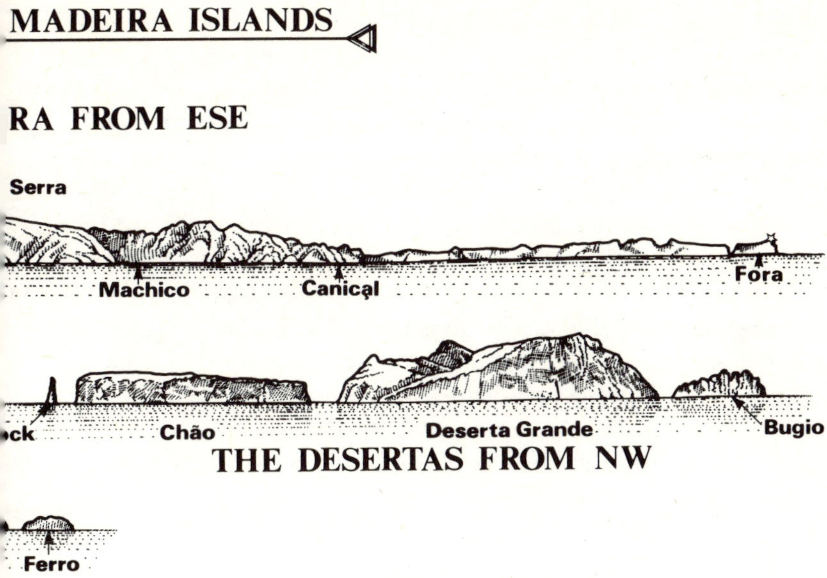

from the crumpled paper than from any description conveyed in words. The same rough model would serve very well for Madeira, the physical geography of which is composed like Jamaica, of hill and hollow in endless iteration.'

Prainha, at the eastern end of the island, has the only natural sandy beach in Madeira, albeit black sand. There are beaches of rounded grey basalt pebbles of varying sizes elsewhere around the island. At the river mouths are stones and huge boulders brought down when the rivers are in flood, although most of the year there is so little water in the rivers that it is hard to imagine.

According to soundings made in the surrounding ocean, there are some very deep ocean trenches in the sea around the island. The shore slopes steeply down into the sea and, if the ocean were to dry up, the island would emerge in a single block some 5,400m above the sea bed.

Porto Santo consists of volcanic rocks (basalt and trachyte) which are located mainly in the north-east of the island, where most of the peaks are. The rest of the island is much lower and flatter and is covered with deposits of sand, calcareous sandstone and clays. The local people call the clays *salão*, and it is traditionally used for covering walls and houses. The island is aligned south-west/north-east, and the whole of the north coast is of cliffs with an average height of 100m. These reach a maximum height in the north-east, at the top of Pico Branco. Porto Santo is not connected under the sea to Madeira but it is of a similar age – Miocene. The island has an eight kilometre long white sandy beach which is one of the last unspoilt natural beaches in Europe.

Geologically the Desertas are similar in formation to the volcanic rocks of the Machico area (post-Pliocene) from which they are separated by a channel 50-100m deep. They are really a southern prolongation of Ponta de São Lourenço.

The Selvagens are geologically similar to Porto Santo. Selvagem Grande is a plateau from which 100m high cliffs plunge into the sea.

The Madeiran archipelago is situated on the African plate in an area tectonically much more stable than the Azores. Occasional earth tremors felt in Madeira are almost certainly reflexes from shocks in the crust affecting the Azores and continental Portugal. The epicentres of these shocks occur on an axis from the Azores to Gibraltar.

Soils

In parts of Madeira (above 800m) the heavy precipitation has made a profound alteration in the basalt to form clays that are reddish in colour. This coloration shows the presence of iron oxides. The forest areas have deeper soils with an organic layer. At the highest level the soils are skeletal. Below 700m many of the soils are man-made – the soils on the terraces having been brought up from the river mouths or down from the bases of the escarpments.

5 *Madeira Wine*

Most people have heard of madeira wine, but few know it. It is a very much lesser-known relative of port and sherry. Such sayings as, 'If it's too late for sherry and too early for the port, ring for the madeira' and 'Have some madeira, m'dear' are well known. However, few people know or appreciate the rich flavours of the four main varieties of madeira wine or are aware of its history.

Production of madeira is very small compared with that of sherry. It is made only on the one small island of Madeira, and production costs are high. There are four main varieties of madeira wine:

Sercial is pale in colour, light-bodied, dry or extra dry and should be served moderately chilled as an appetizer.

Verdelho is golden, medium-bodied, light and elegant. It is a medium-dry aperitif which is ideal with soup, a piece of cake (although madeira cake is a British invention), cheese, fruit or nuts, or as a nightcap.

Bual is a medium to dark dessert wine which is full-bodied and very fragrant.

Malmsey is a medium-dark to dark full-bodied, very fruity, luscious and fragrant dessert wine. Fine old Malmsey is ideal for after the desserts have been cleared away.

The early history of madeira wine is somewhat vague. The early settlers brought vines to Madeira and, according to tradition, Prince Henry the Navigator introduced the superior vine, *Malvasia candida*, into the island from Crete in an attempt to capture the trade in sweet wines from the Genoese and Venetians. In 1455 Luigi di Cadalmosto, an Italian traveller, visited Madeira and noted the excellent wines. There are references to madeira wine at the Courts of sixteenth-century Europe and in the works of Shakespeare. Almost certainly these were table wines for local use or intended as supplies for ships – not madeira wine as we know it today.

The marriage of Charles II and Catherine of Braganza was very important for madeira wine. In 1665 Charles issued an ordinance banning the export of European goods to 'English Plantations overseas' in pursuit of protectionist policies. The ban did not include Madeira, and an important trade opened up sending madeira wine to the Plantations (the West Indies and the American colonies such as Virginia, New England, New York and the Carolinas). The drinking of madeira became very popular in the New World, and the export of wine increased. By 1680 there were twenty-six firms in Funchal exporting wine, and ten of these were English. By 1780 the number of British houses had increased to over seventy.

It was during the eighteenth century that madeira wine as it is known today came into being. In the mid-eighteenth century fortification with brandy was begun. Towards the end of the same century *estufas* (heated chambers) came into use to reproduce the improvements in the wine which had been noted when it crossed the equator in the holds of ships, the changes being caused by the heat and not by the motion of the ship. As a result of these processes, madeira wine gained qualities which made it a rival of port and sherry.

In 1768 Captain Cook, in the *Endeavour* on his first voyage to the South Pacific, called at Madeira. According to records, he took on board some 3,000 gallons of wine for his ninety-four-man crew for the $2\frac{1}{2}$-year journey. Cook again took on wine on his second voyage, in *Resolution*, in 1772. In 1784 a Mr Higgins sold wine to a twenty-six-year-old Horatio Nelson, then captain of the frigate *Boreas*.

During the eighteenth century Madeira's importance grew as a port-of-call for ships *en route* for the Americas and the East, and the market for wine increased. Officers and officials returning to Britain after the American War of Independence took home with them a taste for madeira wine. From Britain the taste spread rapidly to the rest of Europe and to India, where it was very popular in clubs and officers' messes. In 1900 Cossart Gordon & Co issued a list of some 200 messes and clubs in India which they supplied with madeira wine.

In America Thomas Jefferson, George Washington and Benjamin Franklin were all connoisseurs of madeira wine, and the Declaration of Independence was toasted in it. To this day there are many collectors of old madeiras in the United States. The individual members of the Madeira Club of Savannah, Georgia (founded in 1776), own between them probably the finest collection of madeira wines in the world.

During the mid-nineteenth century, the wine trade was hit by a crisis of disease and lack of care and planning. The vines were attacked in 1852 by mildew (*Oidium tuckeri*) and again in 1872 by pest (*Phylloxera vastatrix*), both with very serious consequences. Production declined and exports were made at the expense of reserves accumulated in the warehouses. Many people considered planting coffee, tobacco, sugarcane and sugarbeet instead of vines. Many British and foreign merchants left the island as the wine trade declined. Other events which contributed to the decline of the madeira wine industry were the American Civil War (which meant a temporary loss of the American market) and the opening of the Suez Canal (which meant a reduction in the number of ships calling at Madeira).

With the onslaught of the *Phylloxera* crisis, peaking in the 1880s, American resistant hybrid vines were imported, the first in 1873 by Thomas Slapp Leacock. Not only were the American vines disease resistant: they were also more prolific.

In the late nineteenth and early twentieth centuries, the Krohn brothers (Danish in origin) had a very important market in Russia. Madeira wine was for many years the favourite wine of the Russian Court, and one of the Krohn family had been food-taster to the Tsar. Heather Krohn, widow of Raleigh Krohn, now lives in a converted windmill on the island of Porto Santo.

By the 1880s the chief importers of madeira wine were Russia, Germany, Great Britain, France and Brazil. In 1919, with 'prohibition' in the United States of America, a valuable market was lost. However, Scandinavia rapidly grew up as an important new market.

By 1913 companies began to amalgamate. First Welsh & Cunha joined forces with Henriques & Câmara to form the Madeira Wine Association Lda. In the years that followed they were joined by Donaldson's and Krohn Brothers. In 1925 Blandy & Leacock and other firms joined the Madeira Wine Association within which individual firms retained their separate identities and their own agents. Today the Madeira Winc Co Lda represents many famous names and brands, including all the British names. It has a permanent stock of about 10,000 pipes of wines and ships about fifty per cent of the island's wine exports. In addition the company owns many brand names from companies no longer in the madeira wine business, and these include Rutherford & Miles, Leacock, Bianchi, Ferraz and Welsh Brothers.

Many well-known firms remain independent of the Madeira Wine Co Lda, amongst them Henriques & Henriques, A.E. Henriques Lda, Justinho Henriques Filhos Lda, Veiga França (vinhos) Lda, Vinhos Barbeito (Madeira) Lda, H.M. Borges Sucrs Lda and Companhia Vinicola da Madeira Lda.

At the vineyard of Veiga França (vinhos) Lda in Estreito da Câmara de

Lobos there is an interesting museum of agriculture, and each September here, and in the Madeira Wine Company's lodge in Avenida Arriaga in Funchal, is celebrated the Wine Festival, a very colourful and enjoyable occasion. You can even join in the treading of the grapes – but remember to take off your shoes and socks first. The celebrations are accompanied by song and dance and local food, and the new wine is drunk. Just along from Reid's Hotel on Estrada Monumental is the most recent firm to be established in madeira wine – Vinhos Barbeito (Madeira) Lda. They have one of the most modern lodges in Funchal, with much of their production going to Japan.

The northern slopes of the island produce over half the grapes, but they are not of such fine quality as those of the south side. The best area for vines is around Estreito da Câmara de Lobos. The land is prepared in spring and early summer, and vines are planted in October so that they benefit from the winter rainfall and are well established by the spring.

The vines are propagated by cuttings. A trench one to $1\frac{1}{2}$m in depth is dug, and the base is lined with loose stones to prevent the roots going through to the hard soil beneath. The cuttings are then placed wide apart, to allow room for growth. The vines bear grapes in the third year after planting. They are trained in a corridor fashion over *latadas*, a sun-bleached framework of chestnut wood posts with a lattice of canes on top.

Pruning starts in January and is a skilled art. All non-productive wood must be cut out, and the skill lies in deciding which of the many buds are wood buds and which are fruit buds, and then in deciding which of the wood buds are likely to produce the most fruit buds. This work is often done by an old man of many years experience. In June similar skill is needed to strip some of the leaves from the vine to allow the sun to penetrate to the fruit to improve its richness. Only some of the leaves are stripped, however, as it is through the foliage that the vine breathes, and the cultivator must use his skill to decide which leaves to strip.

The first grapes are harvested from Porto Santo in mid-August, then (on Madeira) Malvasia, Tinta and Verdelho at altitudes up to 200m, then Boal and Tinta at high level, and finally Sercial at around 700m and Muscatel at sea-level in October and early November. The harvest, or vintage, is a family festive occasion. Women, children and old people fill 50kg baskets (increasingly being replaced today by plastic containers) for the men to carry to the lorries which transport the grapes to the wine lodges in Funchal. Only where the grapes are for local wine are they still trodden and pressed where picked.

At the wine lodges the grapes are weighed and graded before pressing. They are destalked and pulped with a light press which produces ninety per cent of the must (juice). Finally a heavy press crushes out the remainder of the must, but this is of an inferior quality. For Sercial and Verdelho, the skins are separated from the juice before fermentation. In the case of all the other varieties, the must and skins go into the fermentation tanks together.

Wine destined as a reserve is fortified before going into the *estufa*. Ordinary madeiras are fortified afterwards. Fine grape alcohol from Portugal, France and some Eastern Block countries is used for the fortification. In the *estufas* the wine is heated for a minimum of three months, but most shippers prefer up to six months at slightly lower temperatures. After the *estufagem*, the wine is cooled carefully. The wine is filtered or fined with bentonite or gelatine and is then put into oak scantling pipes for a period of twelve to eighteen months to rest (*estagio*). It is then racked (*passagem*), when it is pumped up so it can fall into a trough and air can pass through it. Finally it is stored in oak casks, from where it is drawn off for blending.

Soleras are wines which carry the date of the vintage wine with which the solera was begun. No more than ten per cent can be drawn off per year, and this amount must be replaced by old wine of quality. This process is continued until such time as the original solera would no longer exist, i.e. ten years. A solera is a blended wine made through a topping-up process and bridges the gap between a vintage and a blended madeira.

All madeiras are blended and the blender is an artist, giving the blend its distinctive characteristics. He is the most important man in the wine lodge and can smoke or drink spirits only in moderation so as not to spoil his palate. Usually he can spend only a limited time at one session in the tasting room as his work involves so much keen concentration. The tasting room needs an even temperature and good natural lighting, with silence and no distractions or interruptions. Smell and sight tell the taster everything, and taste confirms his ideas. Most tasters of Madeira rely almost entirely on their sense of smell. Once the taster has made his decisions, the lodge workmen carry out the blending process. This may take several weeks, depending on the volume of wine to be blended.

A number of wines are retained for blending only. Among these are Canteiro, Tinta and Arrobo. Canteiro is a wine which has been matured over many years without going into an *estufa*, and it is of a good age. Tinta is made from the *negra mole* grape and is used for colouring and for sweetening. Arrobo is used for sweetening as well as for giving body. The must is heated in a cauldron and boiled until it is reduced to one third of its volume to make the Arrobo. Whether or not the wine has been blended by the *solera* method or by actual blending, it is made up in *lotes* and left to rest until the parts have 'married'.

The whole production process is under the careful control of the inspectors of the Madeira Wine Institute, the official regulating body for all matters concerning madeira wine. The Institute also has a small museum, with many interesting photographs and equipment concerned with the production of madeira.

Madeira wine is relatively expensive and should not be used in basic cooking to give richness or tenderness where a cheaper red or white wine would suffice. However, it is well worth using in dishes which require the wine to be added at a later stage to give flavouring.

It is a very durable wine. Only a small minority of the wines are kept for a long time as vintage wines. Madeira wine need not be kept in a cellar but should be kept away from bright light and hot water pipes. Ordinary madeira has no sediment and does not need to be decanted. The wine needs re-corking every twenty years. A thin, plain, uncoloured glass best shows off the colour and richness of the wine.

Most of the wine lodges in Funchal welcome visitors and are willing to offer samples of the various blends. A very pleasant morning or afternoon excursion, whilst on holiday, is a visit to the Madeira wine lodges.

6 *Agriculture and Island Industries*

Levadas

This lush green mountainous island, with one of the best all-year-round climates in the world, is also a huge self-regulating reservoir which holds up to 200 million cubic metres of water. The rain seeps into and is held in volcanic ash above an impervious layer of basaltic clay and laterite. At the junction of these rock types, springs form and the water runs down ravines to the sea unless diverted into *levadas* (drainage channels). There are some 2,150km of *levada* channels, with 40km of tunnels. They were started as early as 1461, and the system is still being extended and improved today. The construction of *levadas* to carry irrigation and drinking-water has always been a difficult feat of engineering, and many men have been killed over the years in their construction. (Errors in calculation have been made at times, but discovered only when the water began to flow and it was found that the *levada* went uphill.) The majority of old *levadas* were built around 1580 and were of short length, bringing water from springs to agricultural land. By the beginning of the twentieth century there were some 200 *levadas* with a total length of 1,000km. Many of these were privately owned and water was unfairly distributed. By the 1930s only two thirds of the island's arable land were under cultivation and only half of that was irrigated.

In 1939 the government began to study and develop new *levadas*. Many of these are 1,000m above sea-level, where rainfall is plentiful. This water goes first to generate hydro-electric power and then to irrigate the land. Each smallholder has the right to receive water regularly for a certain length of time, and the *levadeiro* is the man responsible for ensuring this is done correctly. The water is diverted by ingenious and simple means, with large stones, sods of grass, old woollens and nylon stockings being used to block a channel and divert the water to another one to irrigate the land and fill the storage tanks.

The *levadas* have all been built by hand, in areas where access is impossible men and their picks being suspended by ropes from above. Many of the *levadas* have become tourist attractions. Their paths afford spectacular views, and new vistas open up around every corner. The paths are bordered with many trees and shrubs as well as hydrangeas, agapanthus and belladonna lilies. Many of the walks are suitable for everyone, but others can be risky and suitable only for people who are unaffected by vertigo. (There is a good booklet of walks describing over twenty-five of these, written by John and Pat Underwood: *Landscapes of Madeira*.) Some hotels and tour companies arrange escorted walks along the *levadas*. It is also possible to arrange with taxi-drivers to drop you at one point and collect you some hours later from another.

Agriculture

Cultivation extends to about 600m, ending at a lower level on the colder north side of the island. Forest extends up to 1,200m and covers an area of over 19,500 hectares. The main varieties of trees to be found are pine (*Pinus pinaster*) and eucalyptus. There are also significant numbers of acacia and chestnut trees, along with many other varieties. Over the years the weather and man have been responsible for destroying parts of the forested areas and, although some re-afforestation has taken place, large areas have remained depleted for many years. Above the forest the land is rocky and exposed and is left to sheep and goats. There is also cattle pasture on the plateau area of Paúl da Serra. In the Poiso area are to be found wild ponies and, more rarely, small wild pigs.

Almost every slope in Madeira is terraced from sea-level to far up the mountain side. The normal method of construction has always been to build retaining walls between six and ten metres high out of huge basaltic rocks. A dry-stone wall method is used to ensure free drainage. The soil in the terraces is the result of sheer hard work. It either comes from the river beds or is scraped from rock (*tufa*) higher up the mountain – either way it has to be carried a long way over steep slopes.

There is little mechanical cultivation of terraces as they are small and access to them is difficult for machinery. Among the traditional agricultural tools and implements which remain today, you can see in common use the *enchada*, a cross between a pick and a hoe which first came to Madeira in 1440 from the Algarve, and also a serrated sickle (*fouce*) for grass-cutting and a kind of pruning hook (*podão*). Traditionally everything is carried in baskets on the head or shoulders, and you can often see these large wicker baskets full of cabbage, potatoes, oranges, apples or whatever is in season waiting at the side of the road for transport to the market in Funchal.

To a large extent the crops grown vary with altitude – they can be grown to a higher altitude on the warmer, less exposed south side. From sea-level to 300m sugarcane, bananas, mango, papaia, vine, custard apple (*anona*), fig, loquat and avocado pear are common. Above 300m maize, wheat and other cereals are grown, as well as cabbage, runner beans, broad beans, potatoes, apples, pears, cherries, peaches, sweet chestnuts, walnuts and sweet potatoes. In the eastern part of the island grow large crops of onions which are much milder than the British ones and more palatable. Also widely grown are tomatoes and strawberries, nowadays mainly under plastic sheeting.

Bananas are a popular crop. In Madeira the plantain (*Musa paradisiaca*) which is very good in cooking has been grown since the island was first settled. In 1842-3 the 'Cavendish' banana was brought from Demerara (it originated in China). In 1911, in order to secure return freight to Lisbon, ship owners began to export bananas. Today all the bananas exported go to mainland Portugal.

Strawberries have been grown in the island since 1860, but raspberries, gooseberries and currants, tried many times, have never met with success. Coffee was grown successfully in Madeira until 1882 when there were problems of root disease. Today experiments in growing coffee are being made.

Two unusual fruits very much prized in Madeira are the pittanga (*Eugenia braziliensis*) and the tree tomato (*Cyphomandra betacea*). The small ribbed orangy-red fruit of the pittanga has a very distinctive, slightly bitter taste. The fruit of the tree tomato looks like a cross between a red pepper and an elongated tomato. Only the inside, which is full of seeds, is eaten, as the outer skin is very bitter. The taste is somewhere between a guava and a grape.

The island of Porto Santo grows cereals, vines, figs, market garden produce, melons and pumpkins. The vineyards produce table grapes and some very good wine. Over 200m above sea-level barley is grown and there is pastureland for sheep and cattle, with a small amount of woodland. Most of the island is cattle pasture, in great contrast to Madeira. The donkey is the beast of burden, and windmills, originally used for grinding maize, abound.

In Madeira it is a rare sight to see a cow. Most cows are kept in small sheds on terraced land and are taken out for weekly walks on the end of a rope. They need to be manicured regularly because of the lack of exercise. The cowshed has a bed of straw or bracken (or even camellias). When driving in the countryside you often see walking human haystacks – people, who have been out cutting grass for their cows, returning home

The Main Seasons for Locally Produced Fruit

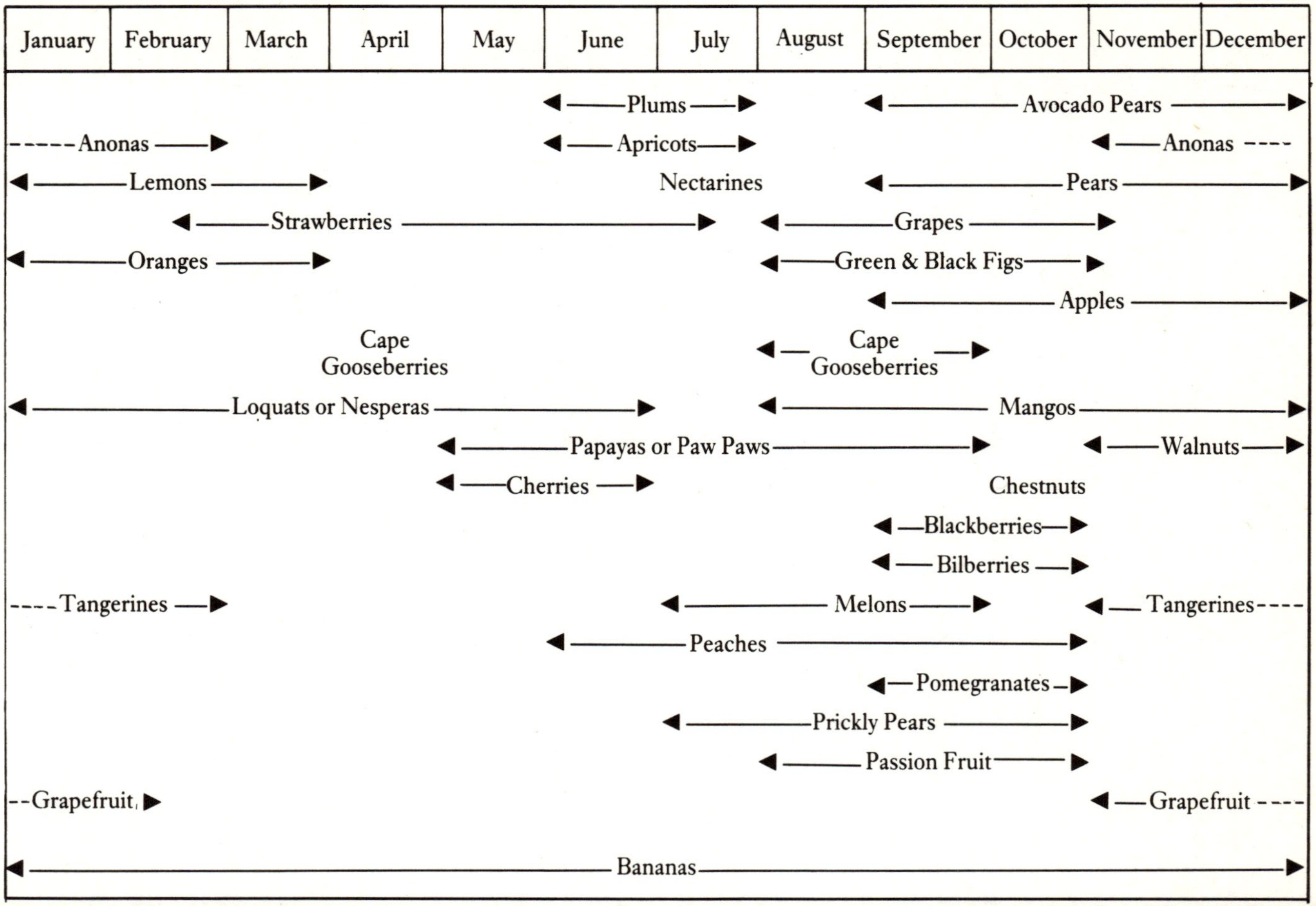

and walking down the road often with only their legs showing beneath their enormous bundles.

The last decade has seen the growth of orchids and other sub-tropical flowers for export. The government is trying to improve fruit and vegetable production, and recently the kiwi fruit, which is known for its prolific yield and good export price, has been introduced.

There is a constant flow of people leaving the land and going into service and hotel jobs, particularly in Funchal. The young people, in particular, as they become better educated are reluctant to work the land – which is very hard work for a low income. In addition much land is being left to go to ruin, especially around Funchal, where it may be sold for building speculation. On the other hand there are beginning to be larger, more profitable units specializing in market gardening, floriculture or cattle or pig production.

Sugar

Sugar was historically a very important crop in Madeira, and many economic and political battles have been fought over its production and monopoly of manufacture. From the earliest times it was said that sugar was brought to Madeira by Prince Henry the Navigator to capture the trade from the Genoese and Venetians.

In 1452 the first sugarmill (water-powered) was constructed. By the end of the fifteenth century, sugar was a large export, Flanders being the biggest market. The importance of sugar production can be judged from a story dating from 1516 when Simon Gonçalves de Câmara, the Governor of the island, whose son had been made a bishop, sent a present to the Pope of a model of the papal palace with figures representing the whole Court and the Cardinals – all made in sugar. Indeed, the Arms of Funchal bear five sugar loaves.

Throughout the history of Madeira, sugarcane and vines have rivalled each other. After the failure of the vines in 1852, the area of sugarcane increased. In 1856 Severiano Alberto de Freitas Ferraz opened a new steam-driven sugarmill in Funchal. Further up a Mr Hinton opened a steam-driven mill at Torreão. In 1873 the Sao João sugar factory opened with the most modern machinery, but it had been driven into bankruptcy by the 1880s. The sugarmill at Torreão outdistanced all its rivals through improved machinery and good management by its owner.

In the late nineteenth and early twentieth centuries, the high import duties on sugar (as much as 300 per cent at times) prevented the import of cheaper foreign sugars. By this time the Hintons more or less had a monopoly on sugar processing, and more and more land was being turned over to sugarcane production. Too much sugar was being produced, so the excess was made into *aguardente* (sugarcane rum) but this was said to be causing alcoholism as the unemployed took to drinking cheap *aguardente*.

Today sugar is no longer processed on the island. The production of sugarcane steadily declined until in 1985 the refinery closed. The sugar consumed in the island is now imported in bulk from mainland Portugal and bagged here.

Wicker

Willows are grown in the damp valleys of the island. Madeiran willow, with its fine supple shoots, is never allowed to grow tall. The shoots are always cut off near the ground. The willow is cut between January and March, left in water until it starts to sprout and then peeled and dried.

The wicker industry began in Camacha, where it is still concentrated today. It was here that the Hintons and other British families had their summer houses. The wicker industry began with the manufacture of copies of cane furniture – popular at that time in Germany and Britain – for the British families, and then for the hotels in Funchal. It proved very popular and from this start began the exportation of wicker furniture. James Taylor and William Hinton brought baskets from Italy to be used as models. Today whole family groups produce basketwork at home in what is very much a cottage industry.

There are now over 1,200 different models made and some 2,500 people are employed. As well as being sold in Camacha and in the Funchal craftwork shops, much production is now exported, especially to the USA and Europe. Over 900 tonnes of wicker are produced annually and exported as bottle-covers, baskets or furniture. A visit to Camacha to see the enormous variety of products and the families skilfully weaving the willow is an interesting half-day excursion by bus or taxi.

Embroidery

Embroidery was introduced to the island by Miss Elizabeth (Bella) Phelps, a British resident, during the period when the *oidium* disease struck the vines between 1852 and 1862. At first the embroidery was sold privately, but then Miss Phelps found agents in London, Robert and Frank Wilkinson, who established themselves in Madeira in 1862, by which time over 1,000 women were employed in the industry. The work became known as 'Madeira fine art embroidery'. Embroidery remains largely a cottage industry with thousands of girls and women employed as outworkers. All the processes other than the actual embroidery are carried out in the numerous 'embroidery factories', most of which are located in Funchal. The materials (thread and Irish and Swiss linen) are imported. Some of the designs are imported, others are composed in the factories by stylists – either an original design or one based on a specific order or according to the article's intended market. The finished design is then transferred onto heavy-duty tracing paper and pierced by a *picador*, a machine which makes tiny holes along the traced lines. The tracing paper is then put on top of the cloth to be embroidered and a stamper wipes the surface of the paper with a cloth soaked in blue dye. The design is in this way transferred onto the material (linen, cotton, silk, organdie, etc). The cloth and thread to be used are then sent to the outworkers who very often work in the open air with their friends, talking, watching the world go by or listening to the radio. The work takes many hours and is done with the type and number of stitches appropriate to the fabric and in the way demanded by the factory. The embroidery is returned to the factory where the open work flowers and patterns are skilfully cut out. It is then carefully washed and ironed. A great deal of embroidery is exported to the USA and Europe, with Italy now the biggest market. All Madeiran embroidery is hand-made and its production, quality and exportation is carefully controlled by the *Instituto de Bordados, Tapeçaria e Artesanato da Madeira* (Madeiran Institute of Embroidery, Tapestry and Handcrafts). It is all good quality and every piece carries a special seal to prove it is genuine Madeiran embroidery. However, for a very fine table set, be prepared for a price shock.

Tapestry

Tapestry is a traditional craft but its commercialization in Madeira is fairly recent. It was introduced by Herbert Kiekeben, who arrived in Madeira to live in 1938. An artist in his own right, he painted pictures onto canvas, and these were then sewn. These pictures were original designs, landscapes, old master copies and floral pieces. Within sixteen years tapestry-making had become an important and interesting local craft industry.

Other manufacturing industry in the island is concerned mostly with the tourist and craft industries and includes the making of straw hats, pottery, ceramics, inlaid wooden items, the traditional Madeiran half-length boots, costumes and hats in the traditional style, plus the manufacturing of food products, such as biscuits, for the local market. One of the few exceptions is a small factory, mainly employing women, which produces electronic components. Service industries predominate for employment in the island offices, shops, banks, garages etc, as well as the whole infrastructure which is associated with tourism.

Fishing

A romantic vista on a moonlit holiday night is across the Bay of Funchal, and most nights it is made more so by the hundreds of flickering lights on the small fishing boats. These boats, the same shape at the bow and the stern and often painted in very bright colours, can stand up to very high seas. They are fishing mainly for *espada* (scabbard fish) which is caught four to five kilometres off shore in depths of over 800m, using lines with about 150 hooks. This very ugly fish, rather like an eel but with large head and many teeth, is versatile and tasty and can be cooked in many different ways.

Tunny fishing is also very important, and many are caught in the waters around Madeira. It is a popular dish, and tunny steak (*bifes de atum*) is tasty served with local onions. In recent years tunny fishing has become a popular sport around Madeira, and there are now many sport fishing boats available for hire. There are also trawlers for net fishing which, as well as fishing around Madeira, work off the African coast. Other fish commonly caught include *cherne*, grey mullet, mackerel and *chicharro*.

The Regional Government has recently opened a new fish-freezer cold store and has replaced the fish landing dock with a new one near the freezer plant and the road entrance to the harbour. The Government of Madeira is also in co-operation with the Norwegian Government undertaking scientific studies of fishing grounds and methods of fishing.

7 *Island Transport*

At one time the best way of travelling between the different parts of the island was by boat. Nowadays there are still tourist boats taking visitors to see Cabo Girão or Machico or to swim in the sheltered coves, but Madeira now has a fine road network stretching to every small hamlet, whether it be on the top of a mountain or in the bottom of a valley. Most of the main roads are in good condition, but driving can be very tiring as there are many bends, and most of the roads are built onto the mountainside with deep ravines dropping away below, and you never quite know what's around the corner – be it a bus straddling the centre of the road to take a corner or a group of children playing football in the road. It would be difficult to average more than 30 km/hr driving round Madeira. It needs a full day to explore just one of the island circuits thoroughly. Many of the roads have laybys with picnic tables and bench-seats, and many places are supplied with wood and simple cooking stoves for barbequeing sardines and *espetada* (chunks of meat on a skewer cooked over an open fire of laurel twigs).

Car hire is expensive in Madeira considering that one cannot travel many miles in a day, but it is not excessive if the car is shared between four people. Taxis are available for hire for full- or half-day excursions, and the cost for four compares very well with hiring a car for a day – without the trouble of driving yourself. Most taxi-drivers also know good simple restaurants in the country for lunch.

There are many buses in Madeira, and all routes start and finish in Funchal, where most buses can be found arriving, departing or just dumped on Avenida das Comunidades Madeirenses (the main road along the sea front). Timetables are sometimes available from the Tourist Office, although the times are not always reliable and many buses and routes are not shown in the timetable. Tell your hotel porter where you wish to go and he will usually know the correct bus. Seeing the island by service bus is the cheapest way and can be the most interesting.

Many years ago we went to Boaventura and back by bus. We caught the bus outside the Savoy in Avenida Infante at six o'clock one winter's morning. The bus was almost full and we had to sit separately, and it was obvious that, as foreigners, we were the object of intense interest. Once we had passed Câmara de Lobos, all the roads were cobbled. When the bus stopped at Ribeira Brava for ten minutes, all the Madeirans got out and many, including the bus driver, crossed the road to the bar for a drink. When it was time to set off again, there was a lot of noisy discussion, live chickens in baskets were moved and we were ushered into the front window seat across from the driver so we could see the view together. This proved a privilege we did not altogether enjoy as, at that time, the road over Encumeada pass was only a very narrow shelf which fell away on our side of the road! We had decided to return by service bus in the other direction so as to complete a round trip. This meant a four-hour wait in Boaventura where we were observed by amused barefooted children, obviously unused to foreigners. For want of a better location, we ate our picnic lunch in the cemetery with superb views of the north coast. The return journey was on a very old bus which picked up people, with baskets of vegetables ready for Funchal market, all along its route. Snow was falling as we drove from Ribeiro Frio to Poiso. We arrived back in Funchal some twelve hours after we had first caught the bus. We should add that animals and farm produce are no longer allowed on public transport.

For those who do not wish to explore the island by bus, hire car or taxi, there are organized coach excursions arranged by both tour companies and hotels, and these visit every part of the island.

Walking is very popular nowadays in Madeira, especially along the *levadas* and mountain paths. It is, however, essential to wear sensible clothes. Just because it is 21°C (70°F) beside the hotel swimming pool does not mean that the weather is the same in the hills – it may well be raining there or the mist may be descending. It is essential to wear good walking shoes and take waterproofs, some food/chocolate and a good map or guide-book. The Tourist Office or your hotel porter can advise you. Care needs to be taken not to start fires in the forests, especially in summer and autumn before the rains begin, when the foliage is tinder dry, and there are many forest fires every year.

Madeira once had its own peculiar forms of transport, but most of these are now seen only on display and not in use. The bullock sledge (*carro de bois*) was a canopied carriage without wheels which slid along the cobbled streets on wooden runners and was hauled by two bullocks harnessed beside each other. This contraption was invented by an

Englishman, Captain Bulkeley of the Second Life Guards, in 1848 for his wife who had difficulty in walking and who felt sick when using the other forms of transport then available. It was really an adaptation for people of the much earlier sledge used for transporting wine casks. This form of transport was available in Funchal until the early 1980s for tourist excursions in the centre of Funchal and near the Savoy and Sheraton Hotels. Sadly these have now disappeared, pushed aside by the needs of the motor car.

The hammock, which was slung from a long pole carried on the shoulders of two men, was used for transporting the sick and infirm across rough country terrain and, in and around Funchal, for the rich and for the tourists who were carried through the dirty, and sometimes muddy, streets. These hammocks were used until the 1920s to carry tourists to Monte and the surrounding countryside, the pole-bearers being human taxis.

The Monte toboggan (*carro de cesto* or *carro do Monte*), unlike the bullock sledge and the hammock which now remain as exhibition pieces, is still in daily use, albeit as a tourist attraction. It was invented by Mr Gordon as a rapid means of transport between his house at Monte and his office in Funchal. The toboggan consists of a wide wicker basket with a cushioned seat, set on wooden runners. Powered by gravity, it transports tourists down the slippery cobblestones from Monte to Funchal. White-suited drivers, wearing straw hats and Madeiran boots, run alongside, pushing the toboggan to gain momentum. They then jump onto the runners behind the toboggan, steering and restraining it with ropes. The descent, like a big dipper, is exhilarating but perfectly safe. Ernest Hemingway is reputed to have considered the descent from Monte in a toboggan one of the strongest emotions of his life. From the bottom, the drivers return to Monte by taxi, and the toboggans by truck, ready for the next ride.

There used to be a rack-and-pinion railway between Funchal, Monte and Terreiro da Luta. Sadly, it was closed in 1939. What an attraction it would have been today. Construction of this short-lived railway was commenced in 1891 and two years later, on 13 April 1893, the Danish boat *Concordia* arrived from Antwerp with the rollingstock. In 1894 the German steamship *Zeus* left Antwerp with another carriage and locomotive. In 1919 one of the locomotives suffered a boiler explosion, resulting in four dead and many injured. The Company struggled on until it finally closed in 1939. The equipment was sold for scrap, and the line was dismantled in 1942. Today you can still see the bridge which carried the railway at Monte, as well as the railway station.

The island of Porto Santo has a regular air link with Madeira by a small Air Portugal plane which only takes a few minutes. Until recently, the sea crossing – in a flat-bottomed former Rhine riverboat, called the *Pirata Azul* – could cause concern to those who were not good sailors as the channel could be very rough indeed. It took between three and four hours, depending on the weather. All passengers were issued with black plastic bags as a matter of course and were sheeted in when the going was really rough. The Madeirans describe the voyage as uphill to Porto Santo and downhill on the return journey, as the outward journey from Madeira is always rougher. In 1983 a new boat, *Independencia*, came into service. This is a modern catamaran with capacity for 244 passengers and makes the journey in about 1½ hours. In winter it makes an early morning crossing, returning in the late afternoon and allowing some six hours ashore in Porto Santo. In summer it makes two complete round trips. The island of Porto Santo has one of the last unspoilt beaches in Europe where, for eight kilometres, you can walk along a white sandy beach washed by the Atlantic Ocean and bordered by sand dunes. The island is beginning to see an increase in foreign visitors, but as yet very little development has taken place.

8 *The British in Madeira*

Wine Merchants

Apart from explorers and travellers, one of the first Englishmen to settle in Madeira was William Bolton, in 1695, when he took advantage of the Act of Charles II which prohibited the export of goods grown or manufactured in Europe to the West Indies and American Colonies, unless shipped from British ports in British ships, with Madeira specifically excluded from its terms. The way was thereby opened for English merchants to establish themselves in the island, and William Bolton came to Madeira as an agent for Robert Heysham of London, who had a brother in Barbados to whom Bolton shipped a large quantity of wine. Bolton's letters (*The Letters of an English Merchant in Madeira, 1695-1714*) are preserved and have been published part in book form and part in duplicated form.

There had been an English career Consul in Madeira since 1658 (although this was not the first foreign consulate), and by 1680 there were ten English wine-shippers in the island. Although, sadly, the archives of the British Consulate in Funchal were lost in a flood in 1803, a few documents were saved, including a notice of the Annual General Meeting of the British Factory on 26 October 1722. There is, therefore, something of a gap in the information available until 1741, when a young man of fifteen years named John Leacock arrived from London where his father, who was a weaver, had died. John Leacock had been educated at Christ's Hospital in London and been apprenticed to a firm of British merchants in the island, Catanach & Murdoch. When this apprenticeship ended, on 11 March 1749, he remained with the same firm as a clerk.

In 1748 a young Scot, Francis Newton, sailed for Madeira from Gravesend. He became a book-keeper to Dom João José da Câmara, one of the largest landowners at that time. During this period both John Leacock and Francis Newton were learning about the wine trade and exploring the possibilities of setting up their own businesses. Francis Newton was to found the firm Cossart Gordon & Co, which is one of the oldest and most respected madeira wine merchants and is today incorporated in the Madeira Wine Company Lda.

In 1757 Mr Murdoch died, John Leacock married his widowed daughter, Mrs Durban, and founded what is now Leacock & Company Lda. Today this is one of the largest companies in Portugal, with very wide interests and over 1,500 employees. It is still very much a family company and is headed by William Leacock, a direct descendant of John Leacock. Its headquarters are in Madeira, and its interests are as varied as embroidery, vehicles, construction, electronics and general import-export, as well as, until recently, tobacco. It no longer has interests in madeira wine, but the name Leacock continues as one of the most distinguished brand names within the Madeira Wine Company Lda. The Leacocks have preserved many letters and documents over the years, including the original indenture of apprenticeship of John Leacock to Catanach & Murdoch in 1741.

Thomas Slapp Leacock, a grandson of John Leacock, was head of the firm during the years the *phylloxera* was attacking the vines. He was one of the leading entomologists of his day and began experimenting with ways of overcoming the disease when it first appeared in Madeira, in 1873, until he finally succeeded (in 1883) in controlling it in his vineyards. He subsequently bequeathed the results of his research to Cambridge University. John Milburn Leacock, the first resident of Madeira to own a motor car and son of Thomas Slapp Leacock, continued to export fine madeiras and win gold medals. He also built up the island's banana trade.

In the early years of the nineteenth century more British names began to appear, all connected with the madeira wine trade. These names are still to be found on prestigious labels on madeira wine bottles.

John Blandy was a quartermaster with General Beresford's force when it occupied the island. He returned to Britain to marry and came back to Madeira in 1811, having opened his commercial house in 1808 and begun to deal in wine. In 1850, at his *quinta* (mansion) in Sto da Serra, John Blandy made the first butter to be sold commercially in Madeira. His grandson, John Burden Blandy, was a great public benefactor and gave land for building the sea wall. In 1882, when the Bourbon sugarcane crop began to fail, he imported other types from Mauritius. The company expanded into coaling, shipping and banking. In the disastrous *oidium* plague of 1852, the company had the good sense to buy up a great proportion of the old wine on the island, thus acquiring excellent stocks. Today Blandy Brothers is a very large and important company on the island with such very diverse interests as madeira wine, Reid's Hotel, engineering, electronics, shipping and insurance agencies, newspaper publishing and tourism. With branches in Lisbon and the Canaries, it is still administered by members of the Blandy family. The present administrator, Richard Blandy, is the Honorary British Consul.

Thomas Gordon of Balmaghie joined Francis Newton's firm in 1758, and the company became Newton & Gordon. His grandson, Russell Manners Gordon, became a partner in the firm in 1850, and in 1857 he married Dona Filomena Gabriela Correia Brandão Henriques of Noronha, Viscountess Torre Bella. The King of Portugal offered to raise him to the title of Count Torre Bella on condition he took Portuguese nationality. Gordon accepted the title and became the largest land- and vineyard-owner on the island. He did, however, have to retire from the firm as he was no longer a British national.

William Cossart arrived in Madeira in 1808 from Ireland, where he had been the agent for Newton, Gordon, Murdoch & Co. The Cossarts were Huguenots but had been living in Ireland for many years. In 1831 the company became Newton Gordon Cossart & Co, and then in 1861 Cossart Gordon & Co. It is still in the madeira trade, and Noël Cossart is one of the foremost experts on madeira wine alive today. He recently wrote an excellent book entitled *Madeira – the Island Vineyard*.

In 1803 William Grant arrived from Nairn in Scotland and in 1814 helped to found Rutherford & Grant, wine merchants. After a series of partnerships and re-groupings, the company became Rutherford & Miles. H.P. Miles had started the brewery in Madeira in 1872. The labels of the wine company are still to be seen today, and their wine is shipped by the Madeira Wine Company Lda. The brewery which H.P. Miles started is still in existence and is run by Anthony Cossart-Miles, his great-grandson who, from a very modern brewery, produces excellent local beers under the 'Coral' label. The brewery also produces a number of soft drinks, and bottles others under licence, as well as being involved in the importation of other drinks.

Other British names which have been associated with the madeira wine trade over the past 200 years include Charles O.L. Power, who came to Madeira in 1878 and lived in Quinta Deão. He was a great horticulturist and introduced many species of rare flowering trees to the island. His son, Charles Power, wrote a famous guide-book to Madeira which was regularly up-dated during the first half of this century. Other names include John Shorbridge, Henry Drury, Robert Donaldson and Welsh Brothers, who were one of the early firms involved in the formation of the Madeira Wine Association. George Day Welsh came to Madeira at the end of the eighteenth century and married the important and rich Vicência Ludovina de Freitas, whose family were large landowners in the Madalena do Mar area.

Traders, Clergy and Characters

One of the most successful families in Madeira at the end of the last century was the Hintons. William Hinton was born in Naples in 1817, the son of a Wiltshire landowner. He came to Madeira in 1838 for health reasons and in 1841 married the daughter of Robert Wallas, a wine-shipper and steam-driven flourmill owner. Some years later William Hinton started a steam-driven sugarmill which his son Harry expanded into a vast sugar empire, with a factory at the Torreão. Today this company is administered by Jimmy Welsh and is a large commercial company with interests in vehicles, fuel oils, electronics and shipping. Harry Hinton was a well-known character of his day. He had been educated in Britain and in 1875, as an eighteen-year-old student, had brought the first football to Madeira – some thirteen years before it was ever played on the Portuguese mainland. The first game played in Madeira was at William Hinton's *quinta* in Camacha.

Elizabeth Phelps, daughter of the scholar and wine-shipper Joseph Phelps, was responsible for the introduction of the embroidery trade in the island (see page 54). She taught women to embroider designs she herself had made as an addition to the income of families hit by the destruction of the vines by the *oidium* disease in the 1850s. Her mother, Elizabeth Phelps, was a driving force behind the re-afforestation of large parts of the island.

Robert Page, who came to the island at the beginning of the nineteenth century in 1804 joined the firm of Joseph Phelps, which later became Phelps & Page. During his short stay in Madeira, he was a great benefactor of the island. Among his public works (mentioned in *Elucidario Madeirense* by Silva and Meneses), he was responsible for building houses of refuge near the exposed mountain passes, and public fountains for thirsty travellers all over Funchal, at his own expense. He also had repaired many of the roads and bridges that were damaged in the great flood of 1803 and built a bridge at Câmara de Lobos, improved the municipal theatre and presented six beds and a hundred blankets to the hospital. He was best known for rebuilding the Milagres Chapel in Machico.

Henry Veitch, from Selkirk in Scotland, was very colourful and a well-liked figure in Madeira. He was appointed British Consul by George

Boys diving for coins thrown by passengers into Funchal Harbour in the late nineteenth century

A busy scene in Funchal Roads in the mid-nineteenth century

Mid-nineteenth century engraving showing traditional Madeiran costume

Loo Rock or the island of Nossa Senhora da Conceição in the mid-nineteenth century – now part of the mole of Funchal Harbour

Zeppelin over the Bay of Funchal in 1932. The Graf Zeppelin made 148 crossings of the Atlantic

Krohn Brothers Wine Shippers in 1900 showing the wine press (*lagar*)

A windmill in Porto Santo around 1900

Wicker workers in Camacha. The craft was introduced to the island British residents in the last half of the nineteenth century

nbroidery and woollens for sale at the viewpoint, Cabo Girão

A picturesque *levada* path near Serra d'Água

Constructing a *levada* in 1949

III in 1809. A wealthy and handsome 'man of many parts', he owned considerable property in Funchal and designed his own town house (the large house, with a tower, which the Madeira Wine Institute now occupies) and his favourite country residence, Quinta do Jardim da Serra, where he built his own mausoleum and was buried. He also designed the English Church.

Although, as we have seen, in 1828 Veitch was dismissed from his consulship for having addressed Napoleon as 'Your Majesty' instead of plain 'General' when he met the vanquished Emperor *en route* for St Helena, he had become such a popular figure in Madeira that, after representations from the island, he was reinstated by Lord Palmerston in 1831. He continued as Consul until 1836.

The famous nineteenth-century scientist William Thomson (who later became Lord Kelvin) was another visitor to Madeira. He came during the laying of the trans-Atlantic cable during 1865-6. He met Fanny Blandy, who is said to have been the only person to understand what he was talking about, and she used flags to signal to him in the harbour from the family Quinta da Santa Luzia. He returned to Madeira to marry her in the English Church in 1874. After this he spent long periods in Madeira until his death in 1907. Some of his inventions in the field of navigational instruments can still be found in the island. A few can be seen in the travel agency of João Silveiro Pires in Avenida Zarco.

Dr Michael Grabham (1840-1938), son-in-law of Charles Ridpath Blandy and brother-in-law of Lord Kelvin was still a practising physician when he died aged ninety-eight. He was a prolific writer on biology and botany and carried out much research in Madeira, including scientific studies into the island's climate, plants and fish. Although he married into one of the long-established British families and lived on the island for so long, Dr Grabham still bemoaned the exclusiveness of the British in Madeira and said he always felt like an outsider.

Mary Jane Wilson was born in Madras, India, on 3 October 1840. She came to live in Madeira in 1880 and two years later opened St George's High School in the Palace of São Pedro (where the Municipal Museum is now housed). This was attended by the daughters of the best society in Funchal until she closed it in 1892. She then rebuilt the old hospital in Santa Cruz and opened a pharmacy there, where she looked after the sick of that area. Mary Jane Wilson founded a religious order in the island, whose members worked in the hospitals and taught in the many parish schools.

During the winter of 1907-8, sick seamen landed from a steamship were found to be suffering from smallpox. Within a few weeks the disease had spread rapidly amongst the poorer people of Funchal, especially among the families of the boatmen. There had been no serious outbreak in the island for over twenty years, so the majority were neither immune nor vaccinated (there was great reluctance to be vaccinated). When things were at their worst and it appeared the disease would spread over the whole island, Sister Mary Jane Wilson offered, if the government would put into good order the hospital at Lazareto (which had been damaged and looted during riots), to take the group of sisters of whom she was in charge to nurse the sick there. Within two weeks the hospital was ready. The sisters had no money for food and medicines, but they received a continuous stream of charitable donations. Because Sister Wilson had spent much of her life nursing the sick and the poor, she had their confidence and they flocked to the hospital. From this date the disease was halted and its final disappearance coincided with a strong *leste*. In recent years a road in Funchal has been named after Sister Mary Jane Wilson.

Dr Robert R. Kalley was born in Mount Florida, Glasgow, in 1809. He became a medical missionary and came to Madeira in 1838, arriving in the island at a time of great social and economic crisis, to which he reacted by opening schools and a hospital where he dispensed free treatment.

Having visited Britain in 1845, where he had meetings with various Protestant groups, on his return Dr Kalley began to use his talents, as a gifted doctor and an eloquent and persuasive orator, to convert the people of Madeira. He began to distribute literature, including readings from the New Testament, to the school pupils and the patients of his hospital. Reaction against him, in the predominantly Roman Catholic island, grew until, on 9 August 1846, the *quinta* where he lived was surrounded and attacked by a large crowd of people. Dr Kalley was forced to flee the island and was smuggled, via the British Consulate, to a British ship in the harbour. He went to Illinois in the United States of America, from where he summoned his closest followers (from Santa Cruz, Santo da Serra and Machico), whose descendants still live in that state, especially in Springfield and Jacksonville. Those remaining in Madeira were subjected to persecution and many emigrated to the West Indies. A short while after his flight, Dr Kalley put in a claim for compensation for £1,574, through the British Government, for the damage the crowd had caused to his house. This claim gave rise to much discussion in the local and national Press, and the Portuguese Government did eventually settle the claim in full in 1853.

The Reverend Richard Thomas Lowe was a Cambridge graduate and eminent naturalist chosen by the members of the English Church to be their minister in 1833. However, matters between him and his congregation gradually deteriorated as he was thought to be very 'High Church', and a bitter dispute broke out between 1845 and 1848 between 'High' and 'Low' Church supporters. Much to the disapproval of the majority of the congregation at this time, a petition was sent to Queen Victoria, and eventually Lowe was dismissed by Lord Palmerston, but he was still supported by the Bishop of London who had issued his licence. In 1848, when the new chaplain for the English Church arrived, Lowe set up a rival church (the Beco Chapel) with his own supporters, who numbered about one third of the English Church members, and took with him communion plate and silver from the English Church. He held rival services until his return to Britain in 1852 to take up a stipend at Lee in Lincoln, when he was succeeded at the Beco Chapel by a Mr Hossmer. However, the Bishop of London refused Hossmer a licence and the following November issued one for the encumbent of the English Church. Thereafter the Beco Chapel closed and was used only occasionally by an unlicensed chaplain until its final closure in 1893 – when six pieces of gilded silver plate were returned to the English Church.

During the winter of 1847-8 Britain's Dowager Queen Adelaide stayed in the island. She attended the English Church until Lowe was dismissed and then tactfully discovered she had her own chaplain and therefore did not need to attend either of the rival churches.

Lowe visited the island several times after his return to Britain, and in 1874 he and his wife were lost at sea when the SS *Liberia* sank *en route* for Madeira. In 1875 a memorial was erected to him in the British Cemetery.

British Influence in Madeira

There was a British Factory in Madeira, but unlike Lisbon and Oporto the island had no British Factory House. It was usual for the British trading community in Portugal to establish a chamber of commerce known as a 'Factory'. The Consul's house was where the meetings were usually held. It is certain that there was a meeting in 1722 but, as almost all the records of the British Consul were lost in the flood of 1803, it is not known exactly when the British Factory began. In the nineteenth century, the British Factory Committee was of vital importance. This Committee met on a regular basis, made rules and regulations, administered charitable funds financed by a tax levied on imports, paid the expenses and salary of a chaplain, physician and surgeon, awarded pensions, buried paupers, assisted shipwrecked mariners and paid the passages of destitute persons stranded in Madeira. It also regulated, amongst the British wine-shippers, the price of wines for export. In 1826, when the members of the British Factory were worried by reports that a daily newspaper was about to be published in Funchal, they decided to set up a fund for the protection of any British subject attacked by the newspaper. The British Factory as such had virtually been dissolved by 1812, although a few 'Select Merchants' continued to hold meetings under the title of 'The Factory' until 1848.

One of the privileges which British residents did enjoy, under the provisions of an old treaty, was the right to choose their own judge, the *Conservador dos Ingleses*, who was, in fact, usually the *Corregedor* (Chief Judge) of the island. He was paid an annual sum by the British and tried any cases where there was a problem between them and the Portuguese. This right disappeared in 1842, and thereafter they had to be tried in a normal Portuguese court, but the jury had to be half British and half Portuguese – this right has also, of course, long since disappeared.

There is still a lot of British furniture, silver and paintings in the island, especially seventeenth- and eighteenth-century works. When Britons came to Madeira, they built themselves houses and then sent home for their furniture and china. There have always been rumours that Thomas Chippendale and George Hepplewhite once resided and worked here, but no proof of this can be found. A surprising amount of work to be found in the island does, however, show their influence. Many of the old families and old *quintas* still have good collections of antiques, augmented over the years by visitors who used to sell china, silver and furniture to pay their bills before leaving the island. For example, the china which Queen Adelaide brought with her from Britain still exists more or less in its entirety in one Portuguese household in Funchal. In the early years of this century, many a collector found Madeira a happy hunting ground. Prices of antiques at auction now, however, are very high.

There has long been a tradition of skilled furniture-making in the island, making copies of British and French pieces. Today this craft industry continues – on an individual basis as well as in a factory which produces copies of British furniture for export.

It may seem from this book that the British have always been in Madeira in large numbers. This is not so, but they have, over many centuries, contributed a great deal in the formation of the Madeira we know today – particularly in the areas of trade, industry and tourism. Although Madeira has always been Portuguese, the British have influenced its thinking and development, but less so in recent years, particularly since the 1974 Revolution and the coming of the island's own political autonomy. Madeira has its own very strong regional identity. Also, as the world has changed and other pressures and influences have appeared, the British influence has lessened. Today Madeira is European, part of Portugal and the European Economic Community, but its geographical position is off the African coast. It has strong emigrant communities in South Africa and Venezuela, and it has its own regional autonomy to balance against the influences of central government in Lisbon.

9 *Tourism*

The history

Madeira can claim to have been in at the birth of modern tourism, along with such famous nineteenth-century resorts as Baden-Baden, the Italian Lakes and the French Riviera. It was both a health resort and a winter retreat for the rich and influential of the day.

Tourism, in fact, really began somewhat earlier, with the island's reputation for having a healthy climate. For example, between 1747 and 1751 the British physician Dr Thomas Heberden kept weather records which showed the excellence of the winter climate – pleasant between October and May, being not too humid and not too dry, with clean, dust-free air. Other members of the medical profession became interested in the winter climate, and the island began to be recommended for the treatment of and convalescence from a whole range of ailments from anaemia to gout. During the nineteenth century it became more specifically recommended for consumptive patients – initially in Funchal itself and later, at the beginning of the twentieth century, at Monte, when the Monte Palace Hotel opened in a magnificent park.

The companions of invalids explored the island on foot, on horseback and in hammocks and palanquins. They took with them their sketchpads, diaries, palettes and easels (later their cameras). Gradually the island became more widely known through picture albums, engravings and travel books. During the mid-nineteenth century the *Illustrated London News* often carried reports about and illustrations of Madeira.

Many people stayed in the island with residence permits for from three to six months on their way to or from South Africa, South America or the Far East. Visitors on their own rented a room with meals and amenities. When the whole family came, with staff (servants, governess and even the private doctor), it was necessary to rent a house.

In the early days of tourism many people spent the winter months in Madeira in private *quintas* (large houses set in their own grounds). These houses were owned by the rich – members of the Portuguese aristocracy or foreigners, mostly merchants. The *quintas* were let for the season, either furnished or unfurnished. This was a good source of income and employment for the island, in providing goods, food and services. By 1887 over 300 people from Britain alone were wintering in the island. The visitors amused themselves with writing, painting, riding, picnics, at social soirées and visiting the various social clubs, such as the English Club which in 1850 had over 2,000 books as well as the daily and weekly British newspapers. Today, though many of these *quintas* have disappeared, most of those in existence are still in use as family homes, some have been restored by the Regional Government and others are awaiting the fate of time. If you explore Funchal, you should be able to see many of these eighteenth- and nineteenth-century *quintas*.

A 'ticket of residence' had to be obtained by people staying in Madeira from the Police Authorities within forty-eight hours of their arrival in the island. The Customs Authorities allowed furniture and household goods in tax-free for the visitors' stay, but they had to pay tax on all goods which they did not take with them when they left. However, many people sold their things when leaving in order to pay their house rent as well as their baker's, butcher's and grocer's bills.

In 1836 William Reid, the founder of the world-famous Reid's Hotel, arrived in Madeira from Scotland, aged fourteen, with £5 in his pocket and a determination to succeed. His father, who had a small farm in Scotland and twelve children to support, had sent him off to seek his fortune. He worked his passage to Lisbon and then to Funchal. In Madeira he first worked in a bakery and then developed a business with William Wilkinson in which they undertook the letting and management of *quintas* (complete with china, linen and furniture) on behalf of their Madeiran and foreign owners. Later Reid turned the Quinta das Fontes into the Royal Edinburgh Hotel and then added the Hotels do Carmo and Santa Clara, as well as some *pensions*. Dreaming of a luxury hotel and the famous people it might entertain, he bought a piece of land across the Ribeiro Seco (a deep ravine to the west of Funchal) and started to build the hotel where today stands Reid's Palace Hotel. William Reid died in 1888, aged sixty-six, before the hotel was finished. The first phase opened in 1891 and was completed in 1900-1901. The hotel opened for the winter and closed for the summer. In 1925 the Reid brothers, William's sons, sold the hotel to a British company, and in 1937 it was sold to the Blandy family who closed it during the Second World War and then modernized it before it re-opened.

The hotel business was a virtual monopoly for the Reid family in Funchal at the end of the nineteenth and the beginning of the twentieth century, the only real rival being Jones' Private Family Hotel (Jones' Bella Vista Hotel) which had been opened in 1880 and had a large garden; it is now the Seminary which overlooks the new Post Office.

Before disembarkation in Madeira, Health Officials would board the ships anchored in the Bay of Funchal. If there were any problems, a yellow flag was hoisted and the ship was put in quarantine off Lazareto. If the ship was given a clean bill of health, Customs Officials went on board. On arrival in Funchal, ships were surrounded by a flotilla of rowing boats with local people selling embroidery and wicker, and youths diving for coins in the harbour. People still exhibit articles for sale on the quayside for visiting cruise ships, but boys no longer dive into the murky waters.

In the nineteenth century, sailing ships or steamships direct from the United Kingdom took between eight and twelve days on the voyage from Southampton to Madeira. Royal Mail Steam Packets spent twelve hours in Madeira on their way to Brazil. The Union Company and Donald Currie Mailboats stopped in Madeira on their way to and from South Africa. They later became Castle Line Royal Mailboats with a fleet of eighteen 'castles' which became very familiar and popular in Funchal.

Royalty arrived by private yacht or steamer. In 1847-8 Queen Adelaide, widow of William IV, visited Madeira on her doctor's advice. In 1849 Prince Maximilian, Duke of Leuchtenberg, arrived in the Russian naval steam frigate *Kamchatka*. In 1852 Empress Amélia, widow of King Pedro IV of Brazil, and her daughter arrived on a Portuguese navy boat, and in 1860 Elizabeth, Empress of Austria, wife of Franz Josef, arrived on the British royal yacht *Victoria and Albert*.

The rich also visited Madeira in their private yachts as part of a grand tour. The British yacht *Sunbeam* arrived in 1876 on a round-the-world voyage with its owner Thomas Brassey MP, his wife, children, guests and thirty-two crew members.

In 1930 the Prince of Wales, later King Edward VIII and then Duke of Windsor, visited the island. Also in the 1930s came Prince Henry, Duke of Gloucester, and Prince George, Duke of Kent. More recent royal visitors have included Saudi princes. In 1985 the royal yacht *Britannia* spent two days in Madeira and Porto Santo with HRH Prince Philip, Duke of Edinburgh, HRH Princess Alexandra and Mr Angus Ogilvy on board. 1986 saw visits from the King and Queen of Sweden and President P.W. Botha of South Africa.

Early visitors to Madeira and Porto Santo were rowed to the beach when the sea was calm and were then carried on the backs of boatmen who rolled up their trousers and waded ashore. All passengers were carried in this way, whether royalty or ordinary mortals. In 1757 the first stage of the harbour was built. It was extended in 1885-9 to the island of Nossa Senhora da Conceição (also known as the Loo Rock) which has the fort on top. The quay was again extended when a tunnel was made through the island in 1934-9, further extended in 1957-62 and achieved its present length in the 1970s, when a storage area for containers was made at the end.

The jetty in the centre of Funchal (long described as part of the 'Entrance to the City') was begun in 1843, but then neglected so that it was almost destroyed by the waves. The reconstruction was completed in 1892. In 1932-3 it was extended by a further 80m and has been a popular promenade for tourists and Madeirans ever since, as well as a good place from which to observe the activity in the harbour and marina.

By the 1890s, Madeira was very popular with the British, French and German upper classes and a few very adventurous Americans. Many Europeans came, to avoid the more northerly winters, on board liners bound for South Africa or South America. They stayed in the luxurious hotels or rented or bought *quintas*, attracted by the low cost of living, low taxation, the hospitality of the people and the beauty of the island – although many people (and this is often still true today) never or rarely left their hotel. This type of person continued to visit the island until the 1960s and the advent of air travel for all.

Many of the famous liners of this century have visited Madeira at some time during their voyages. The number of passengers arriving by ship reached a peak in 1969. Since that time, with the decline in cruising and the opening of the airport in Madeira, the number of ship's passengers has fallen constantly. 1986 saw the sad end of the regular Fred Olsen Line cruises to Madeira and the Canary Islands. These ships were regular visitors for over twenty years. There are, however, still many opportunities to see ocean liners arriving at and departing from the island. Most weeks, in the winter months, you can observe one of the numerous Russian cruise liners entering or leaving port, with occasional visits by the *Canberra, Queen Elizabeth II* or *Europa*, or one of the Italian or Norwegian cruise liners.

On 22 March 1921 the first sea-plane landed in Funchal after completing a flight from Lisbon; in the 1930s a Zeppelin passed over Funchal, and in 1949 Aquila Airways began a regular flying-boat service to the island. These luxuriously equipped flying-boats took only nine hours to fly between Southampton and Funchal, but the service was not entirely dependable as flights had to be cancelled whenever the sea was too rough to land. The service ended in 1958 when a sea plane crashed into the sea between Lisbon and Madeira. From the start of this service in 1949, when 1,591 people were transported by sea plane, the numbers had risen by 1958 to 8,713 passengers.

In 1960 the airport in Porto Santo opened. This covers a large portion of flat land and could take the largest planes available, even by today's standards. It was used for a few emergency landings by Royal Air Force planes during the recent Falklands War. At the present time the runway and airport buildings are being improved.

During 1957 the first (very small) plane landed on an experimental runway at Santa Catarina Airport, Madeira. On 8 July 1964 this airport was officially opened and the first commercial flight arrived in Madeira, bringing eighty passengers and taking away sixty-six. The opening of the airport has affected tourism in Madeira more than any other single factor and has transported an isolated island directly into the latter half of the twentieth century. In 1964 11,204 passengers disembarked by aeroplane. By 1980 this had risen to 330,453 passengers. In the 1960s the opening of the airport opened Madeira to a wider foreign market and to the Portuguese middle class. By the late 1970s and 1980s the increasing numbers of passengers and package tours and growing size of aircraft, as well as the need to comply with international safety standards for larger aircraft, made it essential to extend the runway. This extension was opened in 1985. The largest aircraft that can now land in Madeira is the Boeing 757. There are plans to enlarge the runway yet again to enable jumbo jets to land, but at present all this remains on the drawing board. Such a development would, of course have very significant effects on the tourism of the island. The position of the runway and the topography of the island means that planes normally land and take off over the sea.

The increase in tourism has meant a dramatic change in the number of hotel beds. In the 1930s accommodation consisted of a thousand beds in twelve hotels. By 1960 there were still only 1,300 beds but by 1985 they had risen to 12,000. This still, however, gives the island a quality tourist trade.

Tourism Today

After 200 years in the tourist business, Madeira provides a service few places in the world could rival. Tourism, although one of the biggest sources of income to the island, is not oversold. Indeed, one of the attractions of Madeira is that it does not outwardly appear to be specifically geared to tourism. The visitor is not greeted with the sordid 'home-from-home' bar or the multitude of signs advertising pots of tea, fish and chips, egg and bacon, smorgasbord, German beer garden etc which are found in Spain, the Canary Islands and even the Portuguese Algarve. The quality and style of the restaurants here are very Portuguese or Madeiran, offering a taste of local speciality dishes as well as the standard international ones.

Just by stepping out of your hotel, you are more than likely to find a tree-lined road and a hand-made mosaic stone footpath. A short walk by day or night and you realize you are in a different world. During the day the main streets are full of activity, as people go about their work or shopping in the supermarkets or in the main fruit and fish market in the centre of Funchal. Many a road-side café provides a good vantage point to watch the world go by. But don't sit too close to the road, as some of the old buses and trucks leave a trail of black smoke as they struggle up Funchal's twisting, narrow streets.

At night, after dinner, it is very pleasant to stroll from hotel to hotel or to the many bars and small restaurants or, later, to the discothèques. You are not likely to encounter any problems on the streets in Madeira, apart from the occasional drunk trying to find his way home.

Nor does the island appear to be over-full of tourists, not even in Funchal where over ninety per cent of the hotels are located. At present there are some 12,000 hotel beds, nearly all in Funchal, compared with 200,000 in the Canary Islands and over 36,000 in the Algarve. The government policy is to expand the total number of beds in the island to around 20,000 and to encourage this expansion to be outside Funchal, thereby opening up the wonderful countryside and expanding the economy of the many small villages. A number of new small hotels/*pensions* have recently opened in Ribeira Brava, Porto Moniz, Santana, Caniço and São Gonçalo. The government is also opening *pousadas* (small country hotels) for walkers who wish to visit the scenic beauty of the island. The existing rest houses (with simple catering facilities) are often fully booked by government employees, so it is best to check with the Tourist Office first.

There are also ideas and schemes to purchase and renovate many of the eighteenth- and nineteenth-century *quintas* around the island and to re-open them as small hotels. These *quintas* are large houses in their own spacious grounds which often include a small farm.

For the size of the island, Madeira must have one of the highest concentrations of five-star hotels anywhere in the world . Before the 1974 Revolution, as well as having the world-famous Reid's Palace Hotel and the Savoy Hotel, the island boasted a Sheraton, Hilton (now Madeira Palácio), Holiday Inn (now Atlantis) and the then under construction Casino Park Hotel designed by Oscar Niemeyer – a total of six luxury five-star hotels. In addition to these, there is a good selection of four- and three-star hotels and apartment hotels from which to choose, as well as *pensions*. In recent years a great number of two-, three- and four-star hotels and apartment hotels have opened. Many of them offer an excellent service at a more economical price than the five-star hotels and most of them have a swimming pool, tennis courts and gardens along with night-time entertainment and a relaxed family atmosphere. A good example would be the Hotel Duas Torres, a little way out of Funchal, just before the Hotel Madeira Palácio on the road towards Câmara de Lobos. It has a family restaurant, friendly bar with draught beer and *pregos* (steak sandwiches), discothèque and swimming pool as well as self-catering facilities. Also to be recommended are the Hotels Girassol and Quinta do Sol, both close to Reid's, and the Hotel São João in the centre of Funchal itself. The São João has a varied programme of nightly entertainment and games to amuse its guests.

In the centre of Funchal are a number of relatively inexpensive, budget-priced hotels which, while of a basic and simple nature, are very clean and comfortable. The Hotels Madeira and Carmo are both used by tourists and Portuguese businessmen from the continent. Very good value can also be found in a *pensão* or boarding-house and several of these are situated in Funchal. These are excellent if you are considering a long stay of two or three months.

Madeira has not been left behind in the present craze for time-sharing apartments. There are a number of existing and planned developments in this area with, we regret, the usual sales touts pestering tourists on street corners.

Most visitors stay in the hotels, where service is the finest in Europe.

Visitors to Madeira in 1984 (by country)

Portugal	82,705	Netherlands	10,322
United Kingdom	57,310	Finland	9,182
Germany	36,152	Switzerland	8,702
France	29,466	Belgium	6,295
Sweden	24,853	Austria	4,729
Denmark	17,179	Canada	4,546
Norway	16,680	Italy	3,415
USA	13,820	Brazil	2,015
Spain	12,553	Other countries	6,103

TOTAL: 346,027

Traditionally, the time to visit Madeira was in the winter months (October to April), to escape the cold northern European winters, and the low season was in the summer months. This pattern now appears to have been broken, and Madeira experiences an all-year-round trade with those who want summer sun tans as well as those who want to get away from cold winters.

There has also been a change in the holiday habits of the Madeirans themselves, who used to retire to their summer villas at Monte or Santo da Serra to escape the heat or flocked to the rocky shoreline around Funchal to bathe every day. Today, with the regular air and sea link to Porto Santo, it seems, in the traditional holiday months of August and September, as if the entire population of Funchal has moved to Porto Santo. Regular faces that greet you in the banks, shops and offices in Funchal are to be seen on the eight-kilometre long beach of white sand. Apart from these two months the beach at Porto Santo is almost deserted.

There is a good hotel in Porto Santo, complete with swimming pool and garden leading directly to the beach. There are also small hotels, pensions, private villas and apartments. Increasing numbers of foreign visitors are finding their way to Porto Santo to stay for one or two weeks (as well as the more traditional one-day visit) and a number of tour operators now offer two centre holidays in Funchal and Porto Santo.

Returning to Madeira, we find that the island is catering for the demands of a new breed of tourists who wish for a more active holiday than the traditional visitor who relaxed in the comfort of the luxury hotels or lazed around the swimming pool or at the lido. In recent years there have been increasing numbers of visitors who enjoy the facilities which have been developed for windsurfing, scuba diving and game fishing (tunny, marlin, barracuda etc). There are also many tennis courts, some squash courts and a nine-hole golf course which is very slowly being extended to eighteen holes. Horse riding is also now available at Choupana and Sto da Serra.

Over recent years the Tourist Office has re-vamped certain traditional festivals so they appeal more to both tourists and locals. As well as the traditional Christmas and New Year festivities, the Wine Festival, Flower Festival, Apple Festival and Carnival all now embrace activities to interest visitors.

Christmas and New Year have long been the high point for visitor and Madeiran alike. During this festive season, the population of the island is swollen with Madeirans returning home for their festivities from all parts of the globe, as well as a vast influx of tourists. Every hotel, apartment and *pension* bed is filled by tourists, and there are hundreds of special planes arriving, culminating on New Year's Eve with eight or nine cruise ships filling the harbour.

The build-up towards New Year's Eve starts around 23 December, when the fruit and vegetable market is open all night, with singing and dancing. Christmas is traditionally a family time for the local population, but all the hotels put on special Christmas dinners and parties. By now the whole of Funchal is a mass of colour from over 100,000 coloured light bulbs. Every tree, building, statue and fountain is a blaze of light, and there are tasteful set-pieces strung across the main thoroughfares. The public buildings are floodlit and on all the main roads in and out of Funchal appear strings of white light bulbs. The churches on the hillside are floodlit and, over towards São Gonçalo, appears the year in giant numbers formed by white light bulbs on the hillside, ready to change to the New Year at midnight on 31 December. After Christmas, the build-up towards New Year's Eve continues. More and more planes and people arrive. Accommodation is at a premium in hotels and private houses alike. Bands appear in the streets, and folklore groups are dancing and singing in the central reservations and gardens of Funchal.

As midnight approaches on New Year's Eve, the whole of Funchal is a solid traffic jam as cars, buses and trucks journey from all parts of the island to Funchal bringing everyone, from nought to ninety years old. Some select vantage points in the town, others in the hills up to Monte, some on the harbour or in the gardens and parks. Each family group has food and wine. On New Year's Eve people in long evening dresses or in dinner jackets mingle in the streets of Funchal side by side with 'mountain men' in their woollen hats who have come to Funchal with their wives and children in the family's lorry – which is often decorated with Christmas tree, paperchains and balloons. The householders of Funchal add to the colourful spectacle by opening their doors and windows to show more lights. Occasional firecrackers herald what is to come. Then, at midnight, the ships sound their sirens to welcome the New Year. What a lovely sight the ships make, decked out with their own coloured light bulbs, the tugs and cargo boats as well as the eight or nine cruise liners. The year in lights on the hillside changes to the new as the ships sound their sirens and launch their pink flares. Champagne glasses in hand, people wish each other a 'Happy New Year' ('*Bom Ano Novo*'). And then comes the most gigantic, impressive firework display in the world. From over thirty locations around the natural amphitheatre of Funchal, the whole sky is lit with rockets, cascading Starlights, 3-D effect gigantic flowers, the entire spectacle lasting for over ten minutes. Then it's all over for another year. The crowds begin to disperse – some home to bed, others to drive back to Porto Moniz or Caniçal, and still others to attend the numerous parties, supper buffets, dances and discothèques until time for breakfast and bed.

Carnival in Madeira is not to be confused with Carnival in Rio de Janeiro. Here it is a much more simple affair. It is an elaboration of an old tradition when people used to throw soot and flour and eggs on each other in Rua da Carreira. Nowadays there is a big procession through the streets, on the Saturday night before Shrove Tuesday, of theme groups in fancy dress with bands and streamer-throwing. This is followed on the afternoon of Shrove Tuesday by processions of individuals in fancy dress – adults and lots of children. There are also big festivities in all the hotels, and fancy dress parties.

Another famous event is the Car Rally (*Rally Vinho da Madeira*) which takes place on the first weekend in August. It now attracts international drivers from all over Europe and is worth points in the European Championship. There are many special mountain sections and night drives, and the routes cover the whole island.

The old town (*zona velha*) of Funchal, which is at the far (eastern) end of Avenida das Comunidades Madeirenses (the sea-front road) past the power station, is the oldest part of Funchal, dating back to the sixteenth century. The road through this area has been closed to traffic, and many of the buildings have been restored and turned into restaurants and bars. It all looks very attractive, particularly on a warm evening when you can dine outside.

Slowly parts of Funchal are being given a facelift, partly with tourists in mind and partly just because many of the old buildings are in danger of crumbling away. It is now very difficult to park a car in Funchal as areas are being made into pedestrian streets and the central reservations in Avenida Arriaga are being restored to walking areas, as they used to be before cars took them over.

In 1983 a questionnaire given out by the Tourist Office asked visitors what pleased them most about Madeira: 35.7 per cent of those questioned said the natural beauty of the island, 13.6 per cent the friendliness of the residents, 12.4 per cent the climate, 8.4 per cent good hotels and 7.8 per cent the flowers. They were then asked what they liked least about Funchal: 31.7 per cent said the pollution and 15.8 per cent the noise and confusion in the city. There are plans for multi-storey car-parks to get cars off the streets and restore the pavements to pedestrians and for a major ring-road round Funchal. Maybe in the next few years these projects will come to fruition and achieve the hoped-for and much-needed improvements in the city of Funchal.

The Great Hotels

Because Madeira has been involved in tourism for so long, a tradition of service in hotels has long been established. The hotels of Madeira, in particularly the *de luxe* five-star hotels, are among the best in Europe.

Reid's Hotel is located on Estrada Monumental. The fame of this hotel was as great amongst those generations of the 1920s to 1950s as Raffles in Singapore, Shepheard's in Cairo and The Ritz in London. Here in Madeira, at Reid's you can still savour that luxury. You can enjoy afternoon tea with cucumber sandwiches, lounge in chintz-covered chairs, play billiards or bridge, or dine in tuxedo. It has over four hectares of terraced gardens leading down to the rocky shore where you can swim in the sea or swimming pool. At a higher level in the gardens are two more swimming pools and a garden restaurant. In the main hotel there is a two-level dining-room, elegantly furnished and decorated, plus a separate grill room. In spite of its international fame, Reid's is still a relatively small hotel by today's standards (165 rooms), with a family atmosphere and many members of staff who have spent all their working lives in the hotel.

Over the years Reid's has been host to many people, and its visitors' book reads like an international *Who's Who* over the past century. The famous and the infamous, the wealthy and the powerful, the deposed and the exiled of this century have all stayed at Reid's. The Emperor Charles of Austria stayed here after he was deposed until he moved into Quinta do Monte. Lloyd George was another famous guest. (During a lunch given in his honour by the British in the island, the wife of one of the wine-shippers bit her tongue rather painfully and asked Lloyd George if he ever did that. His reply was that he often did but not usually soon enough.) George Bernard Shaw stayed in Reid's in 1927 and, at the age of seventy-one, learned to dance. He signed a photograph for Max Rinder, the professional dancer who had taught him, with the words: 'To the only man who ever taught me anything.'

In January 1950 Sir Winston Churchill stayed in Reid's and did many paintings of the island, especially of Câmara de Lobos. Many of these paintings now hang in Chartwell in Britain. Whilst in Madeira, Sir Winston was loaned the Leacock family's Rolls-Royce, the boot of which he transformed into a bar. In 1959 ex-President (General) Fulgênico Batista of Cuba installed his large entourage on a whole floor of Reid's. Other famous twentieth-century visitors, most of whom stayed at Reid's, include Marshal Pitsudski of Poland, Sarah Bernhardt, Gago Coutinho, Marconi, Princess Helena Victoria, Gregory Peck, Lord Avon, Lord Birkenhead, Lord Halifax, Lord Jellicoe, S.P.B. Mais, Sacheverell Sitwell and Fanny and Johnny Craddock. A list of famous people who have stayed in the various Reid's hotels, appears in a book on Madeira by W. and A. Reid published in 1893.

Hotel Savoy in Avenida do Infante is one of the leading five-star hotels in Europe. Occupying a prominent position, it is like a gigantic land-locked luxury liner, with all the services and accommodation you would expect on one. The original hotel was opened in 1912 and extended in 1926. In the 1960s it was totally re-built, and at that time no expense was spared. It is a happy blend of old and, what was at that time, new. It has 353 rooms, and many of the guests repeat visits every year or several times a year, some for over twenty years and more. At Christmas the same faces are to be found in the Almeida Bar year after year. Many of the rich, famous and powerful of this world have stayed in the Savoy but, unfortunately, out of respect for their privacy, no official record has ever been kept.

There is a huge dining-room on the seventh floor, with seating for over a thousand, and the Galaxia Night Club on the ninth floor has panoramic views of the bay of Funchal. On the eighth floor is the Fleur-de-Lys Grill Room, which is undoubtedly the finest place to eat in Madeira – it is very elegantly decorated and the food and service are superb. There are also a restaurant and bar at the swimming pool complex, which is reached through the hotel gardens and then down in a lift. At this level you can sunbathe or swim from a stone jetty (connecting off-shore rocks) or in one of the two swimming pools. One of the strong points of this hotel has always been the attention of the staff to every detail and the excellence of the quiet, unobtrusive service.

Casino Park Hotel is a modern hotel designed by Oscar Niemeyer, the architect of Brasilia. It is a long, low, curving building typical of his designs, being some five storeys high with ramps connecting upper and lower floors. Situated on a cliff top above the harbour, the complex also includes the Casino and a luxurious air-conditioned cinema. There is a large garden which contains a swimming pool and affords views of the busy harbour below.

The Madeira-Sheraton Hotel is located between the Savoy and Reid's. It is a seventeen-storey-high hotel with the luxurious ambience associated world-wide with Sheraton Hotels. It has direct access to the sea, three swimming pools and a night club situated in a separate building in the gardens of the hotel. There are various restaurants and bars, including a British-style pub. The hotel has recently been extended with the addition of more rooms and restaurants. It has also developed a time-share group of apartments at sea-level – which makes it a very large complex indeed.

Madeira Palácio Hotel was originally built as a Hilton Hotel, a few years before the 1974 Revolution. This luxury hotel is located a little way out of town, past Reid's, on the road to Câmara de Lobos. There are good views to the sea, as well as of Cabo Girão (Madeira's famous high cliff) to be had from the rooms. The entrance and main public areas are spacious and tastefully furnished, and in the gardens are located a large outdoor swimming pool, snack bar and tennis courts. The hotel also has a good restaurant and separate grill room, as well as a discothèque.

The Hotel Atlantis is near the airport, just outside Machico. It was originally built as a Holiday Inn and is part of a complex of hotel and holiday apartments and villas called Matur. There are tree-lined roads and paths, with open-air swimming pools and shops. The hotel itself has 290 rooms in a tower block and is a complete holiday resort hotel. There is a large heated indoor pool with sunroof in the hotel's main entrance lobby, with a large outdoor pool designed in a figure of eight for sunny days. The hotel has many planned activities to amuse its guests and also has a minibus making frequent trips to Funchal and back.

10 *Tours of the Countryside*

Introduction

In the first half of this book we have concentrated on the discovery and history of Madeira, its social and economic development, together with a description of its topography. In the second half we consider the practical side of exploring the island of Madeira.

The archipelago of Madeira consists of the islands of Madeira and Porto Santo, which are the only inhabited ones, the Desertas, which are the islands close to and visible from Madeira, and the Selvagens, to the south-east and nearer to the Canaries than to Madeira. We hope that, during your stay in Madeira, you will find an opportunity to visit Porto Santo with its eight-kilometre long sandy beach and relaxed way of life. If you can manage a visit of two to three days (or even just one day) it is well worth it – the modern boat takes $1\frac{1}{2}$ hours and it is only a matter of minutes in the small jet aircraft.

When planning your excursions in Madeira, let the morning sun be your guide in deciding whether you go east or west because it is quite common for one part of the island to bask in sunshine while another is cloudy. The weather is one thing we cannot plan for as, although Madeira enjoys a good climate all year round, you must remember it is a small island in the Atlantic Ocean.

Given the topography of Madeira, it is understandable that the island roads are full of twists and turns, climbing and descending all the time. If you are hiring a car in the island, you will need three to four days to cover most of the main roads and to savour some of the breathtaking views. There are various maps to show you the way, and we recommend you take a picnic with you, as most viewpoints also have picnic tables and chairs and space to pull your car off the road. Restaurants, with one or two exceptions, tend to be located only in the small towns.

This chapter has been organized so as to describe three main tours of the island, as well as a trip to Curral das Freiras. The three tours suggested are:

1. Câmara de Lobos – Cabo Girão – Ribeira Brava – Ponta do Sol –

Porto do Moniz (via the coastal towns or Paúl da Serra) – Seixal – São Vicente – Encumeada – Ribeira Brava – Câmara de Lobos – Funchal.

2. Monte – Terreira da Luta – Poiso – Ribeiro Frio – Santana – São Jorge – Boaventura – Ponta Delgada – São Vicente – Encumeada – Ribeira Brava – Câmara de Lobos – Funchal.

3. Caniço – Santa Cruz – Machico – Caniçal – Machico – Portela – Santo da Serra – Camacha – Funchal.

The cumulative distance in kilometres is given for each town from Funchal. These tours of the countryside should not be viewed as compulsory itineraries. They are just suggestions for day and half-day excursions to take in the best of the scenery, rather than the villages the tours pass through. Most of these in themselves do not have a great deal of interest to offer the tourist. It is, after all, the beautiful and varied scenery which you are setting out to see.

Tour 1. Funchal – Porto do Moniz – Funchal

On leaving Funchal, climb the Avenida do Infante past the Casino Park and Savoy Hotels and cross the bridge over the Ribeiro Seco. This bridge was built in 1849, thereby opening up the Estrada Monumental (then just called the New Road) past Reid's Hotel and out to the west, through the present tourist zone. This was the first 'modern' road to be built outside Funchal. After a little while, cross the Ribeira dos Socorridos and reach the main electricity generating station in the island. This river gets its name from the time of the first exploration of the island, when some of Zarco's men were nearly swept away by the river but were rescued by other members of the party in a small boat. (*Socorridos* means 'helped' or 'saved'.)

Shortly after this, we arrive in the village of Câmara de Lobos (9km), an attractive fishing village so named because Zarco saw seals here (*lobos* means 'wolves', i.e. 'sea wolves'). Just before a road turns off to the left into the village there is a terrace, the spot where Sir Winston Churchill did his paintings of the village. The village itself is worth a closer look. The Church of São Sebastião was built in the fifteenth century and has fine gilded carving on the high altar. Another church to see in Câmara de Lobos is the Chapel of Nossa Senhora da Conceição, built in the early part of the fifteenth century. It was one of the first chapels to be built in the island. It was restored in 1908 and has a very richly carved baroque altar. Along the side walls are various paintings by Nicolau Ferreira.

This picturesque fishing village has many interesting buildings and views. It also has a good fish restaurant in the square by the bandstand.

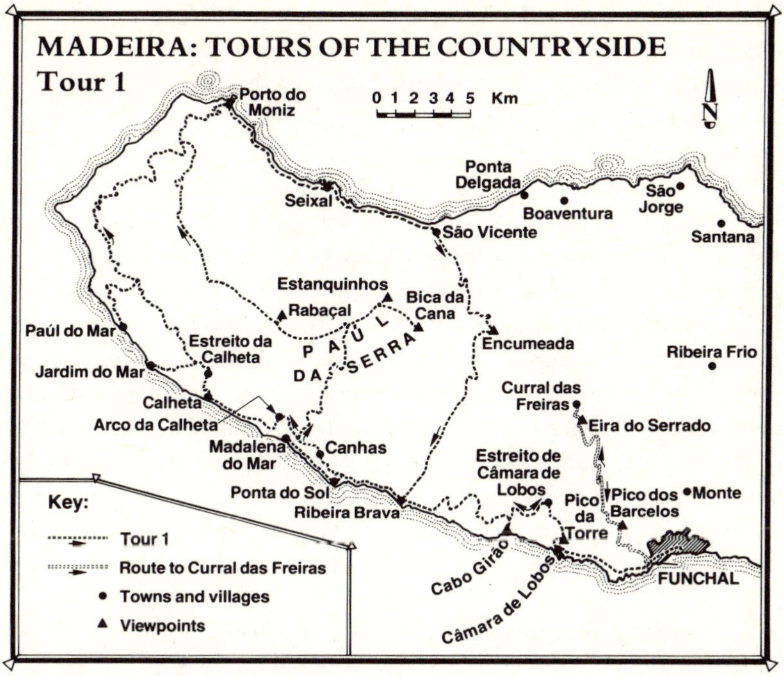

The drawback to spending time in Câmara de Lobos is the hordes of beggar children who appear nowhere else on the island but are a real nuisance here.

Back on the main road, one kilometre out of the village, it is worth turning off and making the short drive up to the Pico da Torre viewpoint which gives a lovely view of Câmara de Lobos. All viewpoints in Madeira are marked by signs which show a pair of binoculars.

The main road now climbs and winds towards the village of Estreito de Câmara de Lobos (14km), past many attractive modern villas and vines growing on trellises. This is the centre of the best vine-growing area on the island. The village of Estreito has one of the best restaurants in the island for *espetada* (meat on a skewer) – the menu and seating are simple, but the meat is very good. From here you can make a side trip to Jardim da Serra (18km) and the *quinta* made famous by Henry Veitch. This is a picturesque wooded place.

Onward again and, after more twisting and turning, there is a left-hand turn to Cabo Girão (19km). This 550m high cliff is one of the highest in the world. There is a coffee bar here and women selling embroidery and woollens line the path to the viewpoint – for all that they are at a good tourist point, the prices here and at other such places around the island usually remain reasonable. Look down from the viewpoint and see the terraced land – minute cultivated pocket handkerchiefs.

The traditional village was centred around the church with its white walls and red or grey stonework. The better houses with two storeys and the public buildings were near the church. Most villages had a sugarmill with a tall, slender chimney, or a modest watermill. Around the village were scattered single storey dwellings with straw roofs and unpainted walls. The old nucleus is still visible in many of the rural settlements.

The main road begins to level off as we pass through Quinta Grande and Campanário, before descending into Ribeira Brava (31km). This is a pleasant town and a major road junction, for it is here that the road forks up to the pass of Encumeada across the centre of the island – and the way we will return. Ribeira Brava used to be like a Wild West or oasis town where buses and cars stopped for the occupants to take advantage of coffee, drinks and food and to fill their vehicle with petrol before venturing into the 'Beyond' or the 'Outback'. Nowadays the island is more developed but this is still a favourite and convenient 'watering hole'.

The Church of São Bento in Ribeira Brava was built in the sixteenth century but completely altered in the eighteenth century. It has a high altar with fine gilded carving and a sixteenth-century sculpture of Our Lady of the Rosary. The pulpit and the arch of the Chapel of the Blessed Sacrament are also splendid, as are the blue-and-white checked tiles on the steeple. There is a tunnel, through the rock at the eastern end of the sea-front, which leads to a small harbour.

There is a story about Ribeira Brava which may or may not be true but which is worth the telling. At one time Ribeira Brava was the only place in Madeira where cherries were grown in large quantities. In 1822, when a new Portuguese constitution was promulgated, the people of the town refused to recognize it and so the Governor sent soldiers to Ribeira Brava, not to use force but with orders to eat all the cherries. The soldiers happily carried out their orders and, having lost their fruit, the inhabitants soon lost their desire for rebellion.

In recent years a new coastal road has been built from Ribeira Brava to Tabua. From here we continue to Ponta do Sol (40km) through a series of tunnels cut into the rock which are lit from the seaward side by sunlit 'windows'. This is yet another fishing village where time seems to have stood still. The ancestors of the famous American writer John dos Passos emigrated from here, and he visited this village when he came to the island in the 1950s. Dos Passos described Madeira as both a paradise and a prison.

A short diversion can be made by continuing along the sea road through yet more tunnels to the tiny village of Madalena do Mar, where the road ends. This village is noted for the amount of sun it receives and for its long pebble beach. Its church (1457) was dedicated to Santa Catarina by Henrique Alemão – 'Henry the German' – who is said to have been a Polish king. Tradition has it that, after King Ladislau lost the Battle of Varna in 1414, he vowed to make a pilgrimage around the world armed as a Knight of Saint Catherine of Mount Sinai. He eventually came to Madeira where Zarco gave him the large area of fertile land around Madalena do Mar. This gift was confirmed by Prince Henry and King Afonso. Henrique Alemão encouraged many people to come and settle to cultivate his extensive land. He married the daughter of Aunes, one of the early colonists, and died when a landslide at Cabo Girão crushed his boat as he was returning from Funchal.

We now retrace our steps to Ponta do Sol and back up onto the road and continue along to Canhas. Here there is a large, imposing statue of Santa Teresa of the Child Jesus. Construction of this was begun in 1955, and it was inaugurated in 1964. Along the roadside leading to the statue are the fourteen Stations of the Cross.

After Canhas there is a road to the right – which it is very easy to miss – which leads up to Paúl da Serra and one of the alternative routes through to Porto do Moniz. On the way up we pass the statue of 'Senhor da Montanha' which was begun in 1962 and weighs six tonnes. The plateau of Paúl da Serra itself is an extensive moorland area where there was once a proposal to build an international airport. There are good or bad weather days here, and nothing in between. On good days there is glorious sunshine with clear, cloudless skies, and in summer the air is pleasantly fresher and cooler than down at sea-level. Then you can picnic, play football or cricket or just walk across the moorland and look at the sheep. On bad days it rains and the mist covers everything in silence – you can see only a few yards in front of you and, if you wander from the road, can easily get lost. The frequency of such bad weather is hardly surprising given the altitude of 1,430m, of this seventeen by six kilometre plateau.

At the start of the plateau a side road leads to Estanquinhos, a forestry station, from which a new road is slowly being built to Ginjas and São Vicente on the north side of the island. Just before the forestry house, a rough road leads off to the rest house at Bica da Cana where picnic tables and benches are to be found. From here the road is slowly being extended to Encumeada. Returning to the main road, which is very good, we cross the plateau and pass a small reservoir on the left-hand side with views down to the south side of the island and the sea. Almost opposite this is a road which turns off to the right down to Rabaçal (64km) at a height of 1,070m. Here there is a rest house with simple but clean accommodation and cooking facilities. In summer a man sells a wide variety of bottles – wine and soft drinks – which he keeps cool in the water fountain. Rabaçal is a popular spot for walkers and close by are the Falls of Rabaçal and the twenty-five *fontes*.

Return to the main road which now follows the spine of a hill and descends to the main coastal road which leads to Porto do Moniz. As it winds atop the spine, the road gives superb views now to the north and now to the south of the island.

There is an alternative route from Canhas to Porto do Moniz, particularly to be recommended if the weather is cloudy up on the moor, although it does wind and twist. After Canhas we pass through Arco da Calheta (immediately above Madalena do Mar) with its Chapel of Our Lady of Loreto which has a sixteenth-century Manueline-style roof.

Calheta (59km), which has been an administrative centre since 1501, has a modified sixteenth-century parish church. In Estreito da Calheta is the Church of Nossa Senhora da Graça which began as a sixteenth-century chapel, although the present church dates from 1791 to 1793. From this road it is possible to make small diversions down into the villages of Jardim do Mar and Paúl do Mar, although the roads in and out of them are more spectacular than the villages themselves. Passing Ponta do Pargo, where the lighthouse was first built in 1922, we come to Porto do Moniz (98km). This is at the north-west of the island and is probably the furthest village from Funchal. It is a very popular summer resort, with sea-water swimming pools in the rocks. There are good fish restaurants and a recently opened camp site with full facilities.

Leaving Porto do Moniz, we are now on the north side of the island, where the road is a narrow shelf cut into the cliffs which rise majestically from the ocean. Here the road is still cobbled, as were all the roads in the island until the late 1970s. This area to São Vicente is very sparsely populated and the road passes through numerous tunnels and past cascading waterfalls, some of which give you a free car-wash, even in the summer when there has been no rain for months. Near Seixal the road goes into a tunnel, and a waterfall cascades dramatically over the top and into the sea. The only village on this section of road is Seixal (108km). Here the vineyards are incredibly steep, and heath tree hedges protect the crops from the wind as well, it is said, as the farmers from falling into the sea below.

The cathedral in Funchal which was built between 1485 and 1514

The mountains at Encumeada illustrating the majestic scenery be found inland

A typical thatched house in Santana

Fireworks over Funchal on New Year's Eve

The beautiful sandy beach at Porto Santo

The Fort of São Tiago

Pico Arieiro (1,818m): the mountain with a road to the top

On the coast where we turn right and inland to the village of São Vicente (116km) there is a tiny chapel which was built into the rock beside the mouth of the river in 1692. São Vicente is set a little way inland where the valley is wider and sheltered from the sea winds. This little town has recently been given a face-lift, and the white walls gleam attractively in the sun above the narrow pedestrianized streets. The road starts to climb and, to our left, we pass a 14m high clocktower – the Church of Nossa Senhora de Fátima – which was built atop precipitous slopes between 1942 and 1953.

Climbing all the way up the valley now, we pass many colourful flowers and trees growing alongside crops in this fertile valley.

Encumeada (117km) is the summit at 1,004m. Just off the main road on the right is a good viewpoint to look down on both the north and south sides of the island. As you start to descend, you pass the Pousada dos Vinhaticos which is a very popular place to spend the night, particularly if you are on a walking holiday. The valley, as it descends towards Ribeira Brava, is probably the most beautiful in Madeira, and it has many picnic tables and pull-offs for the car. The valley has wooded slopes and attractive rock formations. The road into Ribeira Brava has been much improved in the last few years. From here the return journey to Funchal is via Câmara de Lobos, the total trip, without diversions, being about 165km.

Tour 2. Funchal – Faial – São Vicente – Funchal

The vistas on this route are no less impressive than on the first one. We leave Funchal on the Monte road, although more or less any road going up the hill will do, as they nearly all join back *en route* to Monte. From here we continue to Terreira da Luta, where we get a good view of Funchal and see how high we have already climbed. the road leads on up through layers of eucalyptus trees into the pine forest to Poiso, a major road junction with a good restaurant. The height here, some 14km from Funchal, is 1,400m.

From Poiso we make a short diversion to drive to the top of the mountain, Pico do Arieiro, at 1,818m. This area is very popular for camping in summer, and the lower part of the road is through moorland crossed by *levadas* where you may be lucky enough to see small wild pigs or, in the summer months, wild ponies as well as sheep, goats and the occasional deer. On the left of the road on the way to the summit is a small ice house, built about 1800, which has recently been restored. Winter snow used to be stored here from nearby drifts and provided a

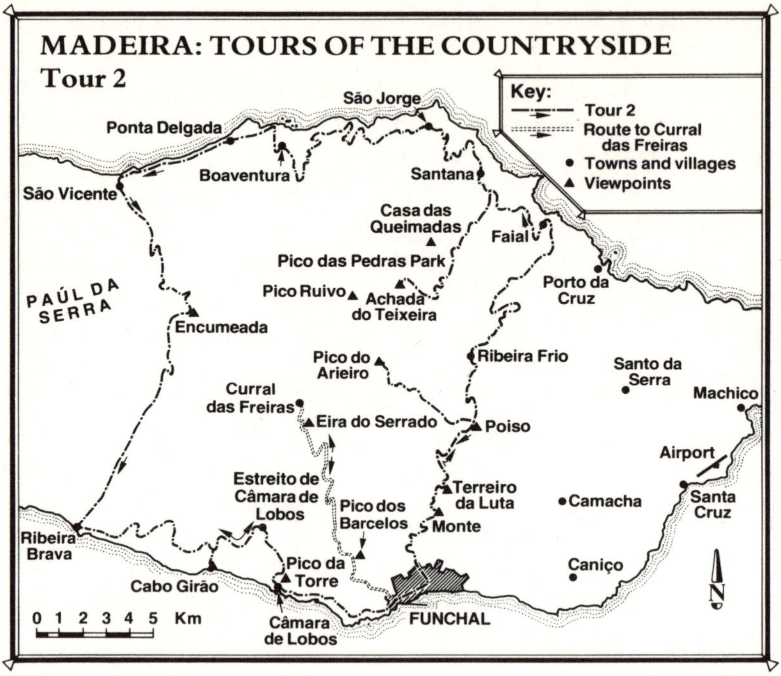

MADEIRA: TOURS OF THE COUNTRYSIDE
Tour 2

supply of caked ice throughout the following summer for the wealthy inhabitants and the hotels in Funchal. The last part of the road to the summit was opened in 1965.

At the summit of Pico do Arieiro (1,818m) there is a snack bar which has been open for many years, and a *pousada* which has been under construction for a number of years. On a clear day there are magnificent views from all along this road as well as from the summit, and you can look down on all sides of the island, even to Porto Santo. Alternatively, and no less awe-inspiring, if the cloud conditions are right, you ascend through the mist until you break out into the sun somewhere before the summit from where you look down on a sea of white cloud with many peaks bursting through. You really feel you are on top of the world. Pico do Arieiro is well worth a visit. After all, how many mountains can you drive right to the top of? There is also a magnificent walk from the top of Pico do Arieiro to the top of Pico Ruivo. This is a good walk for visitors with strong shoes, and it is protected by railings in various parts. The walk, which gives magnificent views, takes about two to 2¼ hours to Pico Ruivo which, at 1,862m, is the highest in the island.

We return to Poiso and head downhill through pine forest and sheep pasture to Ribeiro Frio (29km) at 800m above sea-level. Here there is a government trout hatchery where you can see the fish in all their stages of growth. Across the road are some gardens which are intended to perpetuate every species of flower, plant and tree found in Madeira. Just outside Ribeiro Frio the road is crossed by yet another *levada* walk, that to the right being a particularly nice one to Portela which takes about four hours.

On reaching Faial on the north coast, we turn left towards *Santana* (39km) where you will find the traditional thatched cottages, often with corn cobs hanging out to dry. The cottage consists of the living space on the ground floor divided up into small rooms, with an attic store for beans, grain, potatoes etc. The entrance is through a central door flanked by windows. These cottages (*palheiros*) are now preserved in Santana, and many are still lived in – even the public toilets are disguised as a thatched cottage. Elsewhere in the island most of these cottages have degenerated into cowsheds, and the traditional thatched roof has often been replaced by corrugated galvanized iron.

From Santana a road turns off to the left which winds up into the Pico das Pedras Park. From here it is possible to walk to the government rest house known as Casa das Queimadas – a very pleasant walk alongside a shady *levada*. This is a very popular spot for picnics, and cars are prohibited at the rest house. The main road continues up from Pico das Pedras to Achada do Teixeira (1,592m) from where it is a relatively short walk to Pico Ruivo or even right through to Pico do Arieiro. Sunrise and sunset are particularly breathtaking when seen from these summits.

From Santana we continue to São Jorge along a road lined with arum lilies and Watsonia. São Jorge (49km) has a church with a very imposing interior with decorated gilded carving. The church was built in 1761, and the images of Our Lady of the Incarnation and the Crucified Christ date from the same period. The road winds on to Arco de São Jorge and then goes in and round a deep ravine before it reaches Boaventura (65km). This village has a picturesque setting with the Atlantic rollers below and the mountains towering above. A good viewpoint is the cemetery where a tombstone, above a jagged cliff, bears the name of Miss Turner.

In the early years of this century Miss Turner came to live in Madeira, and managed the flourishing tea-room at Santo da Serra, where Ceylon tea and buttered toast were served. In the evening, after her customers had gone, she would listen to the gardener talking about his village on the other side of the peaks. When she died (about 1925), she left instructions in her Will for her body to be buried in this green paradise about which she had heard so much, and yet which she had never visited except in her dreams. There was no road at that time, and so her coffin was carried from Santo da Serra over the rough mountain tracks to Boaventura. She was buried, as she had wished, beneath the swaying palms in the cemetery of the village whose name means 'Good Luck'.

The last stop on this route is Ponta Delgada (68km) which has a sea-water swimming pool. The present Church of Senhor Bom Jesus was built after a terrible fire on 12 July 1908 destroyed the original building. About the time the original chapel was being built in the sixteenth century, a wooden crucifix was washed ashore in a box. This was badly damaged in the 1908 fire, and the small part which remains is now carefully protected in a glass case at the back of the church. This crucifix is the reason for one of the biggest and oldest religious festivals in Madeira.

From Ponta Delgada we return via São Vicente, Encumeada, Ribeira Brava and Câmara de Lobos – the whole round trip back to Funchal being some 130km.

Tour 3. Funchal – Caniço – Santa Cruz – Machico – Caniçal – Machico – Portela – Santo da Serra – Camacha – Funchal

Leaving Funchal by the airport road, we can take many a backward glance at the town and harbour. After we at last say 'goodbye' to Funchal, turn right for Garajau (so called by the island's discoverers because of the large number of *garajaus* – terns – which nest there). Here a tasteful modern development looks out onto the statue of Christ (similar to but much smaller than those in Rio de Janeiro and Lisbon), which was inaugurated in 1927.

The road continues to Caniço (9km) which is situated on a small plateau some 229m above sea-level. It has a large, imposing church in the recently modernized village square which is complete with fountain and aviary. Caniço has probably the best selection of restaurants outside Funchal and is very popular with both Madeirans and foreigners. A small detour takes you down to Caniço de Baixa or Ponta da Oliveira where there is a small modern development (mainly owned by Germans). You can walk along the pebble beach and watch the Atlantic rollers breaking, before a meal in one of the two very good restaurants here.

From Caniço we go back up onto the main airport road and continue on to Santa Cruz (20km), whose centre is situated off to the right of the main road. The church of Santa Cruz dates from 1533 and is the largest and architecturally most interesting outside Funchal, with good Gothic arches and pillars. There is a sixteenth-century town hall which has been modernized but still retains its charm. The law courts, with their outside

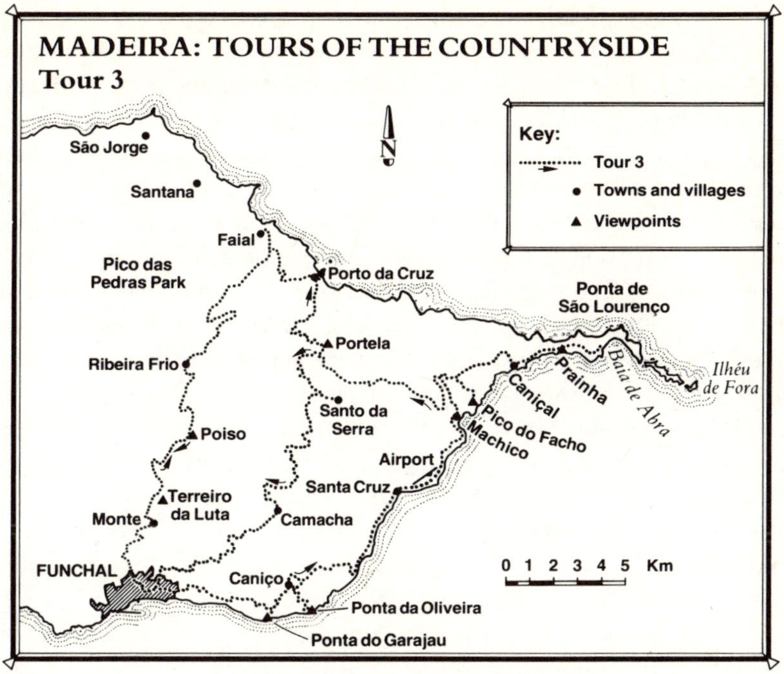

staircase, are also impressive. There is a shingle beach in the town, with bathing facilities.

We continue on past the airport where the road goes under the recent extension of the runway, which is supported on high pillars many metres above the road. The road winds along the coast past the Atlantis Hotel and the Matur Holiday Complex. Just as we enter Machico, we pass the Hotel Dom Pedro on the right, a favourite retreat for a peaceful few days. Machico (26km) was the first capital of Madeira, and the first landings were made here. Today it is an important administrative centre and fishing port. The Church of Nossa Senhora da Conceição dates from the end of the fifteenth century, being built in the Manueline style. The portal was given by King Manuel I. The Cristo Chapel, built soon after the first landing in the fifteenth century, was rebuilt during the sixteenth century and again in 1883. In 1803 the chapel was very badly damaged by flood, and the image of Nossa Senhora dos Milagres was washed out to sea. A crewman on an American ship coming to Madeira saw the image floating and recovered it. It was kept in the cathedral of Funchal until the chapel in Machico was rebuilt and the statue was returned in 1815. The chapel was again damaged by flood in 1956 and restored in 1957. This chapel, also known as the Chapel of Miracles (*Capela dos Milagres*), is situated on the eastern side of the river which divides the city of Machico. Nearby, according to tradition, are the graves of Anne d'Arfet and Robert Machim and the harbour is also on this eastern side. There were once three forts protecting Machico Bay, but only two now remain: the Fort of Saint John the Baptist, near the port; and the Fort of Amparo which is small and triangular and dates from 1706. This fort is in the centre of the city near the sea-front and in front of it is a very pleasant tree-lined road with an open-air café. The third fort, the Fort of São Roque, was next to the existing Chapel of São Roque near to where the Hotel Dom Pedro is now situated. Whenever a pirate attack was imminent a bonfire was lit on the nearby Pico do Facho and the people would flee inland, leaving the soldiers to guard the forts and the city. This is commemorated every September when hundreds of bonfires are lit on the hillsides and hilltops of the immense valley in which Machico is situated.

The road out of Machico towards Caniçal winds steeply up the mountain side. Just before the tunnel it is well worth taking the road to the right which leads to Pico do Facho, from where there is a beautiful view of Machico, the Bay of Machico and the new airport extension. The tunnel through the mountain to Caniçal was completed in the late 1950s. Before then the only way to reach the last village at this end of the island was by boat or along a narrow path which clung to the hillside above precipitous cliffs. Caniçal is some nine kilometres beyond Machico. It has always been a fishing village and trawlers from here and from Machico are used for deep-sea and more distant fishing trips such as to the North African coast. Caniçal was also once the whaling centre of Madeira, and the old whaling factory is now being converted into a Whaling Museum.

The area between Caniçal and the end of the island is very sandy and, indeed, the only natural sandy beach on the island is to be found at Prainha on the road out to Ponta do São Lourenço at the end of the island. At the end of this road, walk a short way over the grassy hillside and look down on the turquoise waters of the bay (Baia de Abra). The Ilhéu de Fora, with the lighthouse on it, is separated from the land by a 165m wide channel through which the boat to Porto Santo passes in all but the roughest weather.

Returning to Machico, we take the road up the lovely valley of the Ribeira do Machico to Portela (35km). Here three roads meet, all of which are signposted Funchal. Fine views can be had looking down on the north side of the island to Porto da Cruz and the Penha d'Aguia (the enormous flat-topped rock) which stands between Faial and Porto da

Cruz. At Portela (625m above sea-level) there is a popular restaurant which specializes in *espatada* and where you can watch your lunch cooking on the fire of laurel twigs. This is also a popular place to stop for hot drinks in winter, cold in summer or coffee and brandy any time.

From Portela, an alternative route is to go along the north coast through Porto da Cruz and Faial. At Faial there is a new bridge over the Ribeira Seca as the old one was washed away in a violent storm a few years ago.

We will take the shorter route from Portela to Santo António da Serra, more commonly known as Santo da Serra (41km). Here there are many *quintas* which were used by the wealthy Funchal merchants in the summer months. The interesting nine-hole golf course affords beautiful views of the mountains and out to Ponta do São Lourenço. The golf course is reminiscent of those in the Scottish Highlands. You don't have to be a member to play – visitors are welcome, and in the week the course is more or less deserted. There is also a small park in Santo da Serra with a good selection of trees and shrubs, a children's play area and small enclosures for wild ponies, deer and even kangaroos.

The last stop on this tour is at Camacha (53km). This village, situated 700m above sea-level, seems to have some kind of festival almost every weekend. It is the centre of the wicker industry, and on one side of the central square is a large warehouse with thousands of items made from wicker – baskets, trays, chairs and more unusually, elephants, lions and giraffes. Camacha is also famous for having one of the oldest and best folk-dancing groups on the island, which has performed in many different countries. Another thing for which Camacha is renowned is its camellia trees, which grow very tall and are covered in blooms. From here we return to Funchal, a total distance of 63km having been covered.

Tour 4. Eira do Serrado and Curral das Freiras

This is a short excursion which does not fit in with any of the circuits mentioned above. From Funchal we take the road out to São Martinho, past the cemetery to Pico dos Barcelos. From this viewpoint we can see that, although the centre of Funchal is very built-up, there is still a lot of green land around the city. From here we take the road marked Curral das Freiras for a short but very scenic and awe-inspiring drive. The whole distance from Funchal to Curral das Freiras is only 15km. It is worth going to Eira da Serrado, just above Curral das Freiras, for an amazing view down onto the village of Curral das Freiras which nestles in a spectacular deep valley. We now descend a winding road into the village.

This was where the nuns from Santa Clara Convent in Funchal fled to during pirate raids in the sixteenth century. Some time later a small permanent settlement grew up there. The village was very isolated in the past, and until the road down into Curral das Freiras was built in 1959, the only access was down the narrow, twisting, tortuous path which you can still see from the village. Television arrived here only in time for Christmas 1986.

11 *Funchal*

Funchal: The City

Funchal, like other historic towns and cities, suffers from the problems caused by the internal combustion engine. Whereas other cities in Europe have tried to combat the disease, little or no progress has been made in Funchal. At the moment the car reigns supreme in the city, although the days of its reign may be numbered if various plans, at present on the drawing-board, come to fruition. In the past few years a number of small streets have been closed to traffic, and car-parking has been prohibited from three out of the four central reservations in Avenida Arriaga. At the present time the best days to walk around Funchal are Saturday and Sunday when it is much quieter and you will have the chance to stop and view the buildings and doorways, many of which have interesting detail. With its narrow streets and lack of parking places, this city is best explored on foot.

According to António Arragão (in *Subsídios para a História da Cidade do Funchal*, 1979), before 1425 a small group of people were living in the area of Santa Maria do Calhau, mainly in single-storey straw-roofed buildings. They were mainly artisans – carpenters, stonemasons, ironworkers, shoemakers, weavers and fishermen. The first street in Funchal was more or less the present Rua Santa Maria, and the flat area of beach was where the Largo do Corpo Santo is now. A tiny chapel dedicated to Santa Maria do Calhau was built here in about 1430 and was enlarged in 1458 to serve the growing population. Unfortunately this church was destroyed by flood and nothing remains of it now. In 1455 Luigi Cadamosto, an Italian navigator in the service of Portugal, had sailed to Madeira. According to him, there were some 800 men living on the island at that time which would suggest a total island population of around three thousand, approximately half living in Funchal.

In general, the buildings in Funchal are of a modest simplicity which make a contrast with the luxuriance of the vegetation. There are two main styles of architecture: the earlier Gothic and the later Renaissance or baroque style. The very austere and pure baroque uses a contrast, in many

Key:

1 Lido Complex
2 Reid's Hotel
3 Sheraton Hotel
4 Savoy Hotel
5 Casino Park Hotel
6 Casino & Cine Casino
7 Quinta Vigia
8 Santa Catarina Gardens
9 Santa Catarina Chapel
10 Hospício Maria Amélia
11 Statue of Prince Henry the Navigator
12 Loo Rock
13 Municipal Theatre
14 Municipal Gardens
15 Madeira Wine Company Lodge
16 Tourist Office
17 Statue of Gonçalves Zarco
18 'Golden Gate' Restaurant
19 Post Office
20 Regional Government Building
21 Pátio & Vicente's Photographic Museum
22 English Church
23 British Cemetery
24 Pico Fort
25 Scottish Kirk
26 Church of São Pedro
27 Municipal Museum & Aquarium
28 Convent of Santa Clara
29 Museum of Quinta das Cruzes
30 Praça do Município
31 Colégio Church
32 City Hall
33 Museum of Sacred Art
34 Cathedral
35 Yacht Marina
36 Quay
37 Beatles Boat Restaurant
38 Palace of São Lourenço
39 Old Customs House
40 Corpo Santo Chapel
41 Fort of São Tiago
42 Market
43 Quinta da Boa Vista
44 Botanical Gardens
45 Quinta Magnolia

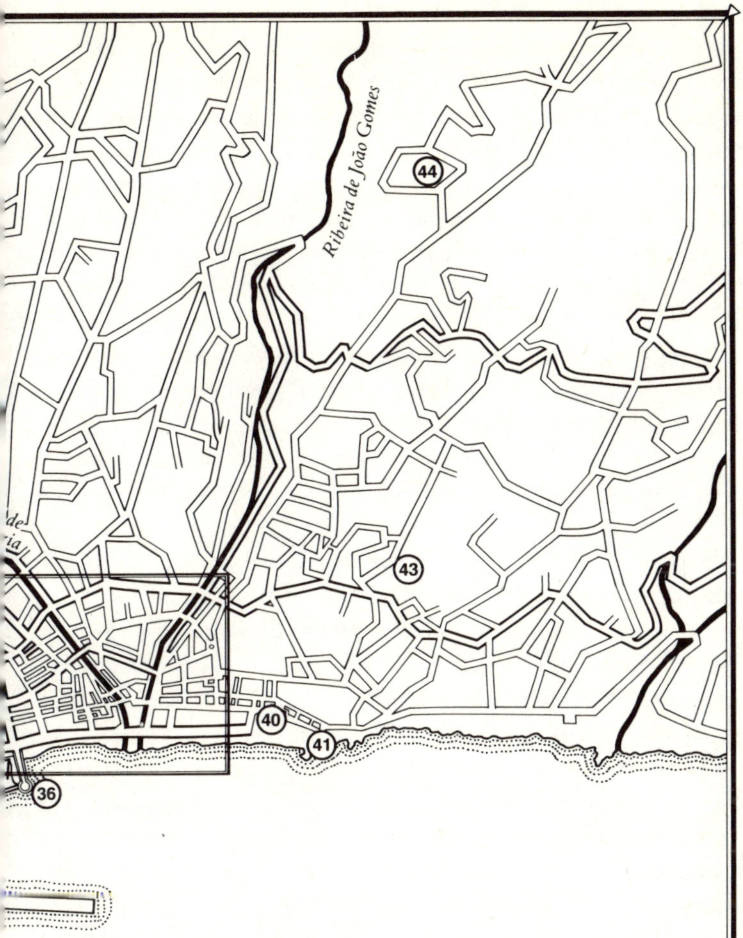

DETAIL OF FUNCHAL CENTRE

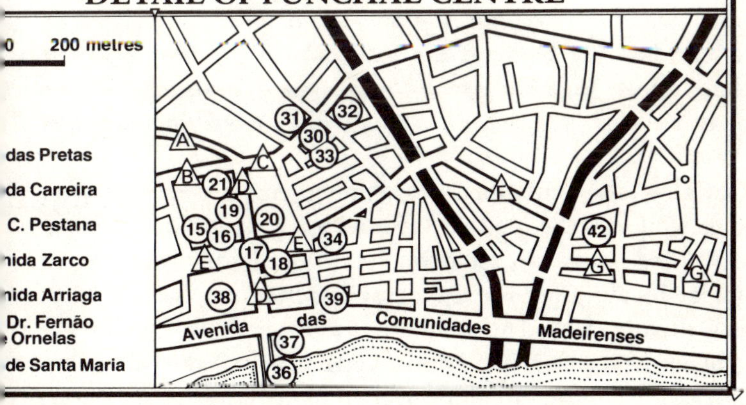

buildings, between whitewashed walls and almost black basalt windows, doorways and angle stones at corners. The traditional colours used in Madeiran houses were white or cream walls, stonework or pale grey paintwork around the windows and doorways, dark green shutters, gates and doors and red tile roofs. In 1986 there was new legislation to restore these traditional colours to houses in the island and banning the use of unpainted aluminium for windows, gates and so on, which have been spoiling many of the traditional buildings. The city has few modern buildings in the central area which do not conform to the height or style of their surroundings. Many modern buildings are in the traditional style and blend in well – as is the case with the Caixa Economica do Funchal building in Rua João Tavira. There are, however, a few blots on the landscape such as the fairly new Centro Comercial do Infante building which towers at one side of the roundabout at the foot of Avenida do Infante.

The large old private houses (*quintas*) are usually to be found behind high stone walls, and an open door in a wall can often reveal a charming old garden with bright flowers and shady paths and, perhaps, even a glimpse of the house itself. Even the smallest garden in Madeira usually has a small courtyard with pergola for vine, passion fruit or rose and numerous pot plants – orchids, anthuriums and ferns.

All the footpaths in central Funchal are made with small black and white stones set in mosaic patterns. Many of the roads are cobbled and the older streets and pavements have rounded pebbles protruding from the cement in which they are set. Shoes with thick soles and low heels are to be recommended for walking round the centre of Funchal. This chapter on Funchal is written in the form of an itinerary in order to include most of the buildings, streets and places of interest in the city in a logical order as Funchal does not signpost or highlight many of its attractions. It can be very hard on the feet and on the nerves in the narrow and busy streets on a hot day without some plan to follow. One of the charms of Funchal, and the island as a whole, is its hidden tourist attractions.

If you are walking down into the centre along Avenida do Infante, after the Savoy Hotel you pass the modern Casino Park Hotel and, behind it, the new Casino. The previous Casino was in an old *quinta* on this site. This new circular building houses a panoramic restaurant, with cabaret and dancing on the top floor. The gambling rooms are below, and there is a discothèque on the lower ground floor. In part of the same complex is the Cinecasino a very modern and spacious cinema, complete with air-conditioning and coffee bar, where most of the latest films are shown. You then pass the official residence of the President of the Regional Government, Quinta Vigia, on your right. The original Quinta Vigia stood where the Casino now is and no longer exists. The presidential *quinta* was originally called Quinta Lambert (after its owner, the French Comte de Lambert) and later the Quinta das Angústias. It is painted pink, which is also one of the traditional colours used on old buildings here.

Below Quinta Vigia are the Santa Catarina Gardens, where there was a cemetery (Cemitério das Angústias) until the late 1940s. These gardens have taken many years to complete and now include a children's play area, a small lake with swans and fountains and a large sloping grassy area surrounded by trees and seats. At the far end of the gardens is the Santa Catarina Chapel which dates from 1425. Originally built by order of Constança Rodriguez, the wife of Zarco, it was rebuilt in the fifteenth and seventeenth centuries. It is the oldest place of worship in Madeira and has recently been converted into a small museum. The terrace outside is a popular spot for watching the activity in the harbour below. From here there is a good view of the fortress of Nossa Senhora da Conceição which was built in the seventeenth century on the Loo Rock to protect ships in the harbour. It contained a chapel, magazine and barracks. Loo Rock no longer stands alone; it is now incorporated in the harbour mole, and a road tunnel passes through it.

On the opposite side of the road to the gardens is the Hospício Maria Amélia, originally a gift by the Dowager Empress of Brazil, whose only daughter the Princess Maria Amélia died of consumption in Madeira in 1853. The building was opened on the ninth anniversary of her death in 1862 and was for the consumptive poor. It was built with two wings, one for men and one for women, separated by a chapel. The beautiful garden is full of rare and interesting shrubs and trees. There is a legend that Maximilian, later Emperor of Mexico, visited the Princess during her stay in Madeira and fell in love with her. It is certainly true that he gave a sculpture of Our Lady of Sorrows, with a gold heart round her neck, to the hospice. In 1880 an orphanage was built at the side of the Hospício, and there is now a primary school housed in a separate building at the back. The Dowager Empress made her sister, Queen Mary of Sweden, a trustee of the hospice, and in 1986, on a visit to Madeira, the present King and Queen of Sweden visited the Hospício.

Down the hill and past the Rotunda do Infante (roundabout with fountains) and the statue of Dom Henrique (Prince Henry the Navigator), we pass the Centro Comercial do Infante, which has a large variety of shops and restaurants. On the right-hand side of the road (Avenida Arriaga) is the municipal theatre (Teatro Baltazar Dias). It was opened in 1888, and inside it is reminiscent of the miniature theatre at Versailles. There is a small circular auditorium with three tiers of boxes rising vertically around it. Completely restored in the 1970s, it is in very good condition and there are also, in the building, a coffee shop, library and art gallery.

Across the road are the municipal gardens, formerly the site of the Convent of São Francisco which had a chapel lined with over 3,000 bones, mainly skulls and thigh bones, but no one seems to know exactly why. In 1834 the monks, along with all other members of religious orders, were ejected from Portugal, and the monastery fell into ruins. When it was demolished, two complete skeletons were found walled up in part of the building. The coat of arms belonging to the fifteenth-century convent is to be found in the gardens. A large variety of plants and trees feature here, including many native trees of Madeira – til, dragon tree and Madeira laurels. At the Avenida Arriaga side of the gardens there is a small pond with ducks and fountains which are illuminated at Christmas time.

Avenida Arriaga was known in former times as the Passéio Público, and there was a tradition of people meeting, talking and walking here. Until recently the central reservation had deteriorated into use as a car-park. In the last few years, cars have been banned from parking in the central areas, and seats and plants have appeared in an attempt to return to tradition. We pass the Madeira Wine Company Lodge, with its museum and tasting room, and the Tourist Office, which also has an art gallery attached, and then comes to the corner of Avenidas Arriaga and Zarco. Here there is a large statue of João Gonçalves Zarco, by the Madeiran sculptor Francisco Franco, inaugurated in 1934.

Diagonally across from the Bank of Portugal is the 'Golden Gate'. Its restaurant and coffee bar are now on the first floor but once were on the ground floor where the bank is now. It used to be called 'the Corner of the World' as it was said that, seated at one of the tables on the pavement, a Madeiran would eventually see all the people he knew and meet people from all over the globe.

We now turn up Avenida Zarco past the Post Office, which has recently been re-modelled inside in glass and marble and with all the latest computer equipment – but the service has not improved and the stamps still have no glue.

On the other side of the street is the Regional Government Building which, from early times, was a hospital. It has two very attractive old patios inside. The alteration of the building into offices was approved in 1946, and the various services of the then Junta began there in 1953.

The Pátio and Vicentes Photographic Museum are reached by entrances in Avenida Zarco and in Rua da Carreira. On entering the courtyard of the Pátio, one may be reminded of New Orleans by the verandah, supported on wrought-iron columns and with ornate roof valences, which is on three sides of the courtyard above the open-air café.

Vicente Gomes da Silva, born on 12 March 1827, was the first commercial photographer in Madeira and one of the first in Portugal. On his return from studying photography in France, he founded his own business here in 1848. In 1866 he was allowed to use the arms of the Empress Elisabeth of Austria, as photographer to Her Majesty. In 1903 his son was given permission to use the Portuguese royal arms as photographer to the royal family. In 1978 the Vicentes Studio was acquired by the Regional Government to make a photographic museum. Helped by Mr Jorge Vicente, they have spent many years sorting and cataloguing the 100,000-plus glass negatives, and further collections from other old photography studios have been added to make a complete photographic history of the island and those who visited it. Downstairs in the courtyard of the Pátio there is also a record shop, health food shop and a bookshop specializing in books in English and other languages. The Pátio is an interesting oasis in which to rest from the hustle and bustle of Funchal.

We continue now along the Rua da Carreira, past the many small restaurants and bread and cake shops until we come to a street on the right called Rua do Quebra Costas which will take us to the English Church, hidden behind a high wall in a large garden. Before the opening of this church in 1822, services had been conducted in the consul's house by the chaplains of ships anchored in the bay. At a British Factory meeting in 1808 it was agreed to ask the British Consul-General to arrange a suitable piece of land for building a British Protestant church. In 1810 the Factory bought the piece of land and opened a fund to raise money for the building of a church. Several ships contributed to the fund, and the subscription list included King George III, the Princess Royal, the Prince of Saxe-Coburg (later King Leopold I of the Belgians), the Duke of Wellington and the Duchess of Bedford.

The church was designed by Mr Henry Veitch and, according to the stipulations of Portuguese law at that time regarding Protestant places of worship, did not look like a church and had no bells. The building looks like a library or similar public building with its classical portico and columns with Ionic capitals. The squat cupola has fan-shaped windows, and the all-seeing eye in the centre of its ceiling suggests a certain Masonic influence.

The inside of the church is friendly and pleasing to the eye. It is usually decorated with a selection of the flowers in season. The organ dates from 1841 and was imported in pieces from Britain. The church is attended by a minority of the foreign residents on the island and relies a great deal on the support it receives from visitors. The chaplain is nearly always a retired clergyman from Britain. The present chaplain, Canon Arthur Walter, was born in South Wales and came to Madeira in 1980, when he was called out of his retirement in East Anglia. The church is part of the diocese of the Bishop of Gibraltar in Europe who is based in London and whose diocese stretches from the Azores to Outer Mongolia and from the Canaries to Finland.

In the large pleasant garden there is a bronze bust of Philippa of Lancaster, daughter of John of Gaunt, Queen of Portugal and mother of Prince Henry the Navigator. The church has a library (with over 2,500 books) that is open to visitors, and informal refreshments are served in aid of church funds after Sunday morning services.

The British Cemetery is a little further up the Rua da Carreira. Before 1765 Protestants were not allowed to be buried on the island and had to be buried at sea off Garajau Point. The earliest part of the cemetery, dating from 1765, was where the Largo do Visconde do Ribeiro Real now stands, all the coffins and tombstones being moved into the present cemetery between 1887 and 1890. It is a beautiful place where visitors are welcome – just ring the bell at the gate. It is interesting to see the gravestones of the numerous people who came here for a cure for consumptive diseases and remained for ever. To the left of the gate in the Middle Burial Ground is a brass plaque in memory of the famous Reverend and Mrs Lowe.

On the hillside above is the Pico Fort (Castelo de São João de Pico) which was built during the Spanish occupation. It has been used by the Portuguese Admiralty as a radio station since 1925.

A few streets away from the English Church, at the corner of Rua Ivens and Rua do Conselheiro beside the municipal gardens, is the Scottish Kirk. It dates from 1861 and was built to look like a church as, by that time, Portuguese law permitted Protestant churches to look like places of worship.

If we go back up to the corner of Rua de Carreira and Avenida Zarco and go up Rua das Pretas, we come to the Church of São Pedro which was completed in 1598 and then extensively restored in 1747-8, when the front was altered. It contains some fine seventeenth-century coloured glazed tiles. The chancel was built in 1733.

Across from the church are the Municipal Museum and Aquarium, in a fine old Portuguese house which used to be the home of the Count of Ribeiro Real. It has a collection of the fish to be found in the waters around Madeira in the aquarium downstairs. Upstairs are examples of birds, fauna and geological specimens from the island. The building also houses the Regional Archives.

Between the museum and the Church of São Pedro is a short, steep hill (Calçada do Pico). Near the top, on the right-hand side, we see a very impressive wrought-iron balcony which is triangular in shape. This used to be the Hotel Santa Clara but is now used by telephone engineers. Across the road is the Convent of Santa Clara which was built at the end of the fifteenth century and rebuilt in the seventeenth century. It has very interesting old cloisters. In the adjoining chapel you will find the tomb of Zarco, the discoverer of Madeira. The chapel is noted for its magnificent tiles.

H.N. Coleridge in his book *Six Months in the West Indies* (1825) tells the story of a young nun, Maria Clementina, the youngest child of Pedro Anostinho, a well-to-do person, born in Madeira. She was said to be the most beautiful girl in the whole island, with a fair complexion, blue eyes and golden-brown hair. She entered the convent at the age of eighteen, at the wish of her parents, and took the veil the following year. One year later, Constitutional Government was established in Portugal, and the Cortes (Parliament) ordered the doors of all religious houses to be thrown open. Maria was released from the convent and fell in love with a dashing Portuguese officer. The wedding had to be postponed because she became ill, and before it could take place, the King dissolved Parliament and revoked its laws. Heartbroken, Maria had to return to the convent and remain a nun for the rest of her life. When Coleridge saw her, she was twenty-one years old. She died in 1850, having been allowed to leave the convent for the last few months of her life to be nursed by her sisters. Many foreign visitors, intrigued by her story, used to visit Maria Clementina.

Just above the Santa Clara Convent is the Museum of Quinta das Cruzes, on the site where João Gonçalves Zarco is thought to have had his house. The present building dates from the seventeenth and eighteenth centuries and was rebuilt in the early nineteenth century. It was the home of the Lomelino family, wine-shippers of Genoese origin. The rooms of the museum are furnished in the style of the period, with important collections of authentic period furniture, silver, china and art. There are Flemish paintings, British furniture (including Chippendale and Hepplewhite), Portuguese colonial furniture and artefacts, Oriental pieces and lithographs of Madeira. In the cellars are cupboards which are unusual in that they are made of the wood from the boxes used in the sugar trade with Brazil. The whole collection shows the many influences on the island of Madeira in the past. The gardens contain many trees and a large collection of orchids, as well as old tombstones, Manueline windows and a fifteenth-century pillory.

We retrace our steps back down Calçada do Pico and Rua das Pretas and turn left along Rua Câmara Pestana to the Municipal Square (Praça do Município). On the left are the Church of Saint John the Baptist and the former Jesuit College (the Colégio). The Jesuits came to Madeira in 1569 and started to construct a church, monastery and college. Although it was begun before the end of the sixteenth century, it was still under construction in 1641. The Colégio Church has a baroque façade, with four marble statues of saints of the Society of Jesus set into it. Inside it is richly decorated and of the typical open style dictated by the Jesuit Order. The gilded retable behind the high altar dates from 1660. After the expulsion of the Jesuits from Portugal in 1759, the building became used as a barracks, and British troops were stationed here during the occupation of the island. Later the college became a school, and it is now used for the embryo of a university for the island.

At the head of the municipal square is the City Hall (Câmara Municipal) which was built as a private residence for the Conde (Count) de Carvalhal at the end of the eighteenth century. It has an agreeable courtyard with an elegant staircase and houses a small museum dealing with the history of Funchal. By 1863 the building was rented by the City Council of Funchal.

Across the square from the Colégio Church is the Museum of Sacred Art (Museu de Arte Sacra), with its entrance just round the corner in Rua do Bispo. Formerly the bishop's palace, it was built in 1600 and rebuilt between 1748 and 1751. Since 1955 it has been used as a museum and now houses many of the best religious paintings, sculptures and vestments from the island's churches, including several fifteenth- and sixteenth-century Flemish works, said to have been obtained in exchange for sugar shipped from Funchal. Many of the paintings have been skilfully restored and are well displayed. We will confine ourselves here to mentioning just four of the works on display.

The Triptych of St James and St Philip is sixteenth-century oil on wood. The central panel shows the two saints, and the two side panels the family of Simon Gonçalves da Câmara (grandson of Zarco) who commissioned the painting.

The Adoration of the Magi is sixteenth-century oil on wood and is probably attributable to the Portuguese master Grão Vasco. This shows Mary, with the baby Jesus on her lap, and Joseph, with the richly dressed three kings. The painting was given to Machico church by Branca Teixeira, wife of Tristão Vaz, one of the discoverers of Madeira.

The Triptych of the Descent from the Cross shows Christ being taken down from the cross on the central panel. The two side panels show Simon Acciaiuoli and his wife (the commissioners of the painting), accompanied by their patron saint.

The fifteenth/sixteenth-century painting of Santana and São Joaquim was originally in Madalena do Mar. It is thought that the saints were modelled on Henrique Alemão (King Ladislau of Poland – see p.87) and his wife, Senhora Anes, who commissioned the painting. The sculptures are almost entirely of Flemish origin and date from as early as the sixteenth century. The very rich religious vestments on display date from the eighteenth and nineteenth centuries and were used for many different ceremonies. There are also a number of gold and silver pieces from the cathedral treasury. One outstanding exhibit is the silver-gilt processional cross which was given by King Manuel I who had ordered the construction of Funchal Cathedral and under whose patronage Vasco da Gama discovered India.

We continue along Rua do Bispo and down Rua de João Tavira to the cathedral (Sé). Occupying a prominent position in the centre of Funchal, the cathedral was built between 1485 and 1514 by two master builders from Portugal, Gil Eanes and Pero Annes. The style is early Gothic, the combination of whitewashed walls and dark red basalt (local stone) being simple but imposing. The portal arch has the Portuguese royal arms on top and a rose window above it. At one stage two large windows were let into the wall each side of the rose window to give more light, but these were removed when the cathedral was restored in the early part of this century as they were not in keeping with the original design. The triangular tower has chequered blue-and-white tiles. The present clock, replacing an earlier one, was presented by Dr Michael Grabham in 1922, and the blessing of the clock was attended by Charles, ex-Emperor of Austria. The designs in the ceiling of the nave are in the *mudejar* style – carved cedar or juniper wood (the various descriptions seem unable to agree on which) encrusted with ivory workings in geometric designs. The carvings depict exotic ideas and discoveries – strange animals, flowers, trees and a round world instead of a flat one. The stalls, carved in cedar, date from the seventeenth century. There are many interesting paintings with a medieval theme, by Portuguese artists, behind the high altar. The sixteenth-century Sacramento Chapel has some interesting work in wood and marble. The acoustics are particularly good, and in recent years the cathedral has played host to International Bach Concerts in June.

Columbus's House was in the part of Funchal near the cathedral and belonged to Jean d'Esmanault (João Esmeraldo) a Flemish merchant. There is, in fact, no proof that Christopher Columbus did stay in the house, only tradition. The house was demolished in 1877, and the windows are preserved in the garden of the Quinta Palmeira. There are plans to re-site the windows in a square in Funchal, between the cathedral and the sea.

A walk along Avenida das Comunidades Madeirenses – or Avenida do Mar, its former and more popular name – takes us along the sea shore from the foot of the Santa Catarina Gardens to the oldest part of Funchal. The promenade is being improved and the road being made into a dual carriageway. At the start of the promenade is a kiosk (a recent construction, based on an old tradition as there were several kiosks in Funchal), open-air café, gardens and seats.

Below us on this first section is the recently opened yacht marina, a very pleasant area to stroll round if you are at all interested in boats. There are yachts from Madeira berthed here, as well as from most European countries and from North America, for Madeira is the natural stopping place for yachts *en route* to and from North America, the Caribbean and Europe. Before the opening of this new marina, yachts had to detour to the south to the Canaries. The marina is a colourful sight and has shops and restaurants. Along one side is the quay, once known as the 'Entrada da Cidade' (Entrance to the City) with fountains and garden at its beginning, still a popular place to promenade. On the other side of the quay is the Beatles Boat Restaurant, a large boat which once belonged to the Beatles pop group which arrived in Madeira in a very sorry state but has now been renovated and, along with many small boats, forms an interesting open-air restaurant complex.

Across the main road is the Palácio de São Lourenço. Construction of this was begun in the first half of the sixteenth century by the Donatory Captain Simão Gonçalves da Câmara. In 1566 it was still incomplete and easily fell to the French corsairs who attacked Funchal in that year. At the end of the sixteenth and beginning of the seventeenth century, in the years of Spanish rule, the fort was completed. Today it is one of the best-preserved examples of Portuguese fortifications. It still maintains the main architectural design of the original, although there have been some alterations – for example, cutting off part of the north bulwark and the covering of the Manueline towers. In the eighteenth century it ceased to be needed as a fortress in the military sense, and in the latter part of that century the conversion of the inside into a palace was begun. It has lofty and spacious reception rooms and a ballroom and has been declared a national monument. Unfortunately, it is not open to the public.

In the gardens on the sea front, just past the Beatles Boat, are a monument to the War Dead, 1914-18, and a monument to the Madeiran Emigrant. Recently re-erected nearby is the base of the Pillar of Banger which was rediscovered during road works. This was an old crane tower built on the shore by John Light Banger, an Englishman, in 1798 to facilitate the unloading of ships. Soon after it was built, it was left high and dry by a storm and thereafter was used as a signalling tower by Blandy's. It was pulled down in 1939 when the Central Government built Avenida do Mar.

On the landward side of the Avenida is the Old Customs House (Alfândega) which is being converted into a new home for the Regional Government. The old Customs House was built at the end of the fifteenth century, having been started around the time Funchal first had its own customs post in 1477. The first-floor room has one of the finest ceilings in Portugal, made of wood carved and painted with shell volutes in the corners. It is not certain at this time whether the small round building, being built in front, as part of the Regional Government complex, will detract from the newly renovated building.

The far end of Avenida do Mar is rather a mess, with parked buses, cars and trucks together with fishermen's huts and boats. Beyond this, and to the left, is the Old Town, where Funchal began. It is now largely restored into an area of restaurants and bars, with narrow cobbled streets. This is a good place to rest for lunch or to visit for an evening out, for there is often live music in the restaurants and bars – folk, *fado* and jazz are all provided for. Standing in the old town is the Corpo Santo Chapel, dating from the sixteenth century, which is open all day for people to view the interior. Beyond the chapel and down to the right is the Fort of São Tiago, named after the patron saint of Funchal. This small fort dates from 1614 and is shortly to be opened to the public.

A colourful ending to our tour of central Funchal would be the market at the end of Rua Dr Fernão d'Ornelas. Fruit and vegetables are on the ground and first floors, with fish on the floor below. It is a very interesting, if noisy, place in which to view the wide variety of produce available and to observe the fishermen as they sell their daily catch of *espada* and tunny.

Shopping in Funchal

Shopping in Funchal for gifts can be a very enjoyable part of your holiday. The tourist bazaars stock a wide variety of embroidery, tapestry, wicker, ceramics, wine and craft items, as well as postcards and foreign newspapers. They will often invite you in to see their stock, and if you make a purchase you may be rewarded with a glass of madeira wine. There are also specialist shops selling only embroidery or wicker. These usually belong to one of the factories, many of which are open to visitors. Flowers are also a popular buy and there are a number of flower shops as well as flower-sellers in the market and by the cathedral. Flowers such as strelitzias, anthuriums and orchids last a very long time and are well worth taking home – some flower shops will pack them specially for export. During the orchid season you can visit the orchid houses at Quinta da Boa Vista of Mrs Betty Garton, one of the leading growers, and see the large variety of orchids available. Also well worth a visit is the Casa do Turista, located behind the municipal theatre, where, laid out in rooms typical of a Madeiran *quinta*, you will see embroidery, table decorations, flower arrangements and ceramics, as you would use them in your own home. The Casa do Turista also has a section with old madeiras and port wines.

Shopping for more mundane items in Funchal can be more of a problem. There are no real department stores as such, most shops being small and specialized. You can buy just about everything you ever need in Funchal, but you may have to search to find it – many shops may just recently have run out of the very product you want, so that you have to search for a shop which still has old stock until more is imported. Or you may return to where you bought an item and the assistant (who served you last time) will tell you that this shop has never stocked whatever it is. Equally well, rather than disappoint you, the assistant may say that the item is not in stock at present but may be in next week – after several weeks of returning to ask about it, you may suddenly realize that the item never is coming in.

As you walk through the streets of Funchal, particularly the small, narrow, side streets, you can see many artisans practising crafts now rarely seen in the mass-production economies of northern Europe and

North America. These craftsmen sit in the open doorways of their small workshops – the tinsmith, the cabinetmaker, the french polisher and the wrought-iron worker.

Funchal: The Environs

Just outside the city centre, on the way up to Reid's Hotel, turn right up Rua do Dr Pita just after the bridge. A short way up, on the right-hand side, is Quinta Magnolia. Until 1980, this was the British Country Club; then it was taken over by the Regional Government and reverted to its original name, being opened as a public park. The house was built by T.H. March (the then American Consul) who was an avid collector of plants and at the beginning of this century it was the home of Dr Herbert Watney, a great horticulturist. There is a valuable collection of palm trees and exotic plants in the gardens which are very spacious and contain a large open-air swimming pool, tennis and squash courts, a keep-fit track and a children's play area. Just at the back of Quinta Magnolia is a small British school which provides a full-time British-style education for foreign and Portuguese children. The original house of Quinta Magnolia has recently been restored and is now part of the Hotel School. A very good-value lunch can be enjoyed here, cooked and served to a high standard by the students of the school.

Past Reid's along Estrada Monumental, going out of Funchal, and down to the left is the lido complex. There are very large sun bathing terraces two swimming pools, sea-bathing, showers, changing-rooms and restaurants in this modern complex. Owned by the municipality of Funchal, the whole facility is kept spotlessly clean. There is a small entrance charge and it is well worth a visit.

A short bus or taxi ride from the city centre takes you to the Botanical Gardens which, until 1936, were the Quinta do Bom Successo residence of the Reid family. Opened in 1960, the gardens portray a living museum of plants and trees. There is a herbarium, as well as a laboratory concerned with scientific research and investigation into plants and crop production. The gardens are situated between 200 and 350m above sea-level and cover a large area. There are terraces and greenhouses with many rare and indigenous plants, all of which are labelled in Portuguese and Latin. There is a terrace with ornamental pools and café which affords excellent views over Funchal.

If you are fond of flowers and gardens, you must not miss a visit to the gardens of Quinta do Palheiro. Situated eight kilometres out of the centre of Funchal on the Camacha road, they can be reached by bus or taxi. The gardens are open in the morning on weekdays, except for public holidays. The gardens were laid out in the eighteenth century by a French landscape gardener for the then owner and founder, the first Conde de Carvalhal. In 1828 he had to flee to Britain when the island was occupied by Miguelist troops but he returned to Madeira in 1834, influenced by British landscape gardening ideas. He died in 1837 and left all his assets to his nephew, who was very extravagant. The property was bought by the Blandy family in 1884, and over the years they have farmed the estate and improved the gardens. Mildred Blandy, mother of the present owner, lovingly supervised the gardens for many years and introduced many plants, many of them (such as Proteas) from South Africa.

A nice half-day excursion would be to Monte and Terreiro da Luta, still within the city of Funchal but a bus or a taxi ride up the hillside at the back of the city. Monte is six kilometres from Funchal at an altitude of 550m. The first church here was built by Adão Gonçalves Ferreira (son of Gonçalo Ayres Ferreira who came to the island with Zarco). In 1741-7 a new church was built but it was destroyed by earthquake in 1748. In 1818 a new Church of Nossa Senhora da Incarnação (or do Monte) was consecrated. It is set on a platform reached by seventy-four basalt steps, and its tall twin white towers, set each side of the main doorway, make it a landmark from Funchal way below. The Emperor Charles IV of Austria was buried here on 5 April 1922. He and his wife Zita had arrived in Madeira on 19 November 1921 aboard the British cruiser *Cardiff*. They lived initially in Vila Victoria, near to and belonging to Reid's, and then moved up to Quinta Gordon (also known as Quinta do Monte), in Monte. There are many large *quintas* in Monte as it used to be favoured by the rich who moved up to their summer houses when it became too hot and humid in Funchal.

In the main square (Largo do Fonte) in Monte there is a shrine with the Virgin of Monte in it, built in 1897 to replace the original one which had been destroyed when one of the large chestnut trees fell on it. The gardens were started in 1894 and have been gradually extended since then. To one side of the square is the former railway station and the bridge over the gardens is a former railway bridge – Monte station was opened in 1894, but the short-lived railway from Funchal closed in 1939. In 1903 a German syndicate began building the present sanatorium and the Hospital of Marmeleiros. At first it appeared a good development for the island – the Germans promised to look after poor patients with tuberculosis and, in return, were given many favourable concessions such as duty-free importation of equipment and the right to expropriate land.

George Bernard Shaw being taught to dance by Max Rinder at Reid's Hotel,
30 December 1924

Sir Winston Churchill at Câmara de Lobos, January 1950

Sarah Bernhardt (1845–1923), the French actress, in a hammock

The Casino Park Hotel and the Casino

The entrance to the Savoy Hotel

The Monte toboggan – a form of transport unique to Madeira

The Madeira Wine Company's Lodge in Funchal

The superbly placed Reid's Hotel and gardens

Sunbathing at the Sheraton Hotel

Machico – where the first settlers landed

Funchal from the Santa Catarina Gardens

The fishing village of Câmara de Lobos

The Palace of São Lourenço

Manueline windows in the garden of Quinta das Cruzes

However, this turned out to be, in reality, another part of Kaiser Wilhelm's expansionist policy, so the concessions were cancelled in 1905 and in 1914, when Portugal joined in the First World War, all German interests were taken over by the Portuguese Government. The sanatorium was opened only in 1941.

Terreiro da Luta (nine kilometres from Funchal at an elevation of 876m) is reached after leaving Monte and following the road through the layers of eucalyptus trees and into the level where coniferous trees commence. This was the terminus of the railway from Funchal, and the Chalet-Restaurant Esplanade was built by the railway company, having been opened in 1912. This has long been a very popular venue for cruise-ship parties, the descent to Monte or to Funchal being made by toboggan. (See p.59.)

Somewhere in the middle of the fifteenth century, legend has it that a little girl was tending sheep here when a young lady came to play with her. Her parents did not believe her story but, when she said it had happened again, her father secretly observed her. He did not see the young lady but found a small sculptured image of Our Lady. This was considered to have been a miracle, and the statue of Our Lady of Monte now stands in the centre of the high altar of the church in Monte.

In 1917, after the bombing of Funchal by the Germans, a large procession of people from all over the island walked to Monte to pray for peace, and the local priest promised in his prayers that, if peace came, he would erect a monument to Our Lady of Monte. After the war the site for the statue was chosen at Terreiro da Luta, near the Fonte da Telha where the Virgin was said to have appeared to the little shepherdess. The statue is 5.5m high and weighs 20 tonnes. Twenty thousand people were present at its inauguration in August 1927. In November 1927 it took 300 men some six hours to carry the giant rosary which surrounds the statue up from Santo António, in Funchal. The rosary is made of stones from the Santo António river and anchor chains from the ships torpedoed in Funchal Bay during the First World War.

Funchal by night

After-dinner entertainment is still largely centred around the hotels. Most have their own band which plays a wide selection of music for dancing. The larger hotels provide an occasional cabaret, and most hotels are visited on a regular one or two nights a week basis by Madeiran folk-dancing groups. Also popular are visits by *fado* (Portuguese ballad) singers and by instrumentalists who play the mandolin. Apart from special occasions, this completes the hotel picture. However, the Sheraton Hotel possesses a fine modern discothèque in its nightclub complete with laser beams, flashing lights and coloured smoke.

The Casino houses a panoramic restaurant on the top floor, complete with floorshow and dancing. On the lower floors, the Casino gambling rooms are open until 3 a.m. There is also a discothèque in the basement of this modern building. Some restaurants in the old town feature musical entertainment while you are dining, including *fado* and piano music. Behind the Savoy Hotel, in and around the Rua da Imperatriz D. Amélia, you can find a number of pleasant cocktail and piano bars that are open until the early hours, including the Prince Albert Pub which is a replica of a Victorian pub, complete with Victorian memorabilia. There are a few discothèques in Funchal for the energetic; they tend to be more frequented by local people than by tourists.

12 *People, Folklore and Festivals*

The Madeiran is an amalgam of descent from the various areas of northern Portugal and the central area around the Alentejo, as well as southern types from the Algarve, together with Moorish influence from the days of the slaves. Over generations of intermarriage, this has produced the Madeiran of today with his own personality and pronunciation of Portuguese words.

Like most Portuguese people, the Madeiran is friendly and polite and, on occasions, very formal. Unless the Madeiran is addressing a close friend or member of his family, he always uses the third person in speech. Formal letters too always appear excessively polite and somewhat 'flowery' to the average British reader.

Family unity is very strong in Madeira, not just amongst the immediate family, but through numerous cousins, aunts and uncles. In the street, when greeting each other as friends or family, there is much handshaking and backslapping between the men and kissing on both cheeks between women, and between men and women.

The Madeiran is very talkative with his friends and family. The coffee bars are full in the late afternoon with discussions about football, politics and the family. Often the women sit separately from the men and discuss their own affairs. This is especially noticeable at cocktail and dinner parties, and it is still not unusual for the ladies to move to a separate room after dinner. Since the Revolution in 1974, women have gradually become more involved in the decision-making processes, and no longer are they confined to the teaching and nursing professions. There are more and more women architects, engineers, journalists, doctors and lawyers.

In the country districts a woman's life is not easy. Apart from looking after the home and having babies, she is still expected to do most of the manual work on the land as her husband may be working abroad or in Funchal or just resting. Before television and feminine liberation, when the men were out drinking or at football, the women on their off-duty moments were usually to be seen at the window, where their social life was to be found. The Portuguese verb *janelar* ('to window') precisely reflects this condition of the woman separated from social life, which she knew only from her window.

The Madeiran changes personality when he is driving and resembles a rally driver or a laid-back Californian, with one arm out of the window dangling a cigarette. It is often necessary to drive with close attention to the car in front, especially if the driver appears to have had a little too much wine or is having a highly excited conversation with his fellow passengers and waving his arms about. It is essential in these cases to toot before overtaking. The Madeiran does, however, excel at parking his car in what looks to be an impossible place.

Like most people outside Britain, the Madeiran does not like queueing. When entering shops it is essential to make a mental note of who is in front of you, and it is the custom when entering a shop to ask if they have the items you want in stock to avoid a pointless wait. When the assistant is serving you, he may also be serving two or three other people at the same time and holding a conversation with yet another. When you have finally made your purchase, it is nearly always wrapped up in brown paper and carefully tied with string or something more elaborate. If your purchase is to be a gift, the assistant will normally offer to giftwrap it for you for no extra charge.

Isabella da França states in her book *Journal of a Visit to Madeira and Portugal 1853-54*:

> The system of washing here is rather different from ours in England … It is always done in a running stream … the rivers contain in ordinary weather but a very small stream of water, trickling through an immense mass of rocks of all sizes. Here the washerwomen find, or sometimes make, by moving some of the smaller stones, a kind of basin through which the water flows, and in which they can dip the linen. When wet they twist it like a rope, and beat some large stone with it, repeating the operation till it is quite clean. If very dirty they lay it in the stream, securing it with a large stone, and let the water flow through it for some time, after which they proceed as before … the linen is spread upon the rocks in the river, or the walls near at hand, and secured, like everything else by a stone at each corner … The linen when dry is as white as snow.

Today, in the country, you are more than likely to see women still washing in this way, although they now use *lixivia* (bleach), sold in bright plastic bottles which, empty and discarded, can often be seen in a river bed or floating out to sea. The maids in houses also wash up under running water, using all the hot water and soap and running up large electricity bills. Even if wages are relatively cheap, electricity is not.

At one time each village had its own traditional dress, and it was possible to see the influences of different regions of mainland Portugal, particularly the Minho district, on the women's clothing. Today the only traditional costumes to be seen are those worn by the flower-sellers and folk dancers. Women wear a wide red woollen skirt with multi-coloured vertical stripes and a band round the hem, a white blouse with wide elbow-length sleeves, a red embroidered waistcoat, and a small red woollen cloak over one or both shoulders. The traditional costume of the men is white baggy knee-length trousers, a white long-sleeved and open-necked shirt with a soft collar and a red sash at the waist. Both men and women wear the *carapuça*, a small dark blue cap, with red trimming and a long stalk in the middle. In the last century the length of the stalk varied with the status and elegance of the wearer, although the upper classes always wore the European fashions of the day. On their feet both men and women wear half-length boots of yellow calfskin trimmed with a red stripe on the turned-down uppers. One traditional piece of clothing still very much used throughout the countryside, particularly by the men, is a knitted conical cap with ear flaps (*barrete de lã*). Traditionally this was always natural brown or cream wool, but bright colours are sometimes used nowadays.

Probably the best known Madeira folk dance group is that from Camacha, which was founded in 1948 under Dr Alfredo Ferreira de Nóbrega. This group is very well travelled and has appeared at many international folk-dancing events. They also, as do the other groups, regularly perform in the hotels and some typical restaurants in the island. Folk dancing is not just a tourist attraction: it is popular amongst all Madeirans, whatever their social background and they start at a very early age to learn the dance steps.

Some of the most well-known folk dances are:

Dance of Ponta do Sol: The dancers move in a circle, taking short steps with their heads bowed in the manner of chained slaves. This dance is named after Ponta do Sol where there were many Moorish and African slaves in the early days of colonization.

Moorish Dance: This is one of the oldest Madeiran folk dances. It was introduced to the island by the Moorish slaves of the early colonists.

Heavy Dance: This is a very old dance with music and rhythm reminiscent of African dances and denotes the crushing of grapes with the feet.

Dance of the Romarias: *Romaria* is the name given to people travelling to church festivals, often many miles across the island. People travelled in groups, dancing and singing as they went.

The Carrier's Dance: Of all the working dances, this one is the most characteristic and represents men being cheered along by music as they carry fully laden baskets or other heavy loads on their shoulders.

Musical instruments typical of Madeira are on exhibition at the *Instituto de Bordado, Tapeçarias e Artesanato* in Rua Visconde Anadia. Although traditional, these instruments are still used to accompany folk dances today. The *rajão* is a five-stringed instrument about 66cm long. It is strung in the same way as a viola and usually has two wire and three gut strings. It was taken by Madeiran emigrants to various parts of the world, including the Hawaiian islands, where it has become the Hawaiian ukelele. The *viola* is 87cm long and is thought originally to have had twelve strings, but now only has nine wire strings. It is of Arab origin. The *braguinha* has four gut strings, although sometimes the first string is wire to give a more strident tone. This is a very popular instrument which gives a lively and happy sound and is always used to accompany singing. The *brinquinho* is a strange but attractive instrument. Wooden dolls are slid up and down a pole in time with the music, and castanets and bells, on the dolls' backs, make a percussion sound. The *bombo* is a small drum which is hit with a leather-bound stick. The *reco-reco* consists of pieces of wood on a string which make a sound rather like someone playing the washboard. Normally a mouth organ or a piano accordion accompanies the music and plays the melody. The singing is full of strident, screechy voices, and one need never worry about being out of tune in Madeiran folk singing.

Fado is music with Arabic roots which comes from continental Portugal. This very popular music with its haunting, melancholy and often monotonous melodies is sung in Madeira but has never become as popular here as it is in Portugal. The songs usually have as themes lamentation, fate, disgrace, love, jealousy, misadventure or *saudades*, a virtually untranslatable word meaning a mixture of fondness and nostalgia. Sung originally by ruffians or sailors, the *fado* of the street is simple accompanied song spontaneously composed, the theme of which is commonly love of mother, town, the sea, etc. Intellectual *fado* is a more stylized form and is sung in the salons and by the students of Lisbon and Coimbra Universities. Sometimes accompanied by a guitar but more often by mandolins, the singer usually has a tremulous voice powerful enough not to need microphones.

The literature of Madeira is dominated, as is the literature of Portugal, by the *Lusiads* of Luis de Camões. These stories of the discoveries made by the Portuguese explorers and told in lyric form were published in 1572.

Camões is the Shakespeare of Portugal and 10 June is a public holiday in honour of him and of Portugal. Also very important are the writings of Fernando Pessoa, dating from the early part of this century.

Madeiran literature has mainly concentrated on the legends and reminiscences of the past. Horacio Bento Gouveia's writings include romantic novels set in Madeira and, although he died a few years ago now, he remains the best known of Madeiran writers. In Madeira, as in Portugal, poetry is very much alive and popular and there are a number of modern poets who publish occasional volumes of poetry, much of it about Madeira. Poems are often published in the daily and weekly newspapers and the Regional Directorate of Cultural Affairs (*Direcção Regional dos Assuntos Culturais* or DRAC) publishes a wide variety of books on Madeira covering history, folklore, reminiscences and poetry. These are, however, all in Portuguese.

Art and art collecting are both very popular in Madeira. There are a number of foreign painters resident in the island, although none is internationally well known. There is also a strong nucleus of contemporary artists centred around the Art College of Madeira (*Instituto Superior de Artes Plasticas da Madeira* – ISAPM) which has students from Madeira and Portugal taking courses in art, sculpture, graphics and visual art. The tourist office and the local artists' community are keen to promote art and there are often exhibitions of some art form in the theatre or the tourist office's art gallery. There are many collectors of modern and classical art in the island. Paintings and old prints of Madeira are always sought after and sometimes change hands for high prices.

Until their dissolution in 1832, the Militia was the most numerous body in the archipelago. They were organized into fourteen sections, each under the command of a captain and a sergeant-major, both of whom were chosen by the municipal council from amongst the most important landowners in the region. The phasing-out of the Militia was not a speedy affair. In 1844 one auxiliary corps of artillery still stood guard on the city walls at night, and they disturbed many people with their noisy alerts. On 29 June 1850 Funchal was awoken in the morning by the sound of music. As the people opened their doors and windows, they saw several uniformed men with four cannons. They gave a 21-gun salute, played hymns and went on board a coastal yacht, where they spent most of the day alternately at anchor or sailing.

The Squadrons of Land Sailors (*Esquadras de Navegação Terrestre*) were formed out of nostalgia for the military service. They had their own uniforms and military codes, and belonging to one of the squadrons became a popular Sunday pastime. The Submarine Squadron (*Esquadra Submarina de Navegaçáo Terrestre*) was the oldest, formed in 1880 by Eduardo Sarsfield, its Admiral. They had many officers, and the uniforms were similar to those of the Portuguese Royal Navy – black uniforms (whites in summer), gold epaulettes or gold braid on both sleeves and gold anchors woven on black cloth on the fronts of their caps.

The houses and *quintas* of the high-ranking officers became the squadron's warships. There, gazing out from the balconies and look-out points, they imagined they were on board frigates and corvettes and that they had cannons and decks. They had a mast on which they raised flags to signal coded orders and instructions. In the grounds of these houses (many of which displayed an old cannon), the men were instructed in marching and the handling of weapons, and bands rehearsed and played. There was always much conviviality and enjoyment and plenty to eat and drink. Sometimes, on Sundays and other holidays, the squadron marched in force, fully armed, through the city to join in some public ceremony or to some *quinta* on the outskirts of Funchal where dinner awaited them. At times they imagined they were a disembarked army and went to Santa Cruz or Machico, which they bombarded and took. They then marched through the village, much to the interest and perhaps fear of the villagers.

Religious festivals (*festas*) are held throughout the year. Nearly every church holds two or three *festas* a year. Some are local saint's days, others are more important and attract people from all over the island. For the *festa*, the church, churchyard and the street leading to them are all gaily decorated with flags – some are coloured striped flags and others are white with red crosses like those used on the sails of Henry the Navigator's ships. The poles along the street are decorated with greenery and festoons of paper flowers, and coloured lights cross the street from pole to pole. The church is also usually decorated with lights.

In the day, there is usually a religious procession consisting of the religious image, the priests, members of the church and other people. Sometimes the streets are decorated with flower petals, although this custom is dying out. Sometimes *xerolas* (vegetables and/or fruits, often in the shape of a gigantic ball and strung on a pole which is carried on the shoulders of two men) are carried in the procession. There are stalls selling sweets, cakes, *espetada* and wine. The silver band plays and there is dancing. Often there are dodgem cars too. Fire crackers are let off during the day. There is much conviviality and noise.

The island has always been predominantly Roman Catholic, ever since the days of the first settlers, and it is still so today. However, since the

1974 Revolution there has been a weakening of the traditionally very strong family ties and a drift away from the Church, particularly among the young and the *intelligencia* of Funchal. The influence of the Church is still very strong among the less well-off in the countryside where it is often allied to superstition. There are minor followings for other Churches such as Church of England, Baptist, Presbyterian and Seventh Day Adventist as well as some Jehovah's Witnesses and Mormons.

As is increasingly true everywhere, many of the old customs in Madeira are dying out. However, there are some which remain strong. On public holidays, including the major religious festivals, carpets are hung over the balconies of public buildings and give a festive air. Bonfires are lit after sunset on the feasts of Santo António (13 June), São João (24 June) and São Pedro (29 June). People often still follow the rather dangerous custom of jumping over these bonfires, especially on the feast of São João. On the eve of the 24 June names are written on paper, folded and put in a bowl of water. The next day, if one is open, it will show the name of the future spouse. 1 November (All Saints' Day) is *Pão-por-Deus* ('Bread for God') when traditionally bread was given to the poor in the city to obtain a blessing on the souls of the departed. This has now become a day when children are given sweets, titbits and fruit.

8 December, the Feast of the Immaculate Conception, is the day when the Christmas preparations begin. The *bolo de mel* is made, the pig is killed and its blood collected, and small pots of lentils, wheat, maize, barley or any other cereal are planted. Some days before Christmas, or even on Christmas Eve, the *lapinha* (grotto) is made. Rocks are grouped together and then crushed paper is put on top of them and painted, to form the grotto. The figures of the main characters of the Nativity are then placed on it along with the pots of cereals, now full of green sprouts which symbolize fertility and plenty for the coming year. Also placed on the *lapinha* are favourite toys (however old and battered), fruits and nuts and models of Madeiran houses. The whole thing is usually lit in some way, be it with a night light, small oil lamp or Christmas tree lights. Christmas trees and other Christmas decorations are popular but the *lapinha* retains its importance in the home and is also to be found in churches, hotels and restaurants.

Some of the Major Religious Festivals held in Madeira
Santo Amaro – Santa Cruz – 15 January
Espirito Santo – Camacha – on the day after Pentecost
Santo António – Santo da Serra – 13 June

São João – Funchal and Câmara de Lobos – 24 June
São Pedro – Ribeira Brava and Câmara de Lobos – 29 June
Santa Maria Madalena – Madalena do Mar and Porto do Moniz – 22 July
Nossa Senhora do Monte – Monte – 15 August
Nossa Senhora da Graça – Porto Santo – 15 August
Nossa Senhora do Livramento – Curral das Freiras – the last Sunday in August
Senhor Jesus – Ponta Delgada – on the first Sunday in September
Nossa Senhora do Loreto – Arco da Calheta – 8 September
Nossa Senhora do Faial – Faial – 8 September
Nossa Senhora do Livramento – Caniço – the second Sunday in September
Nossa Senhora dos Remédios – Quinta Grande – on the second Sunday in September
Nossa Senhora da Piedade – Caniçal – the third Sunday in September
Nossa Senhora do Livramento – Ponta do Sol – the first Sunday in October
Nossa Senhora do Rosário – São Vicente – the first Sunday in October
Senhor dos Milagres – Machico – 8 and 9 October

13 *Food and Drink*

Food is very important to Madeirans and the restaurants of Madeira are often as full of Madeiran families and friends enjoying a meal as they are of tourists. There is now a good variety of restaurants in the island, particularly in Funchal, with new restaurants and bars opening up every month. Twenty years ago there were very few apart from the hotel restaurants. Indeed one of the oldest restaurants in Funchal is the Combatantes which is located behind the Municipal Gardens. It has always given good value for money and continues to do so today. A typical three-course meal with wine would cost about £12.00 for two people. Another long-established restaurant is the Caravela on Avenida do Mar which gives you a panoramic view of the harbour from its windows. Restaurants specializing in fish are Gavinas near the Lido and, not far away, Doca do Cavacas and, in the old town, Golfinhos which is more expensive but has attractive décor. Restaurants that specialize in the local dish of *espetada* (meat on a skewer) include A Brisa, A Seta, Espardarte and Boa Vista. All of these are a short taxi ride out of the centre of Funchal. In Funchal A Brasa in the Centro Comercial do Infante is worth trying.

Good restaurants with an international menu and a sophisticated atmosphere at a more expensive price include the Solar do F, Casa Velha and the Barão, all located within easy walking distance of the Sheraton Hotel. Also close to the Sheraton is the Kon Tiki which is owned and managed by Walter Andresen, a genial German who will welcome you personally to his restaurant. In the old town Romana's and Arsénio's cater for the international taste. For those who are into health foods there is the health food shop (the Alpendre) at the Pátio Esplanade and this caters for vegetarian meals. The large number of restaurants also include those which specialize in Chinese and Italian food, as well as fast foods such as hot dogs and hamburgers. There are also two English restaurants: the Carochinha near the Municipal Gardens is ideal for the traditional English lunch and the Britannia, a little way out of town, is owned and managed by an Englishman, Colin Gedge.

Although Madeira is part of Portugal, there are certain dishes that are typically Madeiran, many of which you would not find on hotel or restaurant menus as they are best prepared in the family kitchen. The recipes we have chosen are those which are likely to be found on many of the menus in the island. We have also included a few typically Portuguese recipes which are popular in Madeiran restaurants.

Soups

Sopa de Tomate e Cebola (Tomato and onion soup)

This is a soup that you will find on nearly every restaurant menu in Madeira – from five-star hotel to the simplest café. It is a simple soup made from a good white stock with lots of finely chopped onions and chopped, skinned tomatoes, salt and pepper. It is served with chopped parsley and croutons on top, an egg is lightly poached in the soup for each person.

Canja de Galinha (Chicken soup)

This is traditionally served in the early hours of the morning of New Year's Day, after the fireworks.

2 soupspoons butter
1 chicken
1 onion
1 medium carrot
2 litres water
150 g fine spaghetti
seasoning
chopped parsley

Boil the chicken in water with the carrot and onion until thoroughly cooked. Allow to cool. Skim fat off stock. Dice chicken and put it in the stock. Bring to the boil. Add fine spaghetti and seasoning. Serve, sprinkled with chopped parsley, as soon as the spaghetti is cooked.

Fish

There are many recipes using the very versatile *espada* fish which is found in such large numbers around the island. It can be boiled, stewed, grilled, fried and served simply or with banana or *provençale*, or even battered for British-style fish and chips. *Espada* is a very white fish which breaks into very large flakes.

Tunny fish (*atum*) in Madeira bears no resemblance to the fish sold in tins, and is usually served as large steaks. Tunny is very meaty, and the average fish weighs around 20 kilos. Contrary to popular belief, it is not caught in tins.

Balcalhau, very popular throughout Portugal, is dried cod fish, imported mostly from Norway, and you can see it hanging up in most food shops. There are a great many recipes for *bacalhau*.

Lulas (squid) are also popular in Madeira when cooked on a skewer with onions and peppers and sometimes with other assorted fish chunks. Octopus (*polvo*) is popular in casseroles and stews and is not at all rubbery if properly cooked. Also popular are *lapas* (limpets) and the inevitable sardines grilled over an open fire. There is a great variety of fish in the market apart from the very common *espada*, tunny, sardines and mackerel. Look out for *pargo, cherne, bodião* and *garoupa*, to name a few – these are usually fried or grilled whole.

Espada com banana (Espada fish with banana)

1 fillet of *espada* per person
1 or 2 bananas, halved lengthwise, per person
butter for cooking

Gently fry the *espada* in butter until cooked, without browning it. Fry the bananas for about three minutes in the hot butter until lightly browned, but not soft. Place the *espada* on a serving dish with slices of banana on each fillet and the butter spooned over. Served with boiled potatoes and/or white rice.

Espada de vinho e alhos (Espada fish in wine and garlic)

750 g *espada* fish
1 dl vinegar
1 tomato
3 cloves garlic (crushed)
1 bay leaf
salt and paprika
flour
olive oil

Cut the fish into slices about 6cm thick. Season with salt, paprika, garlic and bay leaf and leave for half an hour. Add the vinegar and tomato and leave in the marinade for a further half hour. Dip the fish slices in flour and fry in olive oil. Drain fish and put on one side, keeping it warm. Take the pan off the flame and add the marinade to the olive oil. Return to the flame and bring to the boil. Strain the liquid and pour over the *espada*. Serve with boiled potatoes, *milho frito* or *milho cozido*.

Atum Assado (Fried tunny)

1 kg slice of fresh tunny
1 dl olive oil
1 large onion
3 tomatoes
salt and paprika
parsley
500 g small potatoes

Soak the tunny in cold water for several hours to remove the excess blood. Put the olive oil, sliced onion, sliced tomato, parsley, salt and paprika into a frying pan. Drain the tunny and add it whole to the hot mixture in the frying pan. Cook gently until the tunny is golden on both sides, adding a little water as necessary. When the tunny is almost cooked, add the whole peeled potatoes. Continue cooking until the potatoes are ready and golden brown. Cover the pan, take it off the heat and leave it to rest for a few minutes before serving. Arrange the tunny and potatoes on a serving dish and cover with the sauce. White rice (boiled, drained and flavoured with butter) should be served as an accompaniment.

Bifes de Atum Cebolados (Tunny steaks with onions)

750 g tunny
1 dl vinegar or white wine
1.5 dl oil or olive oil
3 onions sliced
1 tsp dried rubbed marjoram
4 cloves garlic (crushed)
1 bay leaf
salt

Wash the tunny well in cold water to remove the excess blood. Make a marinade with the vinegar or white wine, garlic, bay leaf, marjoram and salt and leave the tunny in this for at least three hours. Heat the oil or olive oil and fry the tunny and onions until golden. Add the marinade and simmer until it is reduced. Put the tunny on a serving dish and cover with the onions and the sauce. Serve with *milho frito* or boiled potatoes or white rice.

Caldeirada (Fish stew)

750 g fish of one variety
500 g potatoes
1 large onion
3 tomatoes
1 sprig of parsley
3 tbsp olive oil
6 whole allspice
6 slices of slightly stale bread
salt
sweet potatoes

Put the onion, tomato, parsley, olive oil and allspice in a pan with two litres of water and bring to the boil. Add the potatoes whole (or halved if they are large) and bring to the boil again. Season with salt and add the fish. When the fish and potatoes are cooked, put them on a serving dish and season with olive oil and vinegar. Put a slice of bread on each plate and spoon over the stew remaining in the pan. This dish can be served accompanied by sweet potatoes.

Meat

Traditionally more fish was eaten in Madeira than meat, and so it is not surprising that two of the traditional recipes are for pork and associated with Christmas – the pig is traditionally fattened all year and killed, with much celebration, on 8 December. *Espetada* is a very popular regional meat dish and one that most restaurants include on their menu. It is probably best in the countryside, where it is cooked over an open fire.

Carne de Vinho e Alhos (Meat with wine and garlic)

This is the traditional meal on Christmas Day, Boxing Day and the day after.

600 g loin of pork, fairly fat
8 thick slices bread
600 g small new potatoes
2 dl white wine
1 dl vinegar
coarse salt
6 cloves garlic (crushed)
1 bay leaf

paprika or black pepper
sweet potato (sliced in rings)

Wash the loin of pork in hot water, drain and cut into 2 cm cubes. Make a marinade with the wine, vinegar, salt, garlic, bay leaf and pepper and add the pork which should be well covered with the marinade. Leave in the marinade for at least three days. Then cook the meat in the marinade. While the meat is cooking, soak the bread in the warm marinade but without letting it go mushy. Put the bread on one side and drain the meat and put it on one side. Allow the marinade to cool. Take the fat off the surface of the cooled marinade and use this to fry the meat and the bread in a frying pan over a high flame. If there is insufficient fat, add some lard. Meanwhile cook the new potatoes and rings of sweet potato in boiling salted water and, when cooked, fry until golden in the same fat which was used for the meat. Serve hot with slices of orange and lemon.

Sarapatel

1 kg pig's blood
1 tablespoon lard
2 onions
2 tomatoes
1 sprig parsley
2 pearmain apples
50 g walnuts
50 g raisins
250 g pig's liver
1 tsp sugar
1 tbsp butter
1 tbsp vinegar
salt

Cook separately in boiling water the blood and the liver cut into tiny pieces. Chop the onions, parsley and tomatoes finely; put in a frying pan and cook with the lard. Crumble the blood and chop the walnuts and the pearmains and add to the pan with the rest of the ingredients. Leave to cook on a low heat, stirring continually, until thickened and fairly dry. Serve with slices of bread or boiled potatoes.

This dish is also associated with Christmas.

Espetada (Chunks of meat on a skewer)

Espetada is a very popular Madeiran dish of skewered beef cooked over an open fire which should be kindled from the twigs of laurel to give fragrance and flavour to the meat. The cooking of *espetada*, to many Madeirans, is an art and it can often be seen being prepared at picnics in the countryside, at home for parties or at the local religious festivals. So important is it that many new homes are constructed with an outside barbecue set into a chimney on the side of the house.

4-5 cm cubes of beef
crushed garlic (optional)
coarse salt
laurel twigs

Put the meat on a skewer or skewers (iron or freshly made from laurel) and roll it in garlic (optional) and salt. Cook in a hot fire made of laurel twigs. When cooked, the meat is taken off the skewer and served with chips, salad and country bread and butter.

Accompaniments

The 1974 Revolution made a significant difference in the diet of many Madeirans and today the great majority have a varied diet. *Milho* (cornmeal) was the mainstay of the country person's diet. The ground maize was cooked with water, lard and shredded cabbage in a large iron pot to make a kind of porridge which would be eaten hot when freshly made in the day and eaten cold or deep-fried as *milho frito* in the evening. These variations are now found as regional dishes on restaurant menus. Sometimes the cornmeal was mixed with broad beans or with dried beans or used as the basis of a vegetable soup. *Milho* was so important in the diet because, although only a little was grown locally, it was imported cheaply from the Portuguese colonies in Africa.

Yams and sweet potatoes were also very important in the diet – yams were associated particularly with Lent and had to be left to cook overnight. Sweet potatoes were more widely grown and much cheaper than they are now. Bread, so long as wheat flour was available, was also very important and wheat flour and bread prices have long benefited from government subsidies, although these have now been dramatically reduced. Less traditional but very important was pasta – boiled in salted water and served absolutely plain and without accompaniments. As a warming drink, cocoa was drunk by the country people, again being cheaply available from the Portuguese colonies. It was made with hot water and milk was only added by those families who owned a cow and had been able to reserve a little milk for themselves. Meat only formed part of the diet at Christmas when the pig was killed (sometimes one family owned a pig, but more often it was shared by several). The meat was preserved in salt, although this was often not very carefully done and the meat often became 'high'.

Agricultural workers were always given their midday meal by the landowner and this would be served on one communal dish to which each person applied himself with a spoon. In homes in the country each member of the family usually had his or her own dish, but the only cutlery each person usually had was a spoon. It was customary for each person to cross themselves at the beginning and end of a meal but grace was seldom said.

Batata doce (Sweet potato)

1 kg sweet potatoes

Scrub well and dry. Bake in the oven in the same way as baked potatoes are cooked in Britain.

Inhame cozido (Boiled yams)

I kg yams

Soak the yam in water for 1½ to two hours. Grate off the skin of the yam, taking care not to scratch your hands. Put in a pan, cover with water, add a pinch of salt, put a cloth over the pan and then the lid on top. Bring to the boil and simmer for about two hours. Serve with the grated skin or with molasses (*mel de cana*).

Milho cozido (Cooked maize or cornmeal)

500 g white maize flour
2.5 l water
2 tbsp butter or lard
salt

Mix the flour into a smooth paste with a little cold water. Put the water and fat in a pan and bring to the boil. Add enough salt to season and stir in the flour paste. Leave to simmer, stirring occasionally, until the mixture begins to thicken, and then stir all the time. Continue to cook until it loses its roughness on the tongue (a similar consistency to cooked semolina). When the cornmeal is cooked, put it into a large dish or individual dishes (which have previously had cold water in them), smooth the surface with a knife and leave to solidify. Thyme or garlic can also be used in the cooking, as can smoked fat bacon. (If the latter is added, fat is omitted from the recipe.)

This is generally served as an accompaniment to fish or meat instead of potatoes or rice. Only a small amount of the maize used in Madeira is grown in the island (around São Jorge and Santana where the cobs can be seen drying on the roofs), the majority being imported. Traditionally the white maize flour is considered best, the yellow being used for the animals. Maize flour has always been a staple part of the diet of Madeirans, and in the past the poor relied on cornmeal which they ate just with onion slices.

Milho frito (Fried cornmeal)

500 g white maize flour
2.5 l water
2 tbsp butter, marge or lard
250 g shredded cabbage (type used in *Caldo Verde*)
salt
oil or olive oil for frying

Mix the maize flour to a smooth paste in a little cold water. Put the water, fat and salt (to taste) in a pan and bring to the boil. Add the shredded cabbage and half the cornmeal and simmer until the cabbage is almost cooked. Add the rest of the cornmeal and simmer, stirring occasionally, until the mixture thickens and then stir continuously. Cook until the mixture has the consistency of cooked semolina and feels smooth to taste. Put into shallow dishes (which have previously had cold water in them), smooth the surface and allow to solidify and cool. When cold, turn the meal out of the dishes and cut into 2 cm cubes. Put into boiling oil or olive oil (about a centimetre deep) in a frying pan and cook until pale golden and lightly crisp, turning the cubes until all sides are cooked. Drain and serve hot. *Milho frito* is usually served with fish and is delicious with *bifes de atum*.

Bread

The bread bought from bakeries and shops in the island is very good and is often baked twice a day, morning and afternoon, and sometimes more often. There are several different varieties to be bought in the shops, but because it is non-synthetic it does not keep well for over a day. There are also country breads which can be bought warm and fresh from the covered baskets of the women selling by the roadside in the country, especially on the airport road near Santa Cruz and on the road between Camacha and Santo da Serra. The two recipies given below are for these country breads.

Pão de casa (Bread of the house)

1 kg flour
200 g purée of sweet potato
100 g bread dough (5 g baker's yeast, 100 g flour, water and salt)
salt

Cook the sweet potatoes with their skins on in water seasoned with salt. When cooked, peel and purée the sweet potato. Make bread dough by mixing baker's yeast, flour, water and salt, kneading well so that ingredients are well mixed. Knead in the purée of sweet potato and then the flour, adding warm water (seasoned with salt) as necessary, until the dough has an elastic consistency. Cover and leave to rise until the following day. Mould into bread and cook in a hot oven, preferably a wood-burning one. This bread, traditionally, is often covered with cabbage leaves to keep it moist and then cooked in the hot glowing embers of a wood fire in a stone oven.

Bolo de caco (Country bread)

30-50 g baker's yeast per 1 kg flour
Warm water seasoned with salt

Mix the ingredients and knead well on floured board until it has an elastic consistency. Cover and leave to rise until next day. Divide and mould into large flat circles – about 3 cm thick. Cook on an extremely hot stone (usually on the top outside of a wood-burning stone oven) and leave until it has a fine crust. Turn over and cook the other side in the same way. Then hold vertically and gradually turn so sides are cooked. This bread can be eaten hot with butter or with a meal. It is always served with *espetada* at country festas.

Cakes and puddings

There are many types of cakes and puddings. *Bolo de mel* is made commercially, as well as in the home, and is found in most supermarkets and is now exported. Many Madeiran pudding recipes are extravagant with eggs and sugar, as are Portuguese recipes. In addition there are many variations of fruit salad made with tropical and sub-tropical fruits and various types of alcohol, such as Triple Sec.

Bolo preto (Black cake)

250 g sugar
250 g flour
2 tbsp molasses
1 tsp cinnamon
1 tbsp butter
1 egg
1 level tsp bicarbonate soda
milk (as needed to moisten mixture)
250 g mixture of following fruits (very finely chopped): crystallized citrus fruits, crystallized cherries, almonds (with their skins) and walnuts

Mix the eggs, sugar, molasses, butter and cinnamon together well. Mix the flour and bicarbonate well and then add the chopped fruits and nuts. Fold in the dry ingredients. Put in a round cake tin lined with greaseproof paper. Bake in a hot oven 425°F (Gas Mark 7) until tests done (1-1½ hours).

Bolo de Mel (Honey cake, but more correctly Molasses cake)

2.5 kg flour
1 kg sugar
750 g lard
500 g butter
25 g powdered aniseed
50 g cinnamon
12 g powdered cloves
1 wine glass madeira
250 g bread dough (made with 10 g baker's yeast, 250 g flour, warm water and salt)
1 tsp mixed spice
2 kg walnuts (unshelled weight)

250 g blanched almonds
5 tbsp bicarbonate soda
50 g crystallized citrus peel
1.8 l molasses
4 oranges

The day before preparing the cake, make the bread dough, roll it in flour wrap it in a napkin and leave in a warm place until the following day. To make the cake, first mix together the spices, and finely chop the almonds, walnuts and citrus peels. Dissolve the bicarbonate of soda in the madeira wine. Melt the fats in the hot molasses. Grate rind off oranges and squeeze out juice. Sift together flour and sugar and put in mixing bowl. Make a well in the centre and put in bread dough. Knead flour into dough and continue kneading until well mixed. Gradually mix in warm molasses mixture. Add fruit, madeira wine and bicarbonate mixture, orange peel and orange juice. Knead well until dough no longer sticks to bowl. Cover with thick cloth and leave to rise for three or four days in a place with warm, even temperature. Divide mixture into 250, 500 or 750 g sizes, make into low, round shapes and decorate tops with halves of blanched almonds. Put on a well-greased baking tray. Cook in very hot oven, 450°F (Gas Mark 8), until done. Leave to cool and then wrap in greaseproof paper or cellophane. These cakes keep well for up to a year.

The tradition is for *bolo de mel* to be made on 8 December (Day of Nossa Senhora da Conceição) to be ready for the Christmas festivities with which this cake (although eaten all year) is particularly associated. This is also the day on which the preparations for the Christmas festival begin and any *bolo de mel* left from the year before is eaten up. 8 December, therefore, is a day of bustle and enjoyment.

Pudim de Veludo or Pudim de Ovos (Velvet or Egg Pudding)

5 dl milk
6 eggs
grated rind of 1 orange or 1 lemon
100 g sugar for the caramel
1 dl water for the caramel
250 g sugar

Mix the sugar and water in a thick-bottomed pan over a low heat and stir until the sugar caramelizes (i.e. turns golden-brown). Put the caramel in the base of a pudding basin which has a lid. Separate the egg yolks and whites. Beat the yolks with the sugar until the mixture is thick and fluffy. Add the warmed milk a little at a time, and the orange or lemon rind. Beat the egg whites into peaks and fold gently into the other mixture. Put the mixture on top of the caramel in the pudding basin, cover with the lid and put in a *bain-marie* in a hot oven until cooked (when the outside is firm). Leave to cool and then turn out of the basin.

Panquecas de Abóbora (Pumpkin Pancakes)

500 g pumpkin (weighed without its rind)
500 g plain flour
1 egg
oil for frying
sugar and cinnamon

Cook the pumpkin in salted water. Reserve the cooking water and purée the pumpkin. Add the flour a little at a time, mixing well, and add in the egg. The mixture should not become too wet, but if it is too dry, add a little of the water used in cooking the pumpkin. Fry spoonfuls of the mixture in hot oil, allowing it to become golden-brown on both sides. Serve sprinkled with sugar and cinnamon.

Queijadas da Madeira (Cottage Cheesecakes)

For the dough:
250 g flour
250 g butter
2 tbsp castor sugar

For the filling:
500 g cottage cheese
500 g sugar
12 egg yolks
2 egg whites

Sift together the flour and sugar and rub in the butter until the mixture sticks well together. If necessary, add a few drops of water but the results are better if you can avoid this. Leave the dough to rest for four to five hours. Meanwhile pass the cottage cheese through a fine sieve. Add the sugar and mix well. Add the egg yolks one at a time, mixing well, and then the whites. Beat well until a smooth mixture is obtained. Stretch or roll the dough out very fine and cut into squares. Put one spoonful of the filling in the centre of each square. Fold over the corners of the squares so as to leave some of the filling visible. Put on a tray covered with buttered greaseproof paper. Cook in a hot oven, and spread a little butter on the cooked dough when you take the cakes from the oven.

Dishes from Mainland Portugal

We have included a few dishes here which are from mainland Portugal, because these are commonly found on restaurant menus in Madeira.

Soups

Caldo Verde (Green Broth)

As can be seen from the title, there is no meaningful translation of *caldo verde*. The soup gets its name from the type of cabbage which is used. The stalks and tough part of a large dark green cabbage are removed and then the cabbage is shredded very finely. If this type of cabbage is not available, turnip tops or spring greens provide a good substitute. The cabbage must be very finely shredded as it is cooked for only a very short time.

1.5 l water
500 g peeled sliced potatoes
2 tbsp olive oil
1 large onion
350 g finely shredded dark green cabbage
salt and pepper
few slices *chouriço* (a kind of smoked sausage)

Bring the water to boiling and cook the potatoes and onion in it. Remove and mash the potatoes and onion and then return to the cooking water with the olive oil, seasoning and cabbage. Boil for three minutes – without a lid, to preserve the green colour. Ladle the soup into the bowls and add a few slices of *chouriço* to each dish.

Fish

The cuts from the middle of the *bacalhau* tend to be the best and are often more expensive. It is said there are enough different *bacalhau* recipes in Portugal to have a different one every day of the year.

Bacalhau a Gomes de Sá (Dried, salted cod in Gomes de Sá style)

750 g *bacalhau*
2.5 dl olive oil
2 onions, sliced
500 g sliced cooked potatoes
50 g black olives
1 clove garlic (crushed)
4 hard-boiled eggs
chopped parsley

Soak the *bacalhau* in cold water for twenty-four hours, changing the water several times. Simmer in just enough water until tender (two to three hours). Remove the skin and bones and flake into large pieces. Heat the olive oil in a heavy casserole, add the onions and cook gently until soft. Add the potatoes, cod, olives and garlic and bake in a moderate oven (350°F, Gas Mark 4) until browned – about ten minutes. Garnish with quartered hard-boiled eggs and sprinkle with the parsley.

Bacalhau à Brás (Fried codfish)

750 g *bacalhau*
6 tbsp olive oil
2 large onions, sliced
500 g cooked potatoes, sliced
50 g black olives
8 eggs, beaten

Soak the cod for twenty-four hours in cold water, changing the water several times, then simmer, in just enough water to cover, until tender (two to three hours). Remove skin and bones and flake into large pieces. Heat olive oil in a large frying pan and fry onions until golden. Add the potatoes, fish and olives and cook for a further ten minutes, turning frequently. Add the beaten eggs to the fish mixture. Simmer until the eggs are cooked.

Meat

Cozido à Portuguesa (Portuguese-style stew)

200 g black pudding
500 g chicken
200 g *chouriço* (smoked sausage)
400 g beef brisket

4-5 pork loin bones
1 pig's ear
250 g dark green cabbage or spring greens
1 pig's tail
1 pig's trotter
5 carrots
3 white turnips
6 potatoes
2 parsnips (optional)

For the rice:
750 g long-grain rice
1 onion
2 cloves garlic, crushed
3 tbsp olive oil
salt and pepper

Prick the black pudding and *chouriço* and cook in plain water. Wash pork loin bones well and put in pan of water to cook. Add rest of meat and bring back to boil. When meats are cooked, take out of water and put on one side. Cook vegetables in liquid in which meat was cooked. Take vegetables out of liquid, cut meat into rough pieces, put meat and vegetables on a serving dish and keep warm. Wash the rice well. Prick the onion and cook with the garlic in the olive oil until golden. Remove garlic and onion. Put the rice in the oil and fry very gently until the oil is absorbed, without allowing rice to become coloured. Season with salt and pepper. Add 1.5 litres of stock in which meat and vegetables were cooked. Bring to boil, cover and simmer gently until rice is dry. Serve on a separate plate, garnished with some of the carrot from the cooked vegetables.

Dobrada à Portuguesa (Portuguese-style tripe)

500 g dried haricot beans
2 onions (finely chopped)
1 tbsp flour
a little water
2 cloves garlic, chopped
125 g belly of pork (finely cut up)
1 sprig thyme
1 glass white wine

1 kg tripe, cleaned, boiled & cut into strips or squares
4 tomatoes, skinned & chopped
2 dl white stock
250 g chopped *chouriço*
200 g *presunto* or Parma ham (chopped)
2 carrots (diced)
salt and pepper
½ glass port

Put haricot beans, onion and a little salt in a saucepan and cover with cold water. Bring to boil and simmer for 2½ hours or until beans are tender. Chop an onion and fry slowly with garlic, belly of pork and *chouriço*. No fat or oil is required as enough fat is contained in the belly of pork. After ten minutes add thyme and white wine. Continue to cook slowly until liquid is reduced by half, then add chopped tomatoes, stock, flour (previously mixed with a little cold water), the *presunto* and diced carrots. Leave to cook for a few minutes and then transfer to a stewing pan and add tripe, haricot beans and port. Season with salt and pepper. Leave to cook slowly for further 2½ hours before serving.

Feijoada à Portuguesa (Portuguese-style bean and pork stew)

500 g black-eyed, red or haricot beans
350 g belly pork
350 g black pudding
100 g *chouriço* (smoked sausage)
salt and pepper
1 small white cabbage, cut into strips
1 tsp ground cumin
1 large onion, sliced
1 tablespoon olive oil

Soak beans in cold water over night. Cut pork into cubes and put in casserole with beans, pork, black pudding, *chouriço*, cumin, onion, olive oil, salt and pepper and just cover with water. Cover and cook in a moderate oven (350°F, Gas Mark 4) until beans are tender – about thirty minutes. Add cabbage and a little more water if there is not enough to cook it, but do not make the mixture too wet. Cook for approximately fifteen minutes more in the oven until cabbage is tender but still crisp.

Beverages

In addition to madeira wine, there are locally made wines, both red and white. Country restaurants serve them with lunch – they are new wines and can be strong.

There are various types of *aguardentes* – made from sugarcane. These are very potent and should be taken in moderation. A local concoction is *poncha* made from lemons, *aguardente* and sugar – a pleasant drink which is deceptively strong.

The local beer, produced for many years by the brewery with the brand name 'Coral', has a distinctive flavour. The 'Coral' beers have won many prizes over the years at international beer festivals.

The brewery also produces a soft drink which is very much appreciated in the island – *maracujá*. This is made from passion fruits (*maracujás*) which are imported as well as being grown locally. This is available as a natural drink, fizzy drink or a squash to be diluted. Many tourists buy bottles of the fizzy *Brisa maracujá* to take home.

14 *Flora and Fauna*

Natural Vegetation

According to Rui Vieira (*Album Florístico da Madeira*, 1974) some 780 species of plants are indigenous to Madeira. Of these sixteen per cent are exclusive to Madeira, ten per cent to the Atlantic islands of Madeira, Azores, Canaries and Cape Verde (Macronesia) and the rest of Mediterranean or Atlantic type. Very little of the original natural vegetation of Madeira remains, because of interference by man. However, many plants and trees are preserved in the parks and gardens of Funchal and in the Botanical Gardens. Appendix III gives a more detailed list of some of the indigenous vegetation, and there are many pictorial flower books available about Madeira.

Plants such as Pride of Madeira (*Echium nervosum*) and the Dragon Tree (*Dracaena draco*) were once common between sea-level and 300m. The Dragon Tree grows to a height of six to fifteen metres and has a very straight cylindrical trunk and a somewhat palm-like habit in that all the branches start from the same place. The leaves are long, narrow and greyish-green. Between August and September it has large bunches of small whitish flowers which are followed by orange-yellow fruits about a centimetre in diameter. A red sap (dragon's blood) flows from the trunk or branches when they are cut, and in the past this was sought after as a medicine (tonic) and for the production of a red varnish prized by Italian violin-makers.

Between 300 and 700m there was a transition zone and then, above this up to about 1,500m, there was the area of laurel woods. Only about 1,000 hectares of these original woods remain intact in the more remote valleys. However, trees typical of these woods can easily be found growing at Ribeiro Frio. Two of the main indigenous trees of this belt are the *til* (*Ocotea foetens*) and the *vinhático* (*Persea indica*). The *til* grows from 15-30m in height and is used in furniture-making. The *vinhático* is another giant of the Madeiran forest, growing up to 25m in height, and gives a reddish wood very similar to mahogany which is also used in furniture-making.

At higher altitudes, the laurel woods give way to shrubs and heaths. Of these the best known are the tree heaths (*Erica arborea* and *E. scoparia*). The Madeira bilberry (*Vaccinium maderense*) is also common at this altitude – it is usually about one to two metres in height and produces masses of bilberries in September and October. The bilberries are about a centimetre in diameter, and this is probably the only bilberry which is *easy* to pick.

In recent years the Regional Government passed a law creating the Natural Park of Madeira. This has three main aims: to protect nature; to define and control areas for recreation; and to make people aware of the importance of the environment and how to protect it. The areas where the original laurel woods remain have been made total reserves and given absolute protection from man. Elsewhere recreation zones, zones of pastureland and partial reserves (where some hunting is permitted) have been created. The Regional Government has also designated areas of coastline and sea (as off Garajau) as worth protecting.

The flowers of Madeira

Funchal itself has been described as one great botanical garden. It is full of shrubs and trees from all over the world, but especially from tropical and sub-tropical areas. Almost every house has its own little garden, and the first impression given by a Madeiran garden (be it small or large) is one of uncurbed profusion in terms of growth, colour and intensity. Pot plants abound – ferns (many varieties of which are to be found wild in the island – Appendix III), orchids, anthuriums, azaleas and bignonias. Walls are covered with wistaria (*Wistaria sinensis*) and Golden Shower (*Pyrostegia venusta*), bougainvillea (of various types) and bignonias. The *quintas* usually have a lawn (often of coarse grass which withstands the sun better) dotted with leafy trees such as camphor, magnolia and coral. Cypress trees are rare in private gardens as they tend to be associated in Madeira with cemeteries.

The main streets and squares of Funchal are bordered by trees which look delightful, unless they have recently been pollarded, when they look like tortured stumps. Many of the trees are jacarandas (*Jacaranda mimosifolia*) whose lovely mauve-blue flowers come out in May. Other streets are bordered by Australian flame trees (*Sterculia acerifolia* or *Brachychiton acerifolium*) and *Tipuana tipu* (from Argentina and Bolivia). The river beds have iron arches over them (erected in the 1940s) where bougainvilleas, ranging from pale mauve to scarlet, are found in profusion. The table gives some idea of which flowers can be expected to be in bloom in the different months.

Many of the more exotic species of flowers are carefully tended in pots in people's homes. There is an increasing export business too for the high-value exotic plants such as strelitzias (available all year), anthuriums, cymbidium orchids and lady's slipper orchids.

*Some of the main flowers of the different months:**

January: Coral tree, Golden Shower, camellia, bougainvillea, Maguey plant, Arum lily, cymbidium orchid, lady's slipper orchid.

February: Coral tree, Golden Shower, camellia, azalea, passion flower, mimosa, tamarisk, karat tree, arum lily, cymbidium.

March: Coral tree, star jasmine, wistaria, camellia, arum lily, Pride of Madeira, Judas tree, azalea, cymbidium.

April: Jacaranda tree, bignonia, star jasmine, wistaria, agapanthus lily, camellia, tecoma, Painted Trumpet, anthurium cymbidium.

May: Jacaranda tree, flame tree, bignonia, star jasmine, wistaria, agapanthus lily, weigandia, plumbago, pink creeping geranium, anthurium, cymbidium.

June: Jacaranda tree, flame tree, *Tipuana tipu*, bignonia, agapanthus lily, hydrangea, magnolia, plumbago, anthurium.

July: *Tipuana tipu*, bignonia, agapanthus lily, hydrangea, plumbago, hibiscus, anthurium.

August: *Tipuana tipu*, oleander, cassia, allamanda (Golden Trumpet), hydrangea, fuchsia, hibiscus, dragon tree, anthurium.

September: Floss silk tree, tulip tree, *Tipuana tipu*, oleander, cassia, allamanda, hydrangea, hibiscus, belladonna lily, podranea, frangipani, anthurium.

October: Floss silk tree, tulip tree, poinsettia, oleander, cassia, allamanda, belladonna lily, plumbago, stiverbush, anthurium.

November: Floss silk tree, poinsettia, oleander, cassia, allamanda, aloe arborescens, bougainvillea, plumbago, kaffir tree, daisy tree.

December: Poinsettia, Golden Shower, aloe arborescens, camellia, bougainvillea, lady's slipper orchid, cymbidium.

Some forty-one species of fern are thought to be indigenous to Madeira, only three of which are peculiar to the island. The ferns are largely tropical or herbaceous, but examples of arboreous *Cyathraceae* are to be found in cultivation. The most common ones to be found almost everywhere are maidenhair, *Adiantum capillus veneris* and *Woodwardia*

* The following flower throughout the year. datura, hibiscus, bougainvillea, strelitzias (Bird of Paradise).

radicans. The visitor will also see fine examples of *Pteris aquilina* and *Asplenium* black spleenwort, as well as *Plypodium longifolium*. A fuller list of ferns is to be found in Appendix III. There are also some one hundred species of mosses to be found in the island, Appendix IV shows a list of herbs and plants found in Madeira and which have traditionally been considered to have medicinal properties.

Fish

The deep Atlantic waters around Madeira host a wide variety of fish species, around 250 in total, many of them noted for the brilliance of their colour or for the singularity of their form and structure. Apart from edible fish, there are different kinds of sharks, eels, rays and flying fish, to name but a few. Whales are sometimes seen, and there are plenty of sperm whales, dolphins and porpoises.

The black *espada* (*espada preta – Aphanopus carbo*) is a fish more or less unique to the waters around Madeira. It is monstrous-looking with no fins, spines down the centre of its back, a large mouth with lots of sharp teeth, smooth shiny black skin, no scales and enormous eyes. It looks rather like a long black eel. There is also a white version which is less popular and not such good eating. The *espada* is about a metre long, ten to twelve centimetres wide at the abdomen, and weighs between one and two kilos. Between November and December the females spawn – about 300,000 eggs per female. The fish lives between 800 and 1,600m below the surface and, when caught, dies of decompression as it comes to the surface.

The tunny (*atum – Thynnus alalonga*) is very plentiful in summer and is caught on long lines with live bait. There are many well-known fishing banks in deep waters around the island. Tunny has always been known here as 'the meat of the people' and, although it is now more expensive, it is still cheaper than meat. There is also a lot of sport fishing for tunny. There are lots of other edible fish caught in these waters, including mackerel, sardines, sea bream, sea perch, swordfish and grey mullet. Most of the edible fish found around Madeira are listed in Appendix III.

Monk seals (*Monachus albiventer*) breed around the Desertas in caves. They are culled by the fishermen to prevent their depleting the fish stocks. In 1908 a seal, captured alive, was offered for sale in Funchal. It was purchased and placed in a garden pond 130m above sea-level. It quickly became tame and took food from the hands of a young lady in the house. However, presumably, it pined for the freedom of the sea as one night it made its break for freedom and set off down the road. It went in the right

The church of Nossa Senhora da Incarnação at Monte

North side of the island near Ponta do São Lourenço

Ribeira Brava with the new road (opened in 1986) along the shore

The chapel of Santa Catarina – the oldest chapel in Madeira dating from 1425

The English Church, Funchal

Porto do Moniz and its terraced hillsides

The gardens of Monte with the olc
railway bridge

A religious festival in the village of Câmara de Lobos

The Colégio Church and Praça do Município, Funchal

Funchal's busy new marina

Black *espada* fish in Funchal market

Vicente's Photographic Museum and the Pátio Restaurant, Funchal

Street game in Funchal

direction but unfortunately fell over a cliff, through a pergola and into a peasant's garden. The seal was taken back to its pond but soon afterwards was returned to the sea for the owners by a British admiral who took it to the Desertas.

Birds

Bannerman, in his book *Birds of the Atlantic Islands*, lists forty-two species of birds breeding in the Madeira Islands. Many migratory and breeding birds prefer the uninhabited islands off Porto Santo and the Desertas and Selvagens, away from the influence of man. On Madeira, one is rarely awakened by a dawn chorus, nor does one see large numbers of birds.

There are many sea birds to be found around the islands, including the Madeira little shearwater, Manx shearwater, Cory's shearwater and the Atlantic herring gull. David Bannerman found two distinct breeding colonies of the soft-plumaged petrel (*Pterodroma mollis*), one peculiar to Madeira and the other to the Desertas (*Pterodroma mollis madeira* and *Pterodroma mollis deserta*). One has a heavier bill than the other and they breed at different times. Appendix III lists the birds which breed in Madeira as opposed to the migratory birds.

The Selvagens were once owned by the Rocha Machado family who, in 1967, leased the hunting rights in the islands to Paul Alexander Zino, an ornithologist resident in Madeira. He began to study the Cory's or Atlantic shearwater (*Calonectris diomedea borealis*), known as *Cagarras* in Portuguese, that were nesting on the island. In 1971 the World Wildlife Fund offered to buy the islands from the Rocha Machados but the Portuguese Government intervened, bought the islands and created a bird sanctuary. In 1976 a group of fishermen went to the islands purely and simply to slaughter birds that were depleting their catches. They succeeded in killing about half the 60,000 birds then in the colony. Since then the islands have had a permanent guard.

Other creatures

When Madeira was first discovered, birds and lizards were the largest life forms on the island. Today there are no reptiles, other than frogs and the ubiquitous lizard (*Lacerta dugessi – lagartixa* as it is called in Portuguese), similar to those found in Europe. That lizards have long been residents of Madeira is shown by the fossilized remains found in the fossil beds at Caniçal. The largest lizards can reach 17cm in length and 1.5cm round the body. They vary from black to brown to greeny-blue in colour. Lizards scamper around everywhere in the sun and peep in and out of the rocks and walls in which they live. They are timid, but they can be domesticated and will learn to eat from the hand. To the farmer, however, they are pests as they eat the grapes and fruits.

Rabbits and rats, which are now found in large numbers, were imported by man. The rabbit was brought to Porto Santo by Perestrelo, the first Governor – his action was well intentioned but soon proved disastrous. Charles Darwin commented on the changes which had taken place in the rabbits on the Desertas because of in-breeding, their bodies being shorter and their colouring more adapted to their environment and the rock colour of the Desertas.

Insects are numerous in the islands – there are about 1,200 different species, excluding spiders. About 555 are species of beetles, all of which are harmless, the cockroach (*Blatta maderae*) is common in and around houses in the autumn. Mosquitoes (*Culex longiareolatus*) are also common. They breed in watertanks and wells and find their way into the bedroom, where they seem to buzz incessantly. They are, however, harmless, as their bite just produces an itchy inflammation on the skin. Flies are common all year round, especially the housefly (*Musca domestica*) and two species of bluebottle (*Lucilia caesar* and *L. sericata*).

There are about ten species of ants in the islands, the most common of which, *Iridomyrmex humilis*, is typical of intertropical America and was brought over with the sugar cane from Demerara in 1886-7. The white ant (which is not really a member of the ant family), *Cryptolermes brevis*, is very widespread in Madeira and lives in wood, which it ravages given the chance. It is, therefore, a very real danger in older houses and to antique furniture.

There are about a hundred species of spiders, nearly all of which are harmless. The *Lycosa* (*Trachosa*) *ingens* is the biggest spider in the archipelago and is found only in Deserta Grande. It is black, poisonous and ferocious, and it is said its bite can cause death. There are several other spiders whose bite can cause discomfort: *Lycosa* (*Trachosa*) *Blackwallii*, a large black spider which hides in holes in the wall or in cracks in the rocks; *Epeira aurelia* (Madeiran Tarantula) which is striped black and silver and is said to 'write its name' on its web because of the extra patterns it weaves in places in the completed web; and *Lycosa tarentuloides maderiana* which is found in Porto Santo and is black with three white spots on its back.

There are about 120 species of butterflies and moths found in the islands, including the Death's Head and Humming Bird moths and the Monarch butterfly. Some of the most notable butterflies in terms of the colours of their wings are *Pieris brassicae, Colias edusa, Lycaena baetica, Vanessa atalanta, Vanessa callirhoe* and *Vanessa cardui.*

There has been much interest among scientists over the years in the snails of the archipelago. There are some 131 species, sixty-one of which are peculiar to Madeira, forty-four to Porto Santo and ten to the Desertas, only sixteen being common to all the islands. One of these snails, the *Helix pisana*, has traditionally been used in Porto Santo to fatten ducks. Along the coasts many different types of molluscs are found – periwinkles, whelks and limpets abound. There are many small crabs, but edible crabs and lobsters are rare.

15 *Useful Information*

Shopping

Shopping and Banking Hours:

The normal shopping hours are 9 a.m. to 1 p.m. and 3 p.m. to 7 p.m. Monday to Friday, and 9 a.m. to 1 p.m. on Saturday. The shopping precincts are open 10 a.m. to 10 p.m. seven days a week. Banks are open from 8.30 a.m. to 11.45 a.m. and 1 p.m. to 2.45 p.m. Monday to Friday, although some branches in the main tourist areas stay open for longer for foreign currency exchange. At the Tourist Office and the American Express Agency they normally open the same hours as the shops. Foreign currency can, of course, also be exchanged in hotels (at a slightly lower rate). Nearly all shops, restaurants and hotels accept Eurocheques and the major credit cards.

What to shop for:

Bolo de mel is a long-lasting Madeiran cake which is made from molasses and not from honey as its name suggests (*mel* = honey).

Boots. You can find versions of the traditional boots for sale for adults or children, as well as miniature versions for ornament.

Embroidery in the form of table linen, napkins, handkerchiefs, dresses, scarves and blouses carries the seal of 'IBATAM' (Instituto do Bordado, Tapeçarias e Artesanato da Madeira) and is all of very good quality.

Flowers. At different times of the year, orchids, strelitzias (Bird of Paradise) and anthuriums are available. They are all long-lasting and can be packed in special boxes for you to put on the aeroplane as baggage. Also, at most flower shops, bulbs of agapanthus and orchids can be purchased year-round.

Fruit is available in season, including large avocados. The tasty Madeiran banana is available all year.

Pottery and porcelain are very brightly coloured and hand painted – plates, platters, jugs, jars etc.

Straw hats are a popular buy and are really old-fashioned boaters.

Tapestry is available for wall coverings or chair cushion-covers, often being copies of old masters. It is for sale completed or for you to work. *Petit-point* bags are also sold.

Wickerwork, from a bread basket to a three-piece suite and all hand made, can be purchased at the many wicker warehouses and can be taken home on the plane without problems.

Wine. Madeira wine is available in bottles which are packed in cardboard cartons for easy carrying, as well as in miniatures suitable for gifts. It is not cheaper at the airport Duty-free Shop, and the selection is larger in the wine lodges and supermarkets.

Woollens. Rugs, blankets, cardigans and the traditional hat with earflaps.

Textiles and Shoes made in Portugal are well worth buying.

Currency

The currency used in Madeira is the same as in mainland Portugal – the escudo. Notes are in 20, 50, 100, 500, 1,000 and 5,000 denominations, although the 20 and 50 escudo notes are being withdrawn and replaced by coins. There are 50 centavo (100 centavos to 1 escudo) and 1, 2½, 5, 10, 20, 25 and 50 escudo coins in general circulation, although the 25 escudo coin is being withdrawn. The money is all very straightforward. What is confusing is that larger priced items are often quoted in contos (1 conto = 1,000 escudos).

Postal Services

There are two main post offices in the centre of Funchal – one on Avenida Zarco and one in Rua Dr Brito Câmara – as well as a smaller one in the tourist zone at Lido Sol. In addition to mail, these handle telegrams, telexes, local and international calls and FAX services. It is possible to dial direct from Madeira to most European countries, USA, Canada, Brazil, Venezuela, South Africa and many other countries.

Over the past few years Madeiran postage stamps have become collectors' items as the postal authorities have published many attractive and commemorative stamps. For passengers arriving by cruise ship there is a mobile post office with telephone facilities which meets ships at the dockside.

Sports

Football is the main spectator sport on the island, and matches are usually played on a Sunday afternoon. The main football stadium, Barreiros, is located in the hotel district and is a short walk uphill past Quinta Magnolia. From this stadium you obtain a wonderful view over Funchal – so, if the game is boring, you can enjoy the vista. There are three main clubs – Maritimo, Nacional and União. They all play in leagues with Portuguese clubs and you may even be lucky and see Benfica or Sporting

Lisbon play. Watching football is often a family outing with many children, some wives and no violence or trouble of the kind associated with matches in Britain. At half-time drinks are served, including coffee and brandy, at the bar. Men also go round the crowd selling beer and soft drinks.

Swimming: Madeira does not possess any sandy beaches, and so most hotels provide swimming pools for their guests. Swimming is also available at the magnificent Lido with its Olympic-sized pool, in Quinta Magnolia, at the Clube Turismo and the Clube Naval. Some hotels also have sea-water bathing from jetties.

Water Sports: Many hotels can arrange wind-surfing and boat rentals. It is also possible to arrange snorkelling or scuba diving.

Tennis: Most of the hotels have tennis facilities. You can also play in the courts of Quinta Magnolia, but it is necessary to book in advance as it is a popular game amongst Madeirans.

Golf: At Santo da Serra there is a nine-hole golf course set amongst eucalyptus trees. The course affords magnificent views of the mountain scenery, and facilities include a clubhouse with bar and changing-rooms. You can also hire clubs and caddies. The caddies, often small boys, can offer good advice on which clubs to use and where to drive the ball.

Fishing: Deep-sea fishing off the island is very popular and you may be lucky enough to catch marlin or spearfish. Some big ones have been caught here – over 365 kg. You may also catch tunny, swordfish or several varieties of shark. If you catch nothing, the sea breeze and the sun will have given you an appetite for dinner.

Walking: The island is a hiker's paradise. Whether you prefer *levadas* or mountains or just a simple hour's stroll, there is plenty to choose from.

Bridge is very popular among the elderly foreign residents, who can often be found in one or other of the five-star hotels, eager for a game.

Other sports to be found in hotels or clubs are squash, table tennis, billiards, etc. The Madeirans also enjoy basketball, handball, volleyball and roller hockey.

Hunting is very popular and sacred to many Madeirans. From September to December partridge, pigeon, quail and rabbit are hunted. When the game is on, the beaters in front beat the ground, shout and blow hunting horns, the dogs chase the rabbits and the men behind shoot. It is a very noisy affair as they move along the hillside, and there is plenty of wine for refreshment.

Eating and Drinking

Restaurant hours are normally: Lunch 12 to 3 p.m. and dinner 7 to 11 p.m., although many restaurants will serve meals all day. In addition, there are many snack bars where you can obtain a snack all day and most of the night. All restaurants and snack bars serve alcohol, and it is possible to drink all day if you wish. Many small bars are open until 4 a.m., some with musical entertainment.

The coffee served in the restaurants and snack bars is good and can be black (*café*) or with milk (*café com leite*). There are also special terms for different kinds of coffee which are used in Madeira. *Uma bica* is a black coffee served in a small cup. *Uma carioca* is a small black coffee which has had water added to weaken it. *Uma chinesa* is coffee with milk and is served in a large cup. *Um garoto* is a small cup of coffee to which only a very little milk has been added. *Um galão* is a tall glass of coffee with milk.

The tap water in Madeira is drinkable but lacks minerals. Various bottled mineral waters are available from mainland Portugal and from the island of Porto Santo. These are available with or without gas.

Public Holidays

Watch out for public holidays if you intend to go shopping or to the bank. Only the shopping precincts are open on public holidays, and most restaurants also stay open, although many do close on Christmas Day.

The main public holidays are:

1 January	Ano Novo	New Year's Day
25 April	25 de Abril	Day of the Revolution
1 May	Dia do Trabalhador	Worker's Day
10 June	Dia de Portugal	National Day
1 July	Dia da Região	Regional Day
15 August	Assunção	Feast of the Assumption
21 August	Dia do Funchal	Funchal Day
5 October	Dia da República	Republic Day
1 November	Todos os Santos	All Saints' Day
1 December	Restauração	Restauratio of Independence Day
8 December	Imaculada Conceição	Feast of the Immaculate Conception
25 December	Natal	Christmas Day

Movable dates are:

	Sexta feira Santa	Good Friday
	Corpo de Deus	Corpus Christi

In addition the shops are usually closed on the afternoon of Shrove

Tuesday and the morning of Ash Wednesday for the Carnival (*Carnaval*) Holiday. Although they are not official public holidays, the shops also usually close on the afternoons of 24 and 31 December and all day on 26 December.

Tourist Information Office

There is a very good Tourist Office located in Avenida Arriaga in the centre of Funchal where you can obtain information, help and advice. A free map of Madeira can be obtained here, as can a bus timetable.

Driving

In Madeira, as in Portugal, you drive on the right-hand side of the road and overtake on the left. You give way to vehicles coming from the right (unless otherwise indicated) – although in practice most side roads have white lines across them and often have stop signs too. The speed limit in towns, although not often adhered to, is 30km/hr and in the country the terrain will limit your speed to below 60km/hr almost everywhere. In Funchal there are car-parks and parking meters. Street parking, where allowed, is on the right. It is not technically allowed on the left, but this is usually ignored in Funchal – although the police do make periodic visits to lines of parked cars and issue parking fines. To drive in Madeira you must have a valid driving licence. For holiday purposes your own national driving licence is sufficient (valid for at least one year) or, better still, an international driving licence as this will have your photograph on it. If you are staying permanently, you will need a Portuguese driving licence. To obtain this is probably the most difficult and complicated task you will undertake in moving here – far more complicated than buying property, moving your belongings or buying a car. You will need the appropriate form, fiscal stamps and have to undergo a medical examination by a Portuguese doctor and a second medical by a government doctor. You will also need proof that you do not have a criminal record and will be asked to give up your own national driving licence or take the local written and practical tests. What is more, this licence is only valid for a few years, after which time the process has to be repeated again.

Always make sure you have enough fuel and oil for your journey before leaving Funchal as petrol stations are few and far between in country areas.

Pedestrians

Walking around the centre of Funchal is the only way to see the city and the surprises round every corner. Wear comfortable shoes and do sit down for a coffee from time to time. The small streets are a jumble of people, cars and delivery vehicles. On pedestrian crossings you do have priority, but don't chance it!

Toilets

Public toilets in Funchal are few and far between and not very pleasant. It is best to use those in the restaurants or in the shopping centres.

Medical Care

There are many English-speaking doctors on the island, and most doctors specialize in one field or another, a relatively small proportion being general practitioners. There is also a very well equipped general hospital and good private clinics. Now that Portugal is in the European Economic Community, there is a reciprocal arrangement for people from EEC countries. Otherwise, without an insurance policy to cover medical expenses, it can be expensive. The cost of a visit to a doctor is between 1,000 and 2,000 escudos.

Chemist shops (*farmacias*) can be very useful for small problems as pharmacists in Portugal are allowed to prescribe a suitable remedy. There are many chemists' shops in Funchal, and one is always open, on a rota system, round the clock seven days a week.

Taxis

In and around Funchal there are many taxis, conspicuous in their bright yellow with a blue stripe down the side (the regional colours of Madeira). A few taxis in the traditional black with a green roof can still be seen. In Funchal all taxi rides are metered, and the costs of the fare from the airport to the various parts of Funchal are fixed by the Regional Government and prominently displayed in the baggage hall at the airport. If you are travelling in the evening or after midnight or have a lot of baggage a surcharge, may be imposed. If you wish to hire a taxi for a tour for a half- or full-day, arrange the price with him before you leave.

Buses

Nearly all the buses leave from Avenida das Comunidades Madeirenses (the main road along the shore). The orange buses (Horário do Funchal) serve the city areas, and other bus companies serve the different parts of the island.

Newspapers

It is possible to find most European and American newspapers on sale soon after 10 a.m. the day following publication. Most hotel shops, tourist shops and newspaper kiosks stock a wide range of foreign newspapers and magazines.

The Madeira Island Bulletin is a monthly newspaper of news, tourist information and 'What's on'. It is a very good way to keep informed and to learn more about the island. It also contains information about hotels and the many restaurants to visit. The newspaper is free and can be found in most hotels in Madeira.

Radio and Television

Radio Televisão Portuguesa is the national TV network, the best of the two mainland television channels being condensed into one channel here. There are many programmes in English with Portuguese sub-titles and an average of three films per week which are usually in English but can be in French, German or Italian.

Madeira has three local radio stations, one of which gives air time in the morning and evening to 'Madeira Tourist Radio' which broadcasts in English, French, German and Swedish. With a suitable short-wave radio you can pick up the BBC external services, as well as those of Europe and many countries throughout the world.

Travel to Madeira

By Sea: There are now no regular passenger ships calling at Madeira, but it is still possible to visit the island either as part of a cruise or by booking a one-way passage on a cruise ship calling at the island. The large fleet of Russian cruise ships often call at Madeira, with occasional visits by *Canberra* and the *QE2*.

By Air: There are regular flights everyday from and to Lisbon, operated by the national airline Air Portugal. In addition there are two direct return flights weekly to London, operated by the same airline. There are many regular charter flights to the island from London, Manchester and most major European cities. Air Portugal also operates flights to Porto, Faro, the Azores and the Canary Islands, as well as the shuttle service to Porto Santo.

Purchasing Property

The purchase of property in Madeira follows the same procedure as in mainland Portugal. There are a few golden rules which should be followed to ensure the purchase of your home in the sun proceeds smoothly. The first is never to buy a property which you have not seen for yourself. You should always use a lawyer, preferably a local one in Madeira, and many of them speak English or French. Obviously the lawyers are familiar with the steps involved in property purchase and can ensure you avoid any pitfalls. Having selected your property, a promissary contract to purchase is drawn up. This is a binding legal contract and at this time usually twenty per cent deposit is paid. If you fail to complete the purchase, the twenty per cent deposit is forfeited. If the seller fails to honour his part in selling you the property, he has to repay double the deposit paid.

You should always obtain Bank of Portugal permission to import the money to buy the property, otherwise there will be problems if you wish to sell later and take the money out of the country. The property you select should have a habitation certificate from the local authority. The deeds are made before a public notary, and this stage requires your presence or the presence of someone with your power of attorney. When you finally purchase your property, an additional ten per cent of the purchase price has to be paid to the Portuguese Government as a tax, called the SISA.

Length of Stay

If you are just visiting Portugal from the USA or Europe, you are allowed to stay for sixty days. You can then arrange for two successive extensions of sixty days each. After this time you must either leave and return again for another visit or, if you wish to stay longer, apply for a residence permit (*residencia*).

If you are staying in a hotel, the hotel will inform the Serviços de Estrangeiros of your arrival and departure. If you are staying privately, you must register your arrival and local address in person within forty-eight hours of your arrival and inform them of your departure forty-eight hours before you leave.

Consulates

For those people needing consular services (lost passport and other problems) there are career consul offices for South Africa and Venezuela in Funchal. There are also honorary consulates for Austria, Belgium,

Britain, France, Brazil, Greece, Holland, Italy, Norway, Sweden, Switzerland, Germany, Finland, Spain and the United States.

Visas

Visas are not required from member countries of the European Community or certain other European countries, Canada or the United States of America.

Time

Madeira follows the European pattern of changing the clocks by one hour for summer and winter. It is therefore the same time in London, Lisbon or Madeira.

Appendices

Appendix I
Some of the Scientists and Explorers Who Visited Madeira

Ackermann, Eugène, interested in the geology of the islands. Published a book on Madeira in Alsace in 1910.

Armitage, Eleonora, British botanist who collected herbs in 1909.

Banks, Joseph, British botanist, with Captain Cook in Madeira. 12-18 September 1768. Collected 255 species of plants.

Bannerman, David, British ornithologist who published a book on Madeiran birds in 1965.

Brown, Robert, British botanist in Madeira, 4-7 August 1802.

Charcot, Jean, French explorer in Funchal, 12 September 1908.

Darwin, Charles (1809-82), Well-known British biologist, who developed theory of organic evolution, visited Madeira several times and mentioned thirteen Madeiran species.

Downe, British botanist who collected plants in 1776.

Estepe, Martin Vahl, Danish botanist and biologist.

Friderichsen, K., Danish scientist whose book on Madeira was published in 1905.

Fritze, R., German botanist in Madeira in 1879 and 1880.

Gagel, C., German geologist and palaeontologist in Madeira at the beginning of the twentieth century.

Garnier, P., French medic interested in climate of Madeira. Spent October 1850 in Madeira.

Gourlay, William, British doctor, in Madeira 1792-1810; wrote on natural history.

Grant, W.R.O., British ornithologist from the British Museum who published articles in 1896.

Hartung, George, German geologist here 1853-4.

Heberden, Thomas, British doctor who collaborated with Banks and Solander in 1768 and wrote about climate.

Heer, Osvaldo, Botanist and palaeontologist here 1850-51. Published books in Zürich and died in Lausanne in 1883.

Heineken, Charles, British doctor who lived in Funchal for nine years. Died here on 4 January, 1830.

Hochstetter, Ferdinand von, Austrian geologist visited in June 1857.

Holl, Frederic, German botanist in Madeira June-August 1827.

Johnson, James Yate, British naturalist who lived in Madeira 1850-1900 and wrote widely about natural history.

Joinville, Prince of (1818-1900), Visited Madeira many times in capacity as French Admiral.

Kirkpatrick, R., Naturalist from British Museum; visited Madeira and Porto Santo. Published a pamphlet in 1911.

Kny, Leopold, German botanist here in 1865.

Langerhans, Paul, Father of modern dermatology. Wrote on Madeiran worms 1879-84.

La Pérouse, J.F.G. de, French navigator, here 13th-16th August 1785.

Lemann, Charles, British botanist, here 1837-8.

Lindinger, Leonhard, German botanist. Book published in 1912.

Lindman, Charles, Swedish botanist here in 1885.

Lippold, German botanist here in 1838.

Luisier, Father Alphonse, Swiss Jesuit priest and scientist. Works published 1907-22.

Lyell, Charles, British geologist here in 1853-54.

Macaulay, James, British scientist here 1839-40.

Major, Richard Henry, British writer and member of Royal Geographical Society of the late nineteenth century.

Mandon, G., French botanist here 1865-6.

Mason, J.A., British doctor who wrote about climate here. Visited the island in 1834.

Masson, Francis, British botanist here in 1776 and 1785.

Openheim, German palaeontologist who studied coral fossils in Porto Santo.

Peacock, G., British; Doctor of Theology, Dean of Ely and Professor at the University of Cambridge.

Piazzi Smyth, C., Wrote about Madeira's climate in 1882.

Ponsonby, British zoologist here in 1908-9.

Renton, British doctor who lived in Madeira and studied the climate, conducting meteorological studies between 1826 and 1831.

Richter, Johannes, German who studied the climate here. Published in 1909.

Robins, British botanist who collected plants in 1774.

Ross, Sir James Clark, British expedition commander, in Madeira in

October 1839 and went to Pico Ruivo. Explored Antarctic 1840-1.

Rothschild, Baron Charles, Rich banker and British entomologist studied here and discovered a type of flea which lived on the Cory's shearwater.

Smith, James, British geologist here in 1840.

Smith, Charles Richard, British horticulturist who, in 1757, started a garden in Funchal for the acclimatization of tropical plants.

Solander, Daniel Charles, Swiss naturalist (1736-82) who came to Madeira with Banks on Captain Cook's first voyage.

Stuebel, Alphons, German naturalist and geologist in Madeira 1862-3.

Torrend, Father Camilo, French Jesuit priest who studied mushrooms in Madeira. Published works in 1909-13.

Vahl, Martin, Danish botanist here in 1901-2 and 1920-21.

Walsingham, Lord, British biologist. Published 1894.

Waters, A.W., Biologist. Published work 1898-9.

Watson, Robert Boog, British; studied marine shells here between 1864 and 1874.

Welwitsch, Frederick, Austrian botanist here in 1853.

White, Robert, Englishman who lived here for several years and wrote about the climate publishing an important book on the island in 1851.

Winter, Hermann, German biologist who collected plants here in 1912.

Wollaston, T. Vernon, British naturalist who came here four times between 1847 and 1855.

Ziegler, J.M., In 1856 published one of best maps of Madeira that there had been.

Zimmermann, Charles, Swedish naturalist.

Some of the Scientific Expeditions Which Have Called at Madeira

1755 Bory came on the *Comet*.

1764 Commodore Byron with the *Delphim* and *Tamar*.

1766 Captain Samuel Wallis (Philip Carteret was an officer on board) with the *Delphim*, *Swallow* and *Prince Frederick*.

1768 Captain James Cook with the *Endeavour* and the naturalists Joseph Banks and Dr Solander and the astronomer Charles Green.

1772 Captain James Cook with the *Resolution* and the naturalists John Reinhold Forster and his son.

1785 Jean Francis Galaup de La Pérouse with the *Bussola* and *Astrolabio*.
1792 John Barrow.
1816 Captain J.K. Tuckey.
1838 Charles Wilkes with the *Porpoise, Vincennes, Peacock, Sea Gull* and *Flying Fish*.
1839 Sir James Clark Ross and Francis Roland Crozier with the *Erebus* and *Terror*.
1857 Commodore Wullerstorf-Urbair with the *Novara*.
1883 Alphonse Milne Edwards with the *Talisman*.
1897 Adrien Gerlache with *Belgica*.
1901 Captain Robert Scott, Wilson and Shackleton with *Discovery*.
1901 Dr Erich von Drygalski with *Gauss*.
1902 Captain Colbeck and Dr Wilson with the *Morning*.
1903 Jean Charcot with the *Le Français*.
1908 Jean Charcot with the *Pourquoi Pas*.
1910 *Terra Nova en route* to the Antarctic but as yet without Captain Robert Scott.
1910 Captain Amundsen with the *Fram*.
1911 Prince Albert of Monaco with the *Hirondelle II*.
1914 F. Nansen with the *Armaner-Hansen*.
1914 Captain Worsley with the *Endurance*.
1920 Dr Johannes Schmidt with the *Dana*.
1921 Shackleton and Dr Johannes Schmidt with the *Dana* and *Quest*.
1922 Professors Hansen and Damas with the *Harmaner Hansen*.
1923 Gerard Belloc with the *La Tanche*.
1924 James Hornell with the *St George*.
1960s Sir Vivian Fuchs.

Appendix II
Glossary of Portuguese Words and Phrases

Portuguese is a phonetic language so it is pronounced as it is written. The stress is always on the penultimate syllable of a word except when there is an accent and then the stress is on the accented syllable. Pronunciation is nasal and the ends of the words tend to be swallowed.

Food and beverages

beer	*uma cerveja*
bread	*um pão*
coffee	*um café*
cutlery	*talheres*
dessert	*uma sobremesa*
fish	*peixe*
fruit	*fruta*
glass	*um copo*
ice-cream	*um gelado*
meat	*carne*
menu	*a ementa*
milk	*leite*
mineral water	*àgua mineral*
with gas	*com gás*
without gas	*sem gás*
napkin	*um guardanapo*
potatoes	*batatas* (locally, *semilhas*)
rice	*arroz*
salad	*uma salada*
sandwich	*uma sanduiche*
soup	*uma sopa*
sugar	*açúcar*
tea	*chá*
iced water	*água fresca*
wine	*vinho*

Clothes

shirt	*uma camisa*
blouse	*uma blusa*
jacket	*um casaco*
trousers	*as calças*
sweater/jersey	*uma camisola*
dress	*um vestido*
skirt	*uma saia*
shoes	*os sapatos*
hat	*um chapéu*

Medical

doctor	*um medico*
dentist	*um dentista*
an upset stomach	*mal de estômago*
sunstroke	*uma insolação*
a fever	*febre*

Numbers

one	*um (uma)*
two	*dois (duas)*
three	*três*
four	*quatro*
five	*cinco*
six	*seis*
seven	*sete*
eight	*oito*
nine	*nove*
ten	*dez*
eleven	*onze*
twelve	*doze*
thirteen	*treze*
fourteen	*catorze*
fifteen	*quinze*
sixteen	*dezasseis*
seventeen	*dezassete*
eighteen	*dezoito*

nineteen	*dezanove*
twenty	*vinte*
twenty-one	*vinte e um*
twenty-two	*vinte e dois*
thirty	*trinta*
forty	*quarenta*
fifty	*cinquenta*
sixty	*sessenta*
seventy	*setenta*
eighty	*oitenta*
ninety	*noventa*
hundred	*cem*
hundred and one	*cento e um*
thousand	*mil*

Useful phrases

What time is it, please?	*Que horas são, por favor?*
How much?	*Quanto é?*
When?	*Quando?*
Where?	*Onde?*
How?	*Como?*
How long?	*Quanto tempo?*
How far?	*A que distância?*
Where's the bus for ...?	*Onde está o autocarro para ...?*
When's the next bus to ...?	*Quando parte o próximo autocarro para ...?*
Do you accept travellers' cheques?	*Aceita cheques de viagem?*
Can I pay with this credit card?	*Posso pagar com este cartão de crédito?*
It is very urgent	*É muito urgente*
Do you speak English?	*Fala inglês?*
What is your name?	*Como se chama?*

Greetings and polite phrases

Good morning	*Bom dia*
Good afternoon	*Boa tarde*
Good evening/Good night	*Boa noite*
Goodbye	*Adeus*
Please	*por favor/faz favor*

Thank you	*Obrigado (obrigada)*
Yes	*Sim*
No	*Não*

Other useful words

yesterday	*ontem*
today	*hoje*
tomorrow	*amanhã*
left	*esquerdo*
right	*direito*
good	*bom*
bad	*mau*
big	*grande*
small	*pequeno*
cheap	*barato*
expensive	*caro*
hot	*quente*
cold	*frio*
old	*velho*
new	*novo*
open	*aberto*
closed	*fechado*
stamp	*um selo*
letter	*uma carta*
bus stop	*paragem*
cigarettes	*cigarros*
cigars	*charutos*
matches	*fósforos*
tobacconist	*tabacaria*
supermarket	*supermercado*
market	*mercado*
butcher's shop	*talho*

Appendix III
Flora and Fauna

*Some trees and plants indigenous to Madeira**

0-300 metres:

Musschia aurea
Euphorbia piscatoria (Jimsonweed datura)
Echium nervosum (Pride of Madeira)
Sideroxylon marmulano (Jungleplum)
Andropagon hirtus
Dracaena draco (Dragon Tree)
Olea ocaster (Wild olive)
Foeniculum vulgare (Fennel)

300-700 metres: Transitional zone

700-1,500 metres:

Ocotea foetens (*Til* tree)
Persea indica (*Vinhático*, a tropical tree of the mimosa family)
Apollonias barbujana (Ironwood tree)
Picconia excelsa (*Pau branco*)
Heberdenia excelsa (*Aderno*)
Ilex perado (Holly)
Ilex canariensis (Holly)
Myrica faya (*Faia*)
Rhamnus glandulosa (Dogwood)
Clethra arborea (lily-of-the-valley tree)
Chrysanthemum pinnatifidum

* The English or Portuguese common name is given where we know it.

Sonchus fruticosus (Sowthistle)
Echium candicans (Pride of Madeira or Madeira viper bugloss)
Isoplexis sceptrum (Yellow foxglove)
Cytisus maderensis or *Teline maderensis* (*Piorno*)
Erysimum mutabile (Stock)

Over 1,500 metres:

Erica arborea (Tree heath)
Erica scoparia (Tree heath)
Vaccinium maderense (Madeira Bilberry)

*Some of the main ferns to be found in Madeira**

Latin – English Names

Asplenium hemionitis – Ivy Leaf Fern
Adiantum reniforme – Curious Liverwort
Woodwardia radicans
Adiantum capillus Veneris – Common Maidenhair
Davallia canariensis – Hare's Foot
Notoclaena lanuginosa
Ceterach officinarum – Scale Fern
Cheilanthes fragrans
Gymnogramma leptophylla
Dicksonia culcita – Great Cushion Fern
Trichomanes radicans – Killarney Fern
Hymenophyllum tunbridgense – Filmy Fern
Hymenophyllum unilaterale – Filmy Fern
Acrostichum squamosum – Cow's-tongue Fern
Asplenium furcatum

The main types of edible fish found in Madeiran Waters

Latin – English (Portuguese) Names

Sardinia pilchardus – Pilchard (*Sardinha*)

* Over forty different species of ferns have been found in the island.

Engraulis encrasicolus – Anchovy
Laemonema yarellii – Cod fish (*Abrótea de natura*)
Laemonema robustum – Cod fish (*Abrótea de natura*)
Physis blennioides – Forked Hake or Greater Fork-Beard (*Abrótea do alto*)
Physis physis – Cod fish (*Abrótea*)
Mora mora – Cod fish – (*Abrótea do alto*)
Merluccius merluccius – Hake (*Pescada*)
Polymixia nobilis – Surmullet (*Salmonete do Alto*)
Zeus faber – John Dory (*Peixe galo*)
Zeus conchifer – John Dory (*Peixe galo*)
Cyttus roseus – John Dory (*Peixe galo*)
Polyprion americanum – Stone Bass (*Cherne*)
Serranus guaza – Dusky Perch (*Mero*)
Paracentropristis cabrilla – Sea Perch (*Garoupa*)
Parecentropristis atricauda – Sea Perch (*Garoupa*)
Mullus surmuletus – Red Mullet (*Salmonete da Costa*)
Pagrus pagrus – Sea Bream (*Pargo*)
Trachurus trachurus – Horse Mackerel (*Chicharro*)
Trachurus picturatus – Horse Mackerel (*Chicharro*)
Sparisoma cretense – Parrot fish (*Bodião*)
Aphanopus carbo – Black Scabbard fish (*Espada preta*)
Lepidopus caudatus – White Scabbard fish (*Espada branca*)
Scomber scombus – Common Mackerel (*Cavala*)
Scomber japonicus – Spanish or Coly Mackerel (*Cavala*)
Xiphias gladius – Sword fish or Broad bill (*Peixe-agulha*)
Mugil cephalus – Grey Mullet (*Tainha*)
Mugil auratus – Grey Mullet (*Tainha*)
Mugil provensalis – Grey Mullet (*Tainha*)
Scorpaena scrofa – Scorpion fish (*Peixe carneiro*)

Birds which breed in Madeira

Latin – English names

Hydrobates pelagicus Linnaeus – Storm Petrel
Oceanodroma castro castro – Harcourt's or Madeiran Storm Petrel
Calonectris diomedea borealis – Cory's Shearwater
Puffinus puffinus puffinus – Manx Shearwater
Puffinus assimilis baroli Bonaparte – Madeiran Little Shearwater
Pterodroma mollis madeira – Soft-plumaged Petrel

Pterodroma mollis deserta – Soft-plumaged Petrel
Bulweria bulwerii bulwerii – Bulwer's Petrel
Falco tinnunculus canariensis – Canarian Kestrel
Accipiter nisus granti – Madeiran Sparrow-hawk
Buteo buteo harterti – Hartert's buzzard
Alectoris rufa hispanica – Red-legged Partridge
Alectoris barbara barbara – Barbary Partridge
Coturnix coturnix confisa – Madeiran Quail
Charadrius alexandrinus alexandrinus – Kentish Plover
Charadrius dubius curonicus – Little Ringed Plover
Scolopax rusticola rusticola – European Woodcock
Larus argentatus atlantis – Atlantic Herring Gull
Sterna hirundo hirundo – Common Tern (Portuguese: Garajau)
Sterna dougallii dougallii – Roseate Tern
Comunba trocaz trocaz – Madeiran Laurel Pigeon
Columba palumbus madeirensis – Madeiran Wood Pigeon
Columba livia (subspecies undetermined) – Madeiran Rock Pigeon
Streptopelia turtur turtur – Turtle Dove
Tyto alba schmitzi – Madeiran Barn Owl
Apus pollidus brehmorum – Brehm's Pale Swift
Apus unicolor unicolor – Little Black Swift
Upapa epops epops – European Hoopoe
Turdus merula cabrerae – Cabrera's Blackbird
Erithacus rubecula microrhynchus – Madeiran Redbreast
Sylvia atricapilla obscura – Dusky Blackcap
Sylvia conspicillata bella – Madeiran Spectacled Warbler
Regulus ignicapillus madeirensis – Madeiran Firecrest
Motacilla cinerea schmitzi – Madeiran Grey Wagtail
Anthus bertheloti madeirensis – Madeiran Berthelot's Pipit
Fringilla coelebs madeirensis – Madeiran Chaffinch
Carduelis carduelis parva – Madeiran Goldfinch
Chloris chloris aurantiiventris – Golden-bellied Greenfinch
Serinus canarius canarius – Canary
Carduelis cannabina nana – Madeiran Linnet
Passer hispaniolensis hispaniolensis – Spanish Sparrow
Petronia petronia madeirensis – Madeiran Rock Sparrow

Appendix IV
Some Herbs and Medicinal Plants found in Madeira

Portuguese	English	*Latin*
Abóbora	Pumpkin	*Cucurbita Pepo*
Agrião	Watercress	*Sisymbrium nasturtium*
Alfavaca	Basil	*Parietaria officinalis*
Alfinetes de Senhora	Silene	*Pyretrum partherium*
Araçá	Strawberry Guava	*Psidium cattleyanum*
Avenca	Maidenhair Fern	*Adiantum capillus veneris*
Azeda	Sorrel	*Rumex maderensis*
Bálsamo	Balsam	*Kleinia repens*
Bolsa de Pastor	Shepherd's Purse	*Oxalis corniculata*
Borragem	Borage	*Borago officinalis*
Carvalho	Oak-tree	*Quercus pedunculata*
Cavalinha or Rabo de Cavalo	Swartzpea	*Equisetum fluviatile*
Cedronha (corruption of Celidónia	Celandine	*Chelidonium majus*
Cipreste	Cypress	*Cupressus sempervirens*
Dragoeiro	Dragon-tree	*Dracaena draco*
Erva Cidreira	Common Balm	*Melissa officinalis*
Erva de Santa Maria or Erva Moira	Wormseed Goosefoot	*Solanum nigrum*
Erva de São Roberto	Crane's Bill	*Geranium robertianum*
Eucalipto	Eucalyptus	*Eucalyptus globulus*
Fedigose (corruption of Fedegoso)	Cassia	*Psoralea bituminosa*
Feto abrum	type of fern	*Dicksonia culcita*
Figueira	Fig-tree	*Ficus carica*
Grama	type of grass	*Agropyrum repens*
Hera Terrestre	Common Ground Ivy	*Sibthorpia peregrina*
Hortelã	Mint	*Mentha silvestris*
Inhame	Edible Taro	*Colocasia antiquorum*
Laranjeira	Orange-tree	*Cytrus aurantium*
Lombrigueira	West Indian Spigelia	*Chenopodium ambrosioides*
Loureiro	Laurel or Bay-tree	*Laurus canariensis*
Macela	Camomile	*Ormenus aureus*
Madre de Louro	Honeysuckle	*Exobasidium lauri*
Mentastro	Apple Mint	*Mentha rotundifolia*
Morangueiro	Strawberry plant	*Fragaria vesca*

Nogueira	Walnut-tree	*Juglans regia*
Orelha de Cabra	Roundhead Plantain	*Plantago lanceolata*
Pelicão (corruption of Hipericão)	St John's Wort	*Hypericum perferatum*
Pereira Abacate	Avocado Pear-tree	*Persea gratissima*
Perpétuas amarelas	Everlasting flower	*Helychrysum orientale*
Pessegueiro	Peach-tree	*Prunus persica*
Rosmaninho	Lavender	*Lavandula dentata*
Sabugueiro	Elder-tree	*Sambucus maderensis*
Segurelha	Summer Savory	*Satureja hortensis*
Silvado	European Blackberry Bush	*Rubus fruticosus*
Tanchagem	Rippleseed Plantain	*Plantago major*
Til	'Til'	*Ocotea foetens*
Trevo de Pé de Pássaro	Bird's Foot Trefoil	*Trifolium maritimum*
Urgebão or Jarvão	European Verbena	*Verbena officinalis*
Verbasco	Mullein	*Verbascum sinuatum*
Verbena	Lemon Verbena	*Lippia citriodora*

Appendix V
Conversion Table

Length:

1 millimetre	0.039 inches
1 centimetre	0.394 inches
1 metre	1.094 yards
1 kilometre	0.62 miles

Surface Area:

1 centimetre^2	0.155 inches^2
1 metre^2	1.196 yards^2
1 hectare	2.471 acres
1 km^2	0.386 miles^2

Capacity:

1 litre	0.22 imperial gallons

Weight:

1 kilogramme	2.204 pounds
1 tonne	0.984 tons

To convert metric to imperial, multiply the metric units by the figure in the imperial column.

Bibliography

Bibliography

Books in English

Bannerman, David A. and W. Mary, *Birds of the Atlantic*, Volume II, (Oliver & Boyd, London, 1965)

Bridge, Ann and Lowndes, Susan, *The Selective Traveller in Portugal* (Evans Brothers Ltd, London, 1949)

Brown, Samler A., *Brown's Madeira and the Canary Islands* (Sampson Low, Marston & Co Ltd, 5th revised edition, 1898)

Cane, Ella and Florence du, *The Flowers and Gardens of Madeira* (Adam & Charles Black, London, 1909)

Castelo Branco, Hugo C. de Lacerda, *The Climate of Madeira: With a Comparative Study* (Delegação do Turismo da Madeira, 1938)

Combe, William, *A History of Madeira* (R. Ackermann, 1821)

Copy of the Record of the Establishment of the Chaplaincy and Notes on the Old Factory at Madeira (from the papers of the late C.J. Cossart of Madeira), re-copied 1959 for Graham Blandy by permission of the Church Committee of the Church of England Chapel and British Cemeteries Trust for Madeira; re-copied 1980

Cossart, Noël, *Madeira – the Island Vineyard* (Christie's Wine Publications, London, 1984)

Croft-Cooke, Rupert, *Madeira* (Putnam & Co Ltd, London, 1961)

França, Isabella da, *Journal of a Visit to Madeira and Portugal 1853-54* (Junta Geral do Distrito Autónomo do Funchal)

Franquinho, L.O. and Costa, A da, *Flores – Fleurs – Flowers – Blumen – Blomster* (Francisco Ribeiro, Funchal, 8th edition 1986)

Fortunate Isles: Madeira & the Canary Islands (Royal Mail, Pacific, Nelson & Union-Castle Lines)

Gordon-Brown, A., *Madeira and the Canary Islands* (issued for the Union-Castle Mail Steamship Company Limited, Robert Hale Ltd, London, 1959)

Grabham, Michael C., *The Climate and Resources of Madeira* (John Churchill & Sons Ltd, London, 1870)

Grabham, Michael C., *The Garden Interests of Madeira* (Wm Clowes & Sons Ltd, London, 1926)

Hutcheon, J.E., *Things seen in Madeira* (Seeley, Service & Co Ltd, 5th edition)

Koebel, W.H. *Madeira: Old & New* (Francis Griffiths, London, 1909)

A Madeira e o Turismo: Pequeno Esboço Histórico (in Portuguese, English, French; DRAC; Funchal, 1985)

Madeira Fragments. I: A Trip to Madeira October 28th 1836 to June 25th 1837. Being the Journal of Edward Atkinson Wells. II: Extract from the Diary of Miss Katherine E. Perry who came to Madeira in October 1844 (re-copied 1971 for Mr Graham Blandy)

Mais, S.P.B., *Madeira Holiday* (Alvin Redman Ltd, 1951)

Marsh, A.E.W., *Holiday Wanderings in Madeira* (Sampson Low, Marston & Co, 1892)

Melo, Luís de Sousa and Farrow, Susan E., *Impressions of Madeira in the Past* (Pátio English Bookshop, Funchal, 1983)

Menezes, C.A., *Madeira Ferns* (translated from the Portuguese by Herbert Gilbert, Diário Popular, 1906).

Miles, Cecil H., *A Glimpse of Madeira* (Peter Garnett, London, 1949)

Murray's Handbook of Portugal, Madeira, Azores and Canaries (John Murray, 1887)

Newell, Colonel H.A., *The English Church in Madeira* (Oxford University Press, 1931)

Nicholas, Elizabeth, *Madeira and the Canaries* (Hamish Hamilton, 1953)

Piazzi Smyth, C., *Madeira Meteorologic* (David Douglas, Edinburgh, 1882)

Power, C.A. le P., *Power's Guide to the Island of Madeira* (George Philip & Son, London, 4th edition 1951)

Reid W. & A., *Guide to Madeira* (1893)

Rendell, J.M., *Handbook of Madeira* (C. Kegan Paul & Co, London, 1881)

Sitwell, Sacheverell, *Portugal and Madeira* (B.T. Batsford Ltd, London, 1954)

Sketches and Adventures in Madeira, Portugal and the Andalusias of Spain (Sampson Low, Son & Co, 1856)

Spain (Galicia), Portugal and Madeira (illustrated guide, Booth Line, Liverpool, 1913)

Stanford, Thomas C., *Leaves from a Madeira Garden* (John Lane, The Bodley Head, London, 1909)

Taylor, Ellen M., *Madeira: Its Scenery and How to See It* (Edward Stanford, London, 1882)

Ultra Marine, *Contents of a Madeira Mailbag or Island Etchings* (Moran & Co, London)

Underwood, John and Pat, *Landscapes of Madeira: A Countryside Guide* (Sunflower Books, London, 2nd edition 1983)

Vieira, Rui, *Flores da Madeira: Flowers of Madeira: Fleurs de Madère* (Francisco Ribeiro, Funchal)

White, Robert and Johnson, James Y., *Madeira: Its Climate and Scenery* (Adam & Charles Black, London, 2nd edition 1860)

Books in Portuguese

Aragão, António, *As Armas da Cidade do Funchal no Curso da Sua História* (DRAC, Funchal, 1984)

Aragão, António, *A Madeira Vista por Estrangeiros* (DRAC, Funchal, 1981)

Caldeira, Abel Marques, *O Funchal no Primeiro Quartel do Século XX: 1900-1925* (Funchal, 1964)

Carita, Rui, *Introdução à arquitectura militar na Madeira: a Fortaleza-Palácio de São Lourenço* (DRAC, Funchal, 1981)

Carita, Rui, *Paulo Dias de Almeida e a Descrição da Ilha da Madeira 1817-1827* (DRAC, Funchal, 1982)

Carita, Rui, *O Regimento de Fortificação de D. Sebastião (1572) e a Carta da Madeira de Bartolomeu João (1654)* (Secretaria Regional da Educação, 1984)

Clode, Luiz Peter, *Descendência de D. Gonçalo Afonso d'Avis Trastâmara Fernandes; O Máscara de Ferro Português* (DRAC, Funchal, 1983)

Gomes, Fátima Freitas e Viríssimo, Nelson, *A Madeira e o Sidonismo* (DRAC, Funchal 1983)

Guia Regional da Madeira (Delegação de Turismo do Funchal, 1956)

Melo, Luís de Sousa, *Vicentes Photographos* (Ilhatur, Funchal, 1978)

Noronha, Adolfo César de e Sarmento, Alberto Artur, *Vertebrados da Madeira – 20 volume – Peixes* (Edição da Junta Geral do Distrito Autónomo do Funchal, 1948)

Nunes, Adão de Abreu, *Peixes da Madeira* (Junta Geral do Distrito Autónomo do Funchal, 2nd edition 1974)

Oliveira, A Lopes de, *Arquipelago da Madeira: Epopeia Humana* (Editora Pax, Braga)

Oliveira, Freitas, Fernandes, Alves e Fernandes, *Antológia de Textos: História da Madeira* (Secretaria Regional da Educação, Funchal, 1984)

Pereira, Eduardo C.N., *Ilhas de Zargo*, 2 volumes (Câmara Municipal do Funchal, 1957)

Pestana, César, *As Esquadras de Navegação Terrestre* (Ilhatur, Funchal, 1981)

Pio, Manuel Ferreira, *O Monte: Santuário Votivo da Madeira* (Funchal, 1965)

Quintal, Raimundo, *Os Jardins da Quinta do Palheiro Ferreiro* (Separata da Revista Atlântico, Funchal, 1986)

Quintal, Raimundo e Vieira, Maria José, *Ilha da Madeira*: Esboço de Geografia Física (DRAC, Funchal, 1985)

Ribeiro, Orlando, *A Ilha da Madeira até Meados do Século XX: Estudo Geográfico* (Ministério da Educação, Instituto de Cultura e Língua Portuguesa, 1985)

Silva, Padre Fernando Augusto da e Meneses, Carlos Azevedo de, *Elucidário Madeirense*, 3 volumes (DRAC, Funchal, 1984 – facsimile of 1946 edition)

Silva, Germano da – editor, *A Nova Questão Hinton* (Typographia Portuguesa, Lisbon, 1915)

Simões, Álvaro Vieira, *Transportes na Madeira* (DRAC, Funchal, 1983)

Soares, João, *A Revolta da Madeira* (Editorial Império Lda, Lisbon, 1979)

Trigo, Adriano A e Trigo, Annibal A, *Guide and Plan of Funchal* (Typographia Esperança, Funchal. 1910)

Vieira, Rui, *Album Florístico da Madeira* (Funchal, 1974)

Indexes

General Index

Index of Recipes